Painted with Love

By Karen Diana Montee

Written and developed by Karen Diana Montee
Ketchum, Idaho

ISBN 978-0-9853307-4-3
First Edition August 2013
Printed in the United States of America

*Dedicated to my supportive
parents
and my loving partner*

Contents

Chapter One: **The World in Picture**

Masai Mara, Kenya September 20, 2005

I woke suddenly, my eyes wide, gasping for air, my heart pounding. I listened intently, afraid to move. Suddenly, I leaped from my cot and flung open the covers checking for a snake, then scanned my body for bites. With shaky hands, I unzipped the tent door.

The camp looked the same as the past few days. The air was warming up and smelled of wet soil, unwashed bodies, monsoon clouds and cattle dung. Masai women and children moved about as if the tiger were not on its front paws ready to strike. My hunches were never wrong, so I stayed alert for the silent steps of a savannah cat. Something's coming.

Climbing out the tent door, I met Brian.

"Good morning sleepy-head," Brian called. I found the predator, I thought smiling.

"Sleepy-head? When did you get up?"

"I was up at five…"

"It's been a rough morning. Be nice."

"I'm just teasing you Dee. What's the matter?"

"I don't know-- yet."

"Talk to me girl. What's on your mind?" Brian asked.

"I have a bad feeling."

"What do you mean a bad feeling?"

"A premonition, you know. Something terrible is going to happen. I need to call home to talk to my daughters."

"I'm sorry Dee, but do you know how far it is to the nearest telephone? Nairobi is a five hour drive on mud covered roads and I have no transportation for you today. Besides, you would need to locate a phone, make an out of country call and hope that you would get someone to pick up. You're a million miles away from home. There is nothing you can do. You are just nervous about the upcoming events. Maybe you don't want to see this girl get her parts cut off."

My stomach clinched.

Brian continued, "Today is a big day for all of us. I will talk to the tribe leaders regarding teaching their youth English. The Masai women are preparing for Kurary's circumcision to celebrate entering manhood in two days and Rata's clitoral circumcision before her marriage. We are all on edge, but I need your attention here. This is big stuff going down. Keep your focus. Don't worry about things at home. Changing your travel plans would take at least a day. We are leaving in a few days anyway."

When I didn't respond, Brian added, "What are you thinking, Dee?"

"You remember that I'm leaving tomorrow to get some pictures of Kilimanjaro?"

"I remember."

"I could stop in Nairobi tomorrow to call and check on the girls."

"Dee, if you're going to make it safely from Mara Reserve to Amboseli Park, you won't have time to stop in Nairobi and travel before dark. It's a nine hour drive if all goes well. Please let this go. You will be home in four days."

"I can't let this feeling go, Brian. Something is wrong."

"Alright. Stop in Nairobi tomorrow if it makes you feel better," Brian said.

"Thank you."

"Are you ready to take some pictures today?"

"One more thing."

"What?"

"You might enjoy coming along," I said raising my eyebrows.

Brian paused. I waited, holding my breath with hope, yet not letting him see how scared I was to go alone. "You know that I'm not a tourist here Dee. I'm here to work."

"I am working too. I cannot travel across the world to photograph a story and not include the wildlife and the largest mountain on the continent. These pictures belong in the story of the Masai. Readers want to see the environment as well as the people."

"So, you need me after all," he said smugly.

My face twisted and tightened into a squinted mess. I saw no way out of this one. I nodded my head once.

"I tell you what. I'll think about it," he said with a warm smile as he turned and walked away.

***

Two year earlier my girlfriend and I walked into The Pike Pub and Brewery in Seattle one November night and she recognized her neighbor Brian sitting with two other guys. We sat down at their table and visited and laughed for hours. Brian had an easy way about him and a great sense of humor. We talked about traveling, great restaurants in Seattle, our favorite wines and places we loved to hike or camp. Occasionally, I shivered from a cold breeze that entered the pub each time the door opened. Brian rubbed his hand up and down my back to keep me warm. He warmed me up better than my Greyhound cocktail. He asked for my number. We dated for a month. I realized, from our long conversations, that we both had passion for the work we did around the world.

Brian wanted to get serious. A relationship with Brian did not feel comfortable to me, although I couldn't decide why. Perhaps my divorce had damaged my ability to take a risk, and Brian was a risk. He'd never been married and didn't have kids. My daughters were a huge part of my world and I didn't see him adapting to that. He agreed to be friends, reluctantly, but claimed that I was making a big mistake by passing up a great guy like him. Maybe I was.

One evening we were sharing dinner and he told me about his mission in Kenya. I listened to his every word with keen interest.

"There's a great need in Kenya to educate the native people. When the Egyptian rule spread south in Africa thousands of years ago, their religion was forced upon the natives. These religious beliefs have been passed down over centuries and include male and female circumcision upon teenagers. Women are forever damaged by the brutal ceremony. Education is the key to save future women from this mutilation."

My heart swelled with pain as I imagined the fate of these young women. I wanted to save them all.

3

"Additionally, the government is limiting the land in which these natives can graze their cattle. Centuries of tradition are threatened more each year. Teaching the youth to speak English provides the tribes opportunities for outside jobs and income to help support the needs of the tribe. Those of us who are brave enough must speak to each chief separately and get permission to educate their youth. We have already been successful with a few tribes."

Faces of youth that I had photographed all over the world flashed in my mind. Beautiful, ambitious smiles, innocent of the trials life can pose. No doubt I would see similar smiles and fall in love with new children.

Brian's conviction showed in his face. From the tone in his voice, I knew he was affected by the needs of these native people. His compulsion to help the Masai was contagious.

Then he shared an opportunity with me. "Do you know of any good photographers?" He asked smiling. I could see this project fitting in nicely with my other photojournalist work.

"Oh, indeed. I know this vivacious, clever lady who loves to travel and is an up-and-coming famous photographer," I replied.

"Do you know if she's available?"

"Let me check her schedule," I said looking off into space thoughtfully. "Yes, she's currently has an opening. When do we leave?"

"Dee, are you sure you want this assignment? It takes a lot of strength and will not be easy."

"Of course I want it." Goosebumps climbed my body as I said the words. "I don't have any photos of African villages. It will be perfect to go into my current series. I have a show coming up the first week of October in San Francisco. I could include the Masai in the exhibit. The diversity will add dimension."

"You have an eye for this work. You can come along, but you will have to do what I tell you. I know these people and the land. Can you listen and follow my lead?"

"Yes," I said reluctant to make such a commitment.

"Okay, if you're sure. I know how independent you are. In Kenya you might need me more than you think. Are you ready for the messy details?"

"Hit me with it," I said.

"Okay. Your photographs will be taken in an effort to show potential supporters the trauma to the young Masai women so we can eventually prevent these mutilations from happening. You will have to take some difficult pictures of bleeding teenagers in terrible pain in order to tell this story."

"I can handle it. I want to make a difference," I replied, cringing slightly.

"Very important…Dee, you must respect your place in the eyes of these people. You cannot be your usual outspoken and direct self. Speaking your mind as a woman from another part of the world will alienate you very quickly."

"I promise to hold my tongue, but I know it won't be easy," I said pursing my lips.

"Good. Having the chance to photograph this fierce tribe is not a simple matter, but it is a privilege. Most Masai keep themselves separate from outsiders. This is not for the faint of heart."

"I'm honored."

"There's more. Kenya has developed into a more educated country with larger cities. The indigenous people living outside of developed areas struggle to keep their customs, and at the same time, adopt a better way of living. My purpose is to convince each tribe to allow their children to be educated. Your job is to document the struggles of a village in transition with pictures, and show the world the challenges the Masai face in trying to save their customs while adapting to a modern world."

"I can do this."

"Don't get ahead of yourself. The greatest danger in Kenya is being mugged, often at knife or gun point. People are killed this way every year. You need to always stay with locals. It's usually foreigners who are targeted. You're one hundred times more likely to be robbed by a local than attacked by a wild animal. The second greatest danger is driving on the roads, but most of the accidents are minor. Of course there are a slew of diseases to catch. Be sure to get all of the recommended vaccinations."

"Yes sir! I will."

"Okay. You can come with me."

"Yay," I said with a big smile.

"I've one request, Brian."

"Oh no, here we go...what might that be?" he asked.

"I would like to photograph Kilimanjaro among other natural land formations in Kenya. It's the largest peak on the African continent."

Brian was quiet for a moment. Then he spoke seriously. "Kilimanjaro is in Tanzania. You can get to it from Kenya and see it from Kenya, but we would need to cross the border to get to the mountain and that would further complicate matters and take away precious time. It's also a long way from where I will be meeting with the tribe in the Masai Mara National Reserve. I will not have time to go that far for leisure travel."

A sad feeling spread through my body.

Brian watched my face, then spoke. "I guess I could arrange for a good guide to take you close enough for pictures. The mountain would be in the distance. Would that work for you?"

"Yes, yes, yes! Thank you."

"It's very dangerous for a white female to travel across Kenya. Perhaps some other locals will go with you and the guide. I will see what I can do."

"You're awesome, Brian."

"Don't mention it. This trip will be good for us. It will give us some quality time together. Did I mention that we will have to share a bed?"

"What? I thought we would be camping?"

"Don't freak out. I'm teasing. But you can sleep next to me if you get scared. You never know Dee, you might decide that I'm not such a bad guy after all."

I think I would have figured that out by now, I thought while I shot Brian a forced smile.

When I packed for the trip, I was acutely aware of the information Brian had shared. I prepared as best I could, knowing I would be without all modern conveniences. During the flights to Kenya, he continued to educate me and prepared me for working around the native Masai. By the time I arrived in Africa, I felt only a little nervous to face the upcoming events.

***

I settled in as quickly as I could, acting comfortable in my strange surroundings. The past three days had gone well, and with the big day almost here, I felt I could interact with the tribe and get the shots that I needed.

The hot sun reminded me that the heat of the day would test my body. I walked back inside my small tent to grab my large brimmed hat and beloved camera before heading out to take some pictures. Then I slipped a protein bar in my pocket to go with the milk I would be served for breakfast.

Outside my tent, I took a few shots of the interior of the Masai camp which was surrounded by a tangled, thorny fence gathered from the dessert and assembled with care to prevent puncturing their skin with the four inches thorns intimidating enough to deter lions and hyenas from attacking the cattle. The eight foot high barrier wasn't pleasant and posed a stark contrast to the vast landscape, including snow peaked Mount Meru.

The thorn gates were open to the wild desert. Far away I saw the men herding cattle outside camp to graze on whatever grass was available, which was little. For the past three nights I watched them bring the cattle back into the safety of camp to protect them from wild predators.

Brian explained to me how the Masai followed the same practice as their great-great-grandfathers, believing that their God, Enkai, had entrusted them with all cattle. They took the responsibility seriously. Wealth was determined by how many cattle each man had. Their women could not own cattle.

My eyes lingered on the dark bodies of strong warriors, respected throughout the region for their skill, strength and hunting prowess, as well as jumping high, leaping straight up several feet. I felt intimidated and excited to be among men who were fast and brave enough to kill a lion with a spear. I observed them guiding their cows and searching for grazing ground while moving to the rhythm of the weather, sun and moon.

The women were fit, agile laborers who cared for their children and men with fortitude. They tended to the animals and meals with a rhythmic unity and patience. They wore long draping, multi-colored dresses that covered their bodies except their arms and lower calves. Most of the women were barefoot in the camp and some wore wood sandals for walking outside of camp. After the women cleaned up from the morning meal of milk, they were ready to hike to the river and retrieve water in preparation for a ceremony in two days where a fifteen year old boy, Kurary, would be circumcised and honored. Brian had arranged for me to tag along to the river. I had already documented the preparations of the past two days and felt confident that the story was coming together in pictures.

On day four of my stay with the Masai, making friends with the women proved more challenging than settling into the dust, mud, strange food, new language and dark nights without electricity. I felt like an orphaned child that was a bother rather than a helpful addition. The camera protruding at my breastbone must have seemed strange to them. I didn't speak their language. I didn't look like them and I didn't work hard in the hot sun like they did every day. Each time I offered to help, I got in the way and couldn't understand the instructions offered in a language I didn't know.

It was slightly easier with the children. Mostly they laughed and pointed at me, or walked cautiously around me. Some of them gathered around to pose for my camera when I took pictures. They loved to watch me pick at my food. I watched them eat in complete appreciation of nourishment and comfort to their bellies. I ate in hopes that lack of running water and proper sanitation wouldn't cause me to become ill and lose my lunch. Quickly I tired of eating their staple foods: fresh, warm milk and curdled milk. I smiled a huge 'thank you' for their hospitality, but felt relief that I had packed my suitcase with snack bars and nuts, as Brian had suggested.

I strolled out of camp towards a tributary of the Mara River along with four women carrying buckets. A mule, five young girls and two young boys joined us. The mule was loaded with a harness and buckets dangling from each side. The women leading us began to sing a simple tune in higher tones than most American songs. Their merriment drowned out the coos of nearby birds. I photographed the singing women carrying the empty buckets on their heads.

I remained alert, hoping to photograph some wildlife. We had no defenses against a lion or rhinoceros, but strangely the Masai didn't seem concerned. They knew how to live safely among the animals on one of Kenya's largest animal reserves.

With my trusty Canon EOS in my right hand, I could see Mt Meru in the distance. The aroma of the moist desert filled my senses. Damp soil, bare feet, beetles and cow dung mixed together, creating an earthy aroma. The mid-morning air was dry, near eighty degrees. We walked on a path with occasional muddy patches. The women traveled this route daily to gather water. The damp soil squished between the children's toes and stuck to my wood sandals, making the walk a clumsy affair.

My new constant companion was Kurary's younger brother Leboo. He walked directly in front of me, never straying. He was quieter than the other kids, and attached himself to me like a duck that had lost its mother. The companionship helped me to not feel lonely in this strange land. I had learned a few words from his language, but he remained quiet and often giggled at my attempt to speak his native tongue.

He loved to pose for my camera. He jumped in front of the lens with a full smile and silly pose as often as he could. At first he wanted to see his picture in the display window each time I snapped a shot. I happily obliged him, knowing that the more pictures I took, the better my chances of capturing something wonderful. Snapping his cheerful smile over and over made me

9

fall in love with his vibrant personality. Little did he understand, at the tender age of seven, that my photos would appear in an exhibition in San Francisco next month. His happy, quiet eyes might be seen by thousands.

Leboo skipped along, enticing me to record his merriment. Through the lens I watched his dance, his funny faces and goofy poses. Peering through the glass window I saw the children in front of Leboo dragging sticks to make lines in the mud and brushing the desert plants with their fingertips. I snapped the shutter again and again, capturing the simplicity of their world. The shutter closed for brief micro seconds with new and magical moments before me. I snapped again, waiting for the blackness to blink in front of my eye and a different picture to emerge. When the shutter opened again, a surreal sight appeared. Without stopping to enjoy the moment, I closed the shutter once, twice, maybe a third time before I peered from behind my lens and looked. We had rounded a corner which opened up to trees, a river bank and water with possibly one hundred zebras. My mouth hung open as I stared at the black and white striped beasts. Their heads reached down as they lapped up water. The group had no reaction to our presence, except to notice that we were there.

Leboo stopped his little dance and froze. He turned to grab my leg. I looked at him to understand his reaction. His face showed an expression of concern that didn't make sense to me. We were looking at zebras; what did he fear? Then I noticed that the women were speaking to the children, directing them to hold still. The women all gathered close to the mule as if they were hiding him. I watched the women scan the river and plains in all directions. They spoke to each other softly, but seriously. I didn't know what was going on.

Ahead of us the path continued along the river, with a steep, eroding sandy bank along both sides. It was obvious that at certain times of the year this river held more water. If we moved forward, there was no quick escape.

The women suddenly directed all of us to turn back in the direction that we'd come. They made the mule go at the very front and we all walked quickly behind. I looked at the leading woman, Tigisi, with a questioning expression. She looked back at me wide eyed and said a word I didn't understand. One of the children looked at me, made claws with his hands and roared in a way that made the hair on the back of my neck stand up. I realized they were looking for a lion.

We left the zebras and river with empty buckets. I couldn't leave without more photos. As the group quickly walked away, I let them pass me. I turned back to snap a few shots. Leboo noticed me, and pulled on my shirt, directing me away from the beautiful animals. I closed my shutter several times in a row before turning to follow.

I walked about two hundred yards before I heard it. I didn't know what it was until I turned. Zebras, far behind us, leaped in every direction. All of the children began to run. The women dropped their buckets and ran in the direction from which we'd come. I followed them, running without looking back. About half the zebras were closing in on us, following the easiest escape route. I ran as fast as I could, but the women and children were much faster. Leboo looked back at me, his eyes wide with terror. He ran towards me and I felt a moment of comfort to see the compassion of this young boy. For an instant I felt safe, saved by a young hero. He reached me just in time to pull me out of the zebra's path.

Hooves thundered on the hard earth. Leboo and I waited quietly together for the zebras to move past us. I protected my camera, wishing I could capture this stampede in still frame. We looked for a lion, but it never appeared. It probably had what it wanted back at the river. Within a minute all the zebras had scattered and it was safe for Leboo and me to head back.

When we reached camp, the women were telling the elders what had transpired. Then two men with spears and two women and the mule left camp again to retrieve water. The children and I stayed behind in the warm sun. Brian was sitting with the elders. He walked toward me and asked, "Are you all right? Did you have quite a scare?"

"I'm fine. Leboo protected me. It was very sweet to have a young man looking out for me."

"I see. It takes a wild animal chasing you for you to need a man's help?"

"Ha, ha, ha. You're very funny. Maybe I just need the right man."

"You wouldn't know the right man if he flew you halfway around the world and proposed to you."

I stopped in my tracks and froze. I thought I better leave that one alone and change the subject. I opened my mouth looking for anything to say to ease the conversation down a notch.

Before I could get a word out, Brian changed the tone. "Lighten up, Dee. I'm just teasing you. Are you okay?"

"Oh yeah…," I sighed. "I'm fine; just a little excitement to keep things interesting."

That night I dropped into bed exhausted. I felt grateful that Brian was coming with me to Kilimanjaro, the highest peak in Africa, at 19,341 feet, with three dormant volcanic cones, Kibo, Mawenzi and Shira. The mountain drew me toward her like a thirsty animal to water, just like when I was a child and would wander off into the vastness away from my parent's campsite in the mountains of Washington and Oregon. Nature pulled at me and filled my soul with a liquid joy that I found irresistible. Decade after decade of my life I felt the pull of majestic places, like a mother's call; I was drawn towards them. I began taking photos to remember the powerful experiences I had. Tomorrow I would photograph the largest mountain I had ever seen. Only I would know the feelings that stirred deep inside me as I looked upon the majestic peak. I could hardly fall sleep. Eventually, I drifted off into quiet slumber, restless and dreamless.

At sunrise I woke up with a jolt. I sat up quickly and scanned the tent. I heard nothing unusual as I became aware of my surroundings. A heavy air remained. My head turned to one side, then the other. My arms automatically lifted the sheets. Deep breaths didn't comfort my tingling skin or relax the hair standing up on the back of my neck. I worried about the trip southward today and the potential threat of muggers.

I freshened up and dressed. Brian was already outside of camp with a van and two men from the tribe packing the vehicle with provisions to be prepared for any scenario we might encounter. The sky was bright on the east horizon and darker to the west.

Brian hired one of the best known guides from the region to take us to see Kilimanjaro and help us navigate Kenya's wilderness. He also arranged for nice accommodations, since we would spend one night in an area he didn't know well. Because we were staying in a hotel, Brian offered that we share a suite. I politely declined. He shrugged it off like he was expecting my answer.

Men from the tribe requested to come to assist and protect us. Then Leboo asked if he could come with us. He explained to me, through Brian's translating, that I would need a subject to be in my photos. I also learned that Leboo had never ridden in a vehicle before. I was pleased to have my young hero and best model along for the long ride.

After we enjoyed some fresh milk for breakfast, we set out in the white Nissan van right. There was a hole in the roof of the van with a raised lid for passengers to stand up and look out. The vehicle was typical of those used on African tours and safaris.

The roads were bumpy due to heavy rains. We had a long way to go. I settled into my seat and tried to fall in rhythm with the bouncing and jostling. The roads were also narrow. Only occasionally did the roads widen enough for our van to pass opposing traffic without slowing down or stopping.

13

Leboo and I sat in the back while he grinned from ear to ear without saying a word. He seemed content just to experience the ride. His smile reflected my excitement. Brian spoke often with the two men from the Masai tribe.

Brian explained to the driver that we were diverting our path towards a phone. I anticipated my calls, hoping for good news. We took the main road from the north into Nairobi. The driver took us straight to one of his relative's hotels and negotiated for me to make two phone calls for a heavy fee. I was happy to pay. I dialed my daughter's cell and let the phone ring.

Much to my relief, she answered. We had a nice conversation and she reassured me.

"Everything's fine Mom. I spoke to Jennifer last night and Clair's coming here for lunch today. Jennifer's excited for you to get home. She just entered her third trimester, so she's feeling pretty good."

"So everyone's doing great?"

"Yes, Mom. All is well. But I want to make sure that you will take pictures at my wedding. I know we hired a photographer, but you're the best. Will you take some also?"

"Yes, honey. I promise I will."

"Thanks Mom. I just want everything to be perfect. I also need your help with some final wedding items. I will pick you up at the airport."

"I love you honey. Give my love to your sisters." I hung up the phone feeling relieved.

Perhaps all of my worry was about my upcoming exhibit. Next I made a call to Paul Brown.

"Hi Paul, it's Dee Coulter."

"Hello Dee, great to hear your voice. You are well I hope?"

"Yes, I am. Thank you."

"I received your sample photos of the people in Panama, Turkey and the District of Colombia. I want to use them, so please send them all. Will you ship the art soon?" Paul asked.

"Yes. In about ten days." I replied.

"How long will your presence grace our fine city?" he asked.

"Oh," I said, "I will be in San Francisco about a week."

14

"You have a free tour guide at your disposal. Please allow me the pleasure."

"I might take you up on that, Paul."

"I hope you do." He paused briefly before clearing his throat and continuing. "In addition to the art, I would like a larger photo of you and a bio you want for the show that is more detailed than the one I used in the ads. You are a remarkable woman, from what I know so far."

"Thank you. I will send you the photo and bio in about a week."

"I look forward to it."

"Paul, I have some new material. Could you squeeze a few more shots into the show?"

"That's perfect really. I was going to invite another artist because I still have room, but if you have more material, I will make the show exclusively yours. Where did you photograph the new material?"

"The pictures are from Kenya, but the details I would like to keep a secret until they are in print."

"Okay, I like surprises! I love how you capture people in their element and show their emotion. Incredible talent you have. I look forward to seeing your smiling face in person. Could we have dinner while you're in town? I would love to treat you to a meal, San Francisco style." His tone was flirtatious.

"It's a date. I'll even dress-up," I replied playfully .

"I'll sneak you off to one of my favorite less-known hot spots. No cameras allowed."

I laughed and heard Paul release a small chuckle. Then I noticed a tap on my right shoulder. I looked to my right and Brian mouthed something. I pulled the phone away from my ear and said, "What?"

Brian replied, "Let's go!"

"Just a second," I replied.

"Let's go," Brian said. "We are burning daylight."

"Paul, I have to run. I will see you in San Francisco in a few weeks," I replied.

"I can't wait," he replied.

As I said good-bye to Paul, Brian piped up.

"Your personal taxi is leaving."

"That was an important business call. Why is it so important to save a few minutes?" I asked flustered.

"Well, let me explain it to you, Dee. You are here on this assignment because of me. You could offer a little respect. It's difficult for me to watch you blushing and flirting with another man while I am standing right here leading you on a far off dangerous journey at your request, putting my own time and resources aside. Your business is my business when we are traveling across the desert together and need to be somewhere before dark."

I gathered my composure as I realized my mistake. "You're right. I'm sorry, Brian. I wasn't thinking. This exhibit it a big deal for me. I want this show so badly. I just…got caught up."

"Alright, thanks for understanding. If I weren't in love with you, it wouldn't matter."

Oh my. What am I supposed to say to that? I froze in place.

"That's fine, don't say anything. I know you're not in love with me, yet. Your problem, Dee, is that you won't let a man get close to you or protect you. If you don't trust a man, and let one love you, you will always be alone."

He looked at my face, waiting for a response. I felt flippant but I toned down my response to sound light and joking, "When I meet one worth trusting, I'll let you know. Until then, I am doing just fine." I shot him a teasing smile.

Brian looked disappointed, so I added softly, "It's obvious that you look out for my best interest and I appreciate that you care. You are a good guy and I'm glad that you are in my life." He shot me a half smile and small lift of his chin.

We climbed back in the van with the rest of our party. I sat quietly noticing the happy feeling in my body that Paul's voice stirred inside of me. I wanted to explore that feeling further. Somehow I needed to keep Brian away from my exhibit in San Francisco next month. It was obvious that Paul and Brian should never meet.

We drove out of Nairobi and began the southeast leg of our journey toward Tsavo National Park in Kenya where we could look across the border into Tanzania at Kilimanjaro. Brian pouted and made his jealousy obvious as we drove south. The road was well traveled with many people accessing the volcano from Nairobi via this thoroughfare. I watched patiently for the mountain to come closer and to see any wildlife along the way. About ten miles south of Nairobi, I spotted something more captivating than the mountain. Five adult elephants and two of their young were walking together. They didn't seem to mind the sporadic parade of vans maneuvering through the mud, revving their engines in the process.

"Stop!" I cried far too loudly.

Brian directed the driver to stop the van. The driver pulled the thin framed vehicle onto the bank of rocks at the edge of the road. I jumped out and began shooting as soon as my feet hit the soil. I zoomed, clicked, refocused, zoomed, changed angles and shutter speed. Mount Kilimanjaro peeked out in the background, making a perfect backdrop for capturing the giants. I quickly changed the filter to one that sharpens the images for bright light. The elephants cooperated, walking towards me.

I knew that elephants were dangerous beasts, causing many human deaths in Africa, but these giants looked happy, playful and non-threatening. Remembering my feeling of dread this morning, I took my steps towards them cautiously, feeling vulnerable in size and speed. I felt very pleased for the photos taken. As I turned towards the van, Leboo pointed behind me, urging me to turn around. I spun my head to see if my life was in peril only to witness an adult elephant brushing a younger one with its trunk. I lifted my camera, but I missed the shot. Disappointed, I reminded myself that many of the best moments in life have to be recorded on the film in our minds, because we won't always be pointing a camera.

Brian switched places with the driver and pulled the van back onto the road. He steadied our speed on the rugged road as a large jeep approached from behind. The driver wanted to pass us, but a truck drove towards us from the other direction. The jeep driver appeared to be impatient. I stood up to see if I could get a shot of the elephants in the distance, testing my trusty camera with the movement. I clicked the shutter and looked in the display window. Not too bad, but definitely a little blurry. I adjusted the shutter speed and pointed my instrument again. I obtained a decent shot.

Brian spoke in a concerned tone, "Sit down Dee. It's not safe to stand while we're on the road."

With the driver of the jeep still impatient on our tail, I decided that before I sat down, I would take a picture of the annoyed driver behind us. I looked through my lens and closed the shutter. The driver gave me a grumpy scowl and stomped his foot onto the gas pedal.

Brian turned around and reached for my leg. He grabbed my shorts. "Dee!" he said pleading. Just then the jeep bumped into the back of our van. I tried to catch my balance so I could sit down, when I heard Brian shout, "Look out!" I turned to the front and realized that the bump from the jeep sent us into the oncoming truck. I thought, "We are going to be hit," before I'd enough time to move a muscle. The delivery truck hit our van head-on. My body flew forward, then back. I felt Leboo hold my legs. It seemed that the van fell onto its side, but I wasn't sure what was happening. My final thought was, I have to make it home. And then everything went dark.

In mere seconds it was over and I knew nothing of Kenya and Leboo; only white light, fractured with changing colors. I floated, drifting like falling snow, in a colorful sea of complete calm and love, without a care. Everything was perfect. I felt no worries, no concerns for getting home, no interest in how my body was or if I were well. I enjoyed the serene pool of euphoria, suspended, weightless, at ease and at peace. It was a place I could stay forever. I had no desire to know what happened. I had no desires at all. I was bathed in happiness.

Without any concept of time passing, suddenly the stillness came to an abrupt halt. I tried to open my sand filled eyes, but nothing came into focus. Through small slits, I detected a bright sun beating upon me. I tasted the rich, wet, gritty earth coating my tongue. My limbs would not move. Thirst scratched at my throat. I couldn't feel my hands or feet. I couldn't tell what was happening. Vaguely it seemed as though people were pulling on me, lifting me, shouting, and moving me. But it was as if that was off in the distance. I didn't know if it was real.

Gradually, I slid sideways down an imaginary slope into a peaceful sea of pleasure. A dreamy sunset appeared, similar to the one I remembered from the Eiffel Tower in Paris. I saw Paris and the view from the Eiffel tower. I heard the sounds and smelled the smells of Paris. In the sky above purples danced and traded places with red and orange. Blue intertwined between shades of pink. I merged with the colors. Together we became one sea of bliss and beauty. Africa faded away as I floated in the waters of tranquility. I wondered, *Is this my last sunset?*

   ***

Chapter Two: **Exploding Sky**

Paris, France. New Year's Eve, 1898

From the Eiffel Tower I floated slowly over the landscape of Paris, peering down upon familiar monuments and parks. This Paris was far different than the one I saw on my recent visit. Instead of new, modern buildings, this Paris was ornate and historic; it was the Paris of the past. Horses with carriages stepped slowly through the streets; a strong juxtapose to the automobiles I saw racing around the city last time I was here. The men wore dark suits and coats while the women donned long skirts and elaborate hats.

Despite the remarkable difference from my last visit, Paris felt incredibly familiar, as if it were native to me. Slowly I floated down to the ground and stood on a sidewalk lined with bare trees facing a beautiful bridge whose sides were made of thick, detailed carved stone. Strolling along the street, I knew I was making my way toward home. I passed the Louvre, while the winter sky dripped a light rain. Strolling merrily along the recognizable streets lined with bare branches and manicured evergreens. I opened my mouth and let raindrops fall cool against my tongue. In the center of the long bridge, I twirled in circles with delight as my long coat and full length skirt spun out wide.

Instinctively, I turned left. The street looked familiar. When I saw the street sign, Quai Voltaire, I knew I was nearly home.

I grasped the door handle and pushed it open, feeling certain that this was my front door. I walked past the parlor to the kitchen where the housemaid was preparing croissants and beef stew. The aroma of the glazed meat caramelizing, whet my ravenous appetite. I took a grape from the counter and popped it into my mouth.

My mother spoke as she entered the kitchen. "Cherie, don't forget about the party tonight. That dinner is for tomorrow. Save your appetite." My name was Cherie. Yes, this felt right.

"I'm not going to the party," I said a little surprised as the words exited my mouth.

"You most definitely are going."

"Do not make me do this Mother. I loathe these ridiculous parties. Why must I be subjected to hours of boasting from YOUR friends? Mother, please grant me this New Year's Eve to myself, I beg you. I'm eighteen. Allow me to make my own choice. This is my life, not yours!"

"My child, you never stop with your selfishness. This whole world is not all about you. There are others to consider. You must not live your entire life as if no one matters except yourself. Think of André, working hard at Law School. He would be happy to attend a party instead of studying for exams. His grandparents shall be attending this evening celebration and they will wish to meet you, their future granddaughter-in-law. What would André want for you to do this night?"

"Perhaps you're content to go about your day pleasing everyone except yourself, Mother. I will not sacrifice my desires for the pleasure of others. My life will be lived differently than yours."

"Cherie, you're childish. You will grow up and learn that in order to survive in the world you must cooperate with the people around you. You cannot have every simple wish of your young, naïve heart. You do not live alone in this world."

"We shall see Mother, if I'm naïve or simply strong enough to follow my own passions."

"Indeed we shall. Now, put on the new dress I bought for you. We leave at seven. Wear your red, long coat. There's quite a chill. Bring your overnight case; we are staying until tomorrow. It's too far to travel home tonight after midnight in this cold."

"Argh!" I looked at my mother with an angry pout, wishing to make her feel guilty. She ignored my expression and walked away. When the argument began I knew I would likely fail to get my way; but it was worth a try.

This Paris dream is amazing. It feels as real as it possibly could.

At seven in the evening, I presented my emphatic pout at the front door where my parents were waiting. They both ignored my look and turned to walk out. This meant that my mother had prepared my father for my resistance. He should at least be compassionate that I was upset. She had obviously requested that he have no reaction. This fueled my anger, for the one thing I appreciated most in my home was my father's soft heart for me. His gentle compassion made life more bearable.

We rode quietly together in the closed carriage that helped guard against the bite of the winter air. The horses pranced obediently forward with their noses cutting through the damp night. I continued to pout while my anger thicken the air in the small, carriage cabin.

An hour later, I entered the country mansion of Jacques and Martine Soule, stepping under a large French flag hung above the double door threshold. Immediately my parents were embraced by familiar guests and the hostess, Martine. Martine embraced me as well, kissing my cheeks. "Darling, I'm pleased to have you. I hope you do not find my little party too boring."

"Happy New Year, Auntie. Your party's a perfect opportunity for me to see you," I lied, dreading the next twelve hours.

"Oh, my sweet child, you must come visit more often. We have much to catch up on. Have you seen the ballet recently?"

"Not recent enough. Would you like to attend the ballet with me?" I asked. "I would much prefer to have you all to myself, rather than just see glimpses of you tonight."

"Of course, I would love to my dear. Let us go next week. I will arrange everything. You don't worry about a thing." Martine and I had a wonderful connection, as if she were my real aunt. We enjoyed many of the same things. She always treated me like family.

I glanced around the estate that I visited occasionally. The mansion was adorned with Parisian finery. Painting by masters adorned every available wall. Richly woven fabric draped the floor to ceiling windows, complementing the Persian rugs covering the tile and wood floors.

Inside I found the same crowd from other parties, clothed in their finery and garb. On this winter evening, some of Paris' wealthiest or most educated citizens moved about the three hundred year old estate. Their elaborate apparel fascinated me.

One woman over emphasized every element of popular dress. The bustle on her bottom stuck out from twin pillows hiding under her skirt, while her bosom protruded, clamoring to escape her bodice. Several feathers from some tropical bird adorned her bright red hat, covering her coiffure, held in place stiffly, as if it were wood. Buttons and pearls on her sleeve cuffs nearly hid the fabric, while lace draped over her velvet skirt, which dragged two feet behind her. Her laughter drowned out even the string quartet.

It amused me to look around the room and watch the party goers reveal themselves with their eyes, lips and clothing. The more outspoken the clothing, the more boisterous it made the wearer. Long, bustled skirts swished to and fro, as if each woman were meant to outdo the others. The men wore variations of the same suit, with white, pressed shirts, tightly drawn ties and dark, long dress coats over slacks.

The large hall echoed with laughter, music and conversation. Well-dressed Frenchmen talked above the sonata while holding their champagne glasses casually. There wasn't a single soul with whom I wished to visit, except the busy hostess. Friends of my parents greeted me politely, before gliding away looking for a peer.

Although I would rather have celebrated the coming of the New Year with a hot bath, writing in my journal, at least attending this party had one advantage, Jacques and Martine ensured that their guest enjoyed the finest of everything. They served Bordeaux, Burgundy, Chardonnay and Champagne with excellent cuisine. On the menu were many of my favorites: beef bourguignon, French bread, pastries, chocolate cake, dates, mints, carrot bread, pound cake and fudge.

I enjoyed a delicious plate of bon bons and a glass of Bordeaux. Afterwards, there was nothing to do except watch the hours pass. The terrace seemed a suitable escape and an opportunity for fresher air. Making my way through the crowd of fine fabric and brandiedy breath, I noticed a man watching. My breath quickened as I felt his eyes scan over me. I straightened my posture and ignored his stare. Jean-Paul Soule stepped back into the shadow at the top of the grand staircase overlooking the parlor. He seemed to perceive my pause. A great distance was between us, but it felt as if there were none.

Slowly I turned my head to look away, and I walked towards the terrace. Just as I'd hoped, he followed after me. As I opened the door to the terrace, I noticed that Jacques and my father interrupted his intended path. The thought of the conversation that might ensue if my father knew that Jean-Paul was following me, made me smile. Stepping into the cool night, I tilted my head back to gaze at the shimmering sky. Moments later I heard the terrace door open. The handsome man took a few steps towards me.

"Are you chilled Mademoiselle?" he asked.

"Not especially, merci. It's more pleasant to stand amidst these frosty trees than in rooms filled with stale air."

He stood staring at me for a moment. Finally he spoke. "It has been a while since I have seen you. You have grown into a young woman."

"What did you expect?"

"True, a wise man might anticipate that a young woman would mature. However, your elegance has caught me by surprise."

"How do you mean, sir? Why are you surprised?"

"I didn't anticipate the effect your maturity would have upon me."

"Oh," I replied casually. "Of which effect do you speak?"

"I have always known you to be a young girl. Now that you're a young woman I feel that I don't know you at all."

"In that case, allow me to introduce myself. I'm Cherish Bourguignon, the only child of Michel and Catherine Bourguignon. You, fine sir, may call me as my parents do, Cherie. Pleased to meet you Monsieur. And you are?"

"Captivated...and delighted to be sure." I smiled and blushed at the same time. Jean-Paul was present on many of my previous visits to see Martine, but we had rarely spoken. He was seven years my senior and we had little reason to converse. Jean-Paul had a strong frame, with distinctive features. He was strikingly

24

handsome. Since I was sixteen I had admired him, with no hope of enjoying anything other than distant fancy. He was a man and I was a girl; a girl betrothed to her parent's best friend's son.

"Your father and I spoke inside. He's quite the stern man and somewhat intimidating. He adores you to be certain. He doesn't seem to think that highly of me it would seem; definitely not enough to allow me to court his now mature daughter."

Jean-Paul's remarks surprised me. Our playful conversation had turned serious quite suddenly. I wasn't prepared to be serious, so I kept the conversation light. "Are you not up for a challenge? It may be easier than you perceive to impress my father. I will share a secret. He intimidates everyone. Perhaps it's his intellect and his reputation of a great professor. It's also his silence. He listens far more than he speaks. He does not always reveal what he's thinking, and this is daunting to many men. It may not be as difficult as you thought. That's of course if there were a reason to make the effort."

"Believe me when I say to you, there's a reason, for you have intrigued me more than anyone I have ever laid eyes upon."

Looking at Jean-Paul, I saw him differently for the first time. Prior to this evening, he seemed like an attractive masculine essence, far from my reach. All at once he was before me, teasing me with the idea of courtship? Could this be real? Could I become the object of Jean-Paul's affection? What about André?

"I regret to tell you that there is an obstacle in your path. It's only fair to tell you."

"Oh? What is this great obstacle which must I face?"

"My parents have fixed in their minds that I must wed André Monet."

Jean-Paul stood silently. He stared at me for a moment, then gazed off into the black night. He looked strong and masculine in the dim light. He turned his gaze straight into mine. "André Monet? Do I know of him?"

"He's the son of Bernard and Astrid Monet. Apparently his grandparents are here tonight. I have yet to meet them."

"I do not remember him. Forgive me for being bold, for this is not my place to ask. Are you pleased with the arrangement?"

"Quite the opposite actually."

"Your parents must have good reason to make the arrangement. I'm sorry, Mademoiselle, it's not appropriate for me to be here. I bid you good night, my fair lady." He turned from me towards the door.

"Monsieur?"

He turned his head around slowly, with his body still facing the door, giving me a kind, thoughtful look, "Yes, mademoiselle?"

"May I ask something of you?"

"Oui, you may."

"Provide me company this night. I haven't a soul with whom to speak and I must be here all night. I do not wish to spend this evening speaking with other guests. My parents and I are staying until morning, as your family tradition allows. I entreat you."

He paused briefly, as if quickly considering all that my request entailed. "As you wish."

My heart jumped with excitement. "Thank you, you are very kind."

"Where is your betrothed this evening?"

"He is away studying law at the University of Aix-Marseille III. He has been away at the university for three years."

"Very well, let us not speak of André. Do you enjoy the stars?"

Something in his voice touched me deeply. I wanted to be near him. "Most certainly I do. I love to watch them sparkle, like a deep sea at night with dancing waves of moonlight." I drew in a deep breath, trying to hide my nervousness. Each time I engaged his eyes, my tongue was tied up in wonder and my breath quickened.

"Have you seen the ocean, at nightfall?" Jean-Paul's eyes left my face and looked down the length of my body and up again. The guilt in his eyes was obvious, but I enjoyed his examining glance.

"I have. My mother's sister lives at Le Havre. We visited her and I stared at the sea for hours while the moon shone brightly."

"Le Havre, I know this place. That's where the great ships leave to cross the sea. I expect to be on one of those boats, perhaps later this year to cross the ocean and live in America."

Suddenly I was intrigued. What a daring thing to do to leave France and settle in a foreign land, I thought. I was an adventurous girl and yet I'd never thought of doing something as courageous. I found myself having new respect for the man. "How spirited of you."

"Spirited? That is not an accurate description."

"Why not? It's a daring thing to consider."

"I'm leaving France to assist my uncle in expanding his tea and coffee trade. He made me a good offer and my new position will help his business a great deal. Martine and Jacques have done much for me. I wish to repay them. You may know that my parents died of influenza when I was eight years old. Jacques and Martine raised me as one of their own children and provided all that I needed. I feel an obligation to help them."

"Then why the heavy heart?"

"You see ma cherie, in my soul, I'm a painter. This is who I am. Paris is the best place in the world to be a painter. I do not wish to leave the most divine, inspirational city in the world."

"I see. However, in France there are many accomplished artists. Your skills are less common in America. Other countries need good artists as well as Paris. The potential to be recognized could be greater."

"Thank you for your encouragement my lady. You are very kind." He smiled again and my heart melted another layer. We stood there on the terrace until my toes froze and my fingers hurt from the cold. He pointed out Orion's Belt, the Big Dipper, the Little Dipper, the Seven Sisters and other constellations. I pretended that he was teaching me something new. Although the cold closed in on me, I didn't want to re-engage with the boisterous partygoers. I did, however, want to see what Jean-Paul liked to paint.

"May I see some of your work?"

"You may. A few pieces are displayed throughout the house. I also have a studio for painting upstairs with some new pieces. I would be honored to show you. We must get an escort. My cousin Marion would be happy to accompany me."

"Must we really have an escort?"

"Mademoiselle, we should not be seen alone. It would be improper under the circumstances."

"Who's to know?"

Jean-Paul was quiet while he contemplated the ramifications. As I watched him shuffle thoughts around in his head, I enjoyed the idea of sneaking off together; doing what I wanted instead of what my mother wished. Jean-Paul answered carefully, speaking as if he were giving directions. "It's possible to enter the home from the north entrance, but that requires going around the east side to the north. We must walk in the dark through the garden. Is this comfortable to you?"

The moon was nearly full and disappeared for only short periods behind sparse clouds. "The moon's bright enough. Please Jean-Paul, guide the way."

We walked to the edge of the terrace. "Be mindful of these stairs, allow me to assist you." When my hand found his, tingling waves pulsed through my body. He held my hand gently and properly, without a full embrace, although it felt as if he held my whole body at once. A soft shudder gently shook my body. I hoped that he hadn't detected it.

After the last step, he let go of my hand and gently took ahold of my left elbow. "It's this way, mademoiselle." He spoke softly as he directed me across the grass to a set of steps leading up to the house. The soft moonlight cast deep shadows of dark, bottomless holes. His hand slid down my arm and found my fingers once again. He led me up the stairs and through a tall wooden door. We walked down a large unlit hallway. The mystery and excitement of tiptoeing through the darkness together was fun, like two lovers stealing time to be alone. We turned down a maze of corridors. I knew I would never find my way out without his assistance. When we arrived at a tall, carved panel door near the end of the hall, he graciously held the door open and allowed me to enter first. He lit several candles in the room. The room grew brighter while the surroundings emerged like children coming out of hiding.

I looked. I studied. His work amazed me. I witnessed magnificent art before me. His style was realistic with a strong talent for showing emotion. "Jean-Paul, your paintings are powerful and cause many emotions to stir." I stood transfixed on one painting in particular. Softly I spoke, "This woman is full of sorrow. Her pain wrenches my heart enough to make me cry. It feels as if…I am looking at myself, although I can't imagine why." My breathing stopped as a cold chill froze me in place. The heart of this woman was breaking, without love to comfort her. Her suffering overcame me, as if her agony could steal my life. I tried to shake the feeling of dread that the painting stirred. I didn't want to own this woman's plight, although perhaps I already did.

Fortunately, Jean-Paul's other paintings didn't pierce my heart as deeply as the first, even though they were inspiring expressions. I caught my breath and shook my head quickly. "Your work is impressive. Your passion is obvious, as well as your skill. Paris is where you belong, among the best artists in the world."

"Perhaps, but it's not meant to be. I must serve my family."

"Forgive me for being direct Jean-Paul. Your uncle would seem to be doing well financially without your assistance. One can merely look around to see this. Why not live your dreams and make your life your own?"

"Do not let your eyes deceive you. Jacques inherited this estate and it was in some disarray. He's a generous man who helps his family in need. His wealth is certainly more than average, but not more, perhaps, than your own family, except for this grand estate given him by his deceased parents. He has done everything for me, provided me a family when I had none. How ungrateful would I be to let him down?"

Jean-Paul paused in deep reflection. Then he spoke in a serious tone. "It's because of Jacques that I paint. When I was a boy living with Jacques and Martine, I desperately missed my mother. I missed her tucking me in to bed at night. I longed for the look she gave me when I said something she didn't quite understand; her inquisitive expression, with a slight tilt of her head and a crease in her brow. I pined for my mother's warm touch and approval, especially went she cupped her hand over the back of my head to pet my hair. I craved her gentleness with me, her voice and her flowing hair.

29

"I also missed walking to the market with Papa to get tobacco and wood. I missed watching him work in his shop creating enchanting things from wood with his tools. I wanted to be like my papa and craft toys magically.

"My presence in her home reminded Aunt Martine of her deceased younger sister. She would tell me, 'You're a big boy. You must be strong and brave. You're lucky to live through this plague. God saved you for a reason.'

"I didn't want to be big and I was certain that I wasn't lucky. Aunt Martine would tell me, 'Mummy and Papa are in Heaven with God. God needed them to go home and he needs you to be here with us. God asked me to take good care of you. I will do my very best.' I began to resent God for having my parents when I did not.

"Over time I forgot how my mother's cooking smelled and the expressions she wore. I forgot what my father's tools looked like and the wonderful things he crafted. I could not remember his shop.

"One day I attempted to draw the pain that was taxing my heart. It felt good to release my ache. The next day I asked Jacques for paint. He traveled to Paris and bought me eight colors and several canvases. 'Paint to your heart's content my boy,' he said with love. The best way to release the deep pain in my soul was to stroke the canvas with reds, grays, black, yellows and blues. I grew up mixing colors in an effort to capture my mother's face, that I might see her again. Although I suffered sadness, I owe everything I have left to Jacques and Martine."

"Forgive me for meddling. Certainly I know nothing of what I speak. Yet I do know that your abilities with a brush are far beyond what an average artist can do. It would be a shame to not have Paris and all the world know of your skill." I may have been selfish in my statements, as I was beginning to feel that Jean-Paul should stay in Paris for my own reasons

"If it be God's will then my work shall grace the walls of museums."

"Well, then I pray that God loves your art. But if God doesn't help you, then I will. I need just such a cause to help me forget my own…" I paused, wondering how that slipped out.

"Yes. You were saying? Forget your own what?"

I wasn't sure if it was safe to share my passion with this man. But what did I have to lose? If sharing my dreams separated me from Jean-Paul, then it were meant to be. He smiled a soft grin at me as if we were sharing a secret just between us that could be communicated with our eyes and quiet lips. I decided to tell him what I'd shared with no one, except my mother. "My passion is dance Jean-Paul. I love ballet and have dreamed of performing."

"Really, ballet, what do you love about it?"

His question was curious to me, but I felt that he was reading my excitement and wanted to hear more. "When I was a small girl my mother allowed me to take ballet classes. She thought it to be an excellent way to develop grace."

"How old were you?"

"I was five. Ballerinas were the most beautiful women that I'd ever seen. I wanted to be like them. I loved going to class. Dancing made me feel beautiful. When I moved my body in slow, graceful motions, I experienced a control that I didn't have when I was with my mother. I entered my own world where I was my own master. Every twist of my hand or tilt of my head was calculated and controlled by my will. It empowered me."

"I see, and your family doesn't support your dreams?"

"Of course not. When I told my mother that I wanted to be on stage, she made me quit as soon as I said it. I was eleven. A lady of my upbringing would never dance, she told me. We are spectators, as my parents said. It's beneath us to parade on stage to be seen in such a way and also be judged by our peers. My only choice was to fantasize." Jean-Paul and I were quiet for a moment, staring off in the soft light of the candles. I finally broke the pensive silence. "I love art, freedom, and creativity. If we cannot express who we are, then we are inauthentic, and life is full of heartache."

"You make such an impression on me Mademoiselle. Your passionate appreciation for art is inspiring. If there is a way in which you may assist me, then I shall certainly be happy to receive it." We both smiled. Uncertain of how I could spread the knowledge of Jean-Paul's considerable talent, I felt happy to be connected to him through my offer. "We should return to the terrace, so that our absence is not noticed," Jean-Paul said.

We made our way back through the maze of corridors and into the dark garden. Once again Jean-Paul politely assisted me up the steps. At the top step to the terrace I thought there was one more and I raised my leg up to reach the non-existing step. We both laughed when my foot came down upon the flat surface next to my other foot. Our laughter was interrupted. "Cherie!" My mother's voice cut the crisp air like a sharp knife. I swallowed hard, nearly choking on my laughter.

"Hello Mother. Happy New Year," I added with cheer.

"Where did you go off to?"

Jean-Paul and I were both silent for a long second. Then we both spoke at the same moment. I raised my voice above his, speaking clearly with confidence. "Mother, you know Monsieur Soule, nephew of Jacques and Martine. He's familiar with astrology and we stepped off the terrace to see if we could find the constellation Aquarius. I apologize for our absence Mother. It was at my insistence, you can be certain."

"I have no doubt Cherie, regarding your insistence. Do you realize the inappropriateness of your absence? André's grandparents have been asking to see you. I took them around the party and to the terrace in search of you. It is unseemly that you are alone in the darkness with a man. You embarrass me."

"You embarrass me at this moment Mother. Nothing untoward has taken place. Please tell André's grandparents that I was in the washroom. There's no need for alarm."

"You may tell them yourself Cherie. They are sitting on the other end of the terrace." My mother walked across the terrace to a couple I'd not noticed. They were bundled together on a stone bench which had a soft cushion cover added for the evening's events. "Monsieur and Madam Monet, please meet my daughter, Cherish Bourguignon." I froze as the couple walked towards me, sober and quite formally. The older man bowed his head and said, "Mademoiselle." I extended my right hand, palm down which he took in his hand and brought to his right cheek, not kissing my hand, but in a gesture of how a stranger greets a child or very young girl.

32

"Monsieur," I replied.

I turned to look at the woman. She didn't turn her face directly at me. Her chin was down. She glared at me with a frown through the top of her eyes. It seemed as though she could look right through me. Perhaps she could see my interest in Jean-Paul. Maybe she could see that I was a rebellious girl, unwilling to have the world constrain me through society's conventions. If I couldn't be free, then I may as well be dead. This woman seemed as if she knew all of that with her disapproving stare. "Madame," I said as politely as possible. She nodded her head and softened her expression.

I could not know what they had heard of our conversation, but had to assume they heard all of it. I tried not to care what they thought. It was not as though my small misbehavior was going to change anything. The fact was that my parents were determined to have me marry André.

They shared this fateful plan with me when I was eleven years old. At that time, André was thirteen. He was changing into a young man. It seemed plausible that he could be my husband. If not André, my childhood playmate, then who would I marry, I wondered? The question of who I would marry seemed far more important, at that tender age, than if I would want to marry André one day. I'd not thought of what it would be like to kiss André, or sit at dinner with him night after night. For my young self it seemed like a simple answer to the perplexing question of my future. It was perfect that our parents were best friends and enjoyed dinners together. Our fathers both taught at the University. But as I approached adulthood, the idea had less and less appeal.

Yes, André was my friend. But spending time with him didn't feel exciting. Kissing him had no appeal to me. Each summer when he returned from the University, he had tried to meet his lips with mine. I would always turn my head and tell him that I wasn't ready. The truth, however, was that I didn't feel attracted to him. Then this last fall as he departed for another year at Aix-Marseille III, he insisted on a goodbye kiss. I didn't see a way out of it and I was curious. I allowed André to draw me in and smother me with his mouth. I attempted my best effort at returned affection, my first ever. The feeling was best described like kissing my cousin, more inappropriate than exciting or lovely. Since that encounter, I dreaded the day that I would be wed to André. What seemed like a simple answer at age eleven, felt like being sent to prison at age eighteen.

I told my mother that kissing André was like kissing a stone. She insisted that love was something that you decided to do and it grew overtime as two people took care of one another. That seemed boring to me. I wanted excitement, passion, desire. I could feel that there was more to love than finances and associations. My body told me that I wanted a man's touch. I craved to close my eyes and allow a man's lips to know every area of my body. I wanted to be vulnerable emotionally and naked before a man who desired me above all others, and not because his parents told him to do so.

I needed to convince my mother to allow me to make my own choice for a husband. If I could not live my own life then life would be hell. My mother was stubborn and followed tradition. I was stubborn too, but we were opposites and we both knew it.

Jean-Paul introduced himself to André's grandparents and the tension in the air thickened. I wanted to run to away. My mother suggested that we all go inside, out of the chill. I requested that I remain outside, but she insisted with her lips firm against one another and her eyes as wide as an owl.

A plan formed in my head. If I sat pouting in the corner for a while she may tire of watching me and leave me be for a spell. I excused myself to sit by the fire to warm up. She allowed me to sit alone, but she watched that Jean-Paul did not follow me. When she wasn't looking, my eyes met Jean-Paul's. I offered a soft smile and slight nod. The opportunity to speak again did not present itself until right before the fireworks. The house was a bustle of commotion as people gathered their fine coats to cover their exquisite apparel and skin against the cold and watch a tradition of Jacques's and Martine's. They always brought in the New Year with a blast of rockets and Roman candles. Jean-Paul walked up to me and said, "You have an adorable pout."

I looked back at him in shock, and then chuckled. He smiled that secret grin at me again.

"Jean-Paul, Jacques is waiting for your help with the fireworks. Hurry," Martine said.

The crowd was enthralled with the pyrotechnics. At midnight people shouted, kissed and clapped in appreciation. I thought the moment was spectacular. The only thing missing was Jean-Paul beside me.

Jacques and Martine had a tradition of inviting guests to stay for the night and enjoy the sunrise rather than take the long ride back to Paris in the cold, dark night. My parents had prepared to stay the night and suddenly that seemed like a wonderful idea. I enjoyed the thought of seeing Jean-Paul the next day.

As the guests made their way into the house to receive their assigned rooms or say their goodbyes, Jean-Paul walked towards me on the terrace. "Is your family staying until morning mademoiselle?"

"We are."

"Very well, I bid you a good night's rest." He took my hand in his and gently held it under his lips. As he lowered our hands he softly folded mine around a note of paper and let go. Then he turned away. I realized the nature of the note was just between us. I was careful not to expose it to anyone. I went straight away to the washroom and held the note under the candlelight. It simply said, "*If you would enjoy watching the sunrise from a particularly beautiful place in the gardens, then join me at 7:00 AM at the back entrance and I shall take you there. Sincerely, Jean-Paul.*"

I held the paper to my heart and smiled, not understanding the full meaning of my emotions. I hid the paper in my coat pocket for safe keeping to read again later. That night I struggled to fall asleep as I reviewed the night's events in my mind. Finally I slept a dreamless night, smiling in anticipation of what tomorrow would bring.

***

Chapter Three: **A Sky Surprise**

Outside of Paris, New Year's Day 1899

In the morning I awakened refreshed, but nervous. Upon lighting the bed lamp, the small clock on the wall announced it was six a.m. There was plenty of time to freshen up and dress while I came up with a good story to tell mother. She would believe me if I told her that I had a headache and I needed some time alone to feel better. She would tell me to consume less wine and would leave me alone while she visited with the guests. I smiled, realizing I had a flawless plan.

Mother visited with Martine in the kitchen. When I told mother and Martine that I was not feeling well and needed to be alone, Martine immediately wanted to nurse my aching head with teas and tinctures. "Quiet is what I need the most," I reassured her. They both were convinced and they went on visiting.

At seven o'clock I stepped out the back entrance of the chateau. Jean-Paul was already waiting. "Bonjour Mademoiselle, I pray you slept well."

"Apparently I did. I do not remember a thing."

"I'm pleased to hear it," Jean-Paul said sounding eager. My whole body tingled. I nearly held my breath. "Follow me." Jean-Paul held a lantern in his right hand at chest level. With his left hand he took my fingers, as if we were dancing, and guided me through the grass. As we walked, the sky began to reveal the horizon with a faint blue-glowing outline. After we walked a few minutes, Jean-Paul stopped and gently took my arm. "There's a log here," he said guiding my arm and shining the lantern at the tree trunk. I examined the log with my hand for a safe place to sit and noticed it was smoothed on top by someone's handy work. I wondered if Jean-Paul had crafted the bench.

Jean-Paul sat next to me. Looking straight ahead, he spoke quietly. "The only person I have ever brought here to watch the sunrise is Jacques." He paused but I didn't say anything. "Thank you for coming this morning."

"Thank you for the invitation."

We sat quietly for a moment. Then Jean-Paul asked, "What do you plan to do about André?"

I was surprised that he broached the topic so quickly. "I plan to convince my mother that I'm not going to marry André."

"You are a resolute young woman," Jean-Paul said.

"What are my options, dear sir? I'm forced to choose between pleasing my family or being happy. I must choose my happiness. I cannot live any other way. Would you not do the same?"

"It is not my place to tell you how to live your life Cherie. How could I advise you? I'm choosing to sell tea and coffee abroad to help my aunt and uncle while my paintings take a second position to my family's needs. I do not say that one road is good or bad. I'm simply observing the courage it takes to lead with your heart."

Silently I contemplated his decision. We were different, Jean-Paul and I. He felt a duty to the people who raised him. I felt a duty to myself.

The sky shifted before us while we sat quietly.

A shiver came over me as my mind contemplated many thoughts in the brisk morning air.

"Are you chilled?" Jean-Paul asked.

"Apparently I am."

"Please, take my jacket."

"No, then you will be cold."

"Perhaps a little, but I would have the reward of chivalry, which is worth the price of a few chills. Please, I insist."

Jean-Paul wrapped his large jacket over my shoulders. His hands lingered at my shoulder. I reached for the collar to pull the jacket down and our hands touched briefly, which quickened my breath.

As the sun neared the horizon, the sky appeared like a normal January morning, with subtle, powerful colors interacting in the atmosphere. But as the orb showed its full disc, I looked more carefully. I closed my eyes to blink and reopened them, bewildered. Jean-Paul and I looked at each other with puzzlement. We stared back at the sky. The sun shone its vibrant yellow, illuminating the dispersed clouds while shooting far reaching rays of light in a great arc. The vapor directly above the sun glowed fiery orange, topped with a purplish gray. Above and behind the grey sat a rich, deep purple. To the left and right of the rising ball of fire, lenticular clouds glowed yellow, orange, pink and purple. Above them were puffs of wide mists. They were purple with a velvet red glowing outline at the bottom. A sea-blue backdrop peeked out behind the rainbow of color woven together like a rich tapestry. Far in the distance, evergreens atop hillsides were illuminated, revealing their presence.

"I've never seen the sky do that," I said.

"This is the most spectacular sunrise I have ever observed."

I glanced at Jean-Paul's face as he stared in a trance at the mesmerizing firmament. I looked back at the sun in wonder. The rest of the world melted away, as if the sky, Jean-Paul and I were all that existed. I didn't remember the home behind us full of guests. My parents never crossed my mind. I was immersed, deep in the beauty of dawn. It was a magic that eluded description. I held myself there, embracing the moment. I wanted to relish and prolong the moment.

All at once, Jean-Paul reached his arm around me, holding my arm in his hand and pressing me close to him. It was a gesture of sharing the enchantment of the moment. But as he realized his proximity to me, he froze. We were suddenly close and swimming in the scent and emotion of each other. He looked into my eyes for a long second. Then he closed the gap between us, finding my lips with his in a brief, gentle, meaningful kiss. My lips responded, receiving his and pressing back. A wave of pleasure rushed through me. In that moment, I understood what a kiss should feel like: passion, desire, surrender, in selfless compassion. Jean-Paul pulled his lips back slowly, still holding me close with one arm.

Gazing into my eyes he said, "Forgive me, mademoiselle. I could not stop myself. The…sunrise…and your…"

"Shhh," I said out of breath, "That was lovely. Please do not apologize."

Jean-Paul nodded. He removed his hand slowly from around me. We sat side by side in silence as blue took over and dominated the heavens.

"There you are."

I heard my mother's voice and I nearly jumped out of my skin.

"You must be feeling better. I see you found someone to keep you company after all."

"Hello Mother. Jean-Paul offered to show me this..."

"We are going home now Cherie. Au revoir, Monsieur Soule," mother said abruptly.

Jean-Paul stood and faced my mother. "Au revoir, Madam," Jean-Paul replied.

I looked at Jean-Paul with a slight smile. "Au revoir Jean-Paul," I said. "Thank you for...this morning." Our eyes locked briefly.

"Come, Cherie."

I walked away with my mother, wishing that Jean-Paul would do something to save me from my fate, but he watched me go, standing still in the garden, without his coat. "His coat, Mother." We turned back.

"Keep it for the ride home. I shall retrieve it another day. Please!" Mother and I turned to go. I was pleased that she didn't say a word.

We barely spoke on the long ride back into Paris. While it was quiet in the carriage, I thought about Jean-Paul. For the past two years I'd noticed him and he finally noticed me. How could I see him again?

***

A week passed. Each day I obsessed about my upcoming nuptial with André. My mind raced with every possible scenario with André as my husband or with Jean-Paul. I thought of dinners together, children, family gatherings and making love. Each image with André as my husband caused me more distress and frustration. My future seemed bleak with my commitment to André. I knew I must speak with my mother.

For hours I sat on my bed to develop a reason to see Jean-Paul. Perhaps he would undo the knot that held me in dark

39

disappointment. Not only might he save me from my doom, but he may also provide the love and passion I desired. The thought of missing out on great romance in exchange for the opposite, tangled my stomach into a tightly knit ball. A numbing panic clouded my head. My room felt dark, as if the walls were closing in on me. No easy solution came to my confused mind.

Seven days after the sunrise with Jean-Paul, fate intervened. Martine sent word that she had tickets for us to see the ballet. She asked me if I could meet her for coffee that day. I showed my mother the letter.

"Perhaps I shall come with you," Mother replied.

My heart jumped into my throat. I wanted to speak to Martine alone and ask about Jean-Paul. "Mother, you always protest that Martine and I discuss the things you don't wish to hear about. How may I have the conversation that I desire if you're complaining?"

"Martine and I can visit and then I shall listen quietly while you discuss the ballet."

"Mother, I did not want to mention this, but Martine told me at her party that she wanted to discuss a party for your fiftieth birthday and a present. I didn't want to mention this to you, but you keep on insisting. Now you're ruining a perfectly good surprise."

"But my birthday is not until June," Mother protested.

"You know Martine. She plans these affairs far in advance. She's to have things shipped in, an must order necessary items in January."

"Very well, if you insist that she wants to surprise me for my birthday."

"Mother, why else would Martine not invite you to join us for coffee?"

Mother relented, much to my relief.

I arrived for coffee at our favorite afternoon restaurant, La Vie en Rose. Martine and preferred the large white and yellow-striped, cushioned chairs that gave us a restful posture. There were only a handful of tables with the chairs we liked, but Martine must have pulled some strings, for without fail we were given a puffy chair in which to enjoy our coffee and cake.

I gave Martine a wide, genuine smile. We ordered our favorite coffee and began to visit. Once we had discussed the latest news and updates about our families, we talked about the upcoming ballet. Then I had the courage to ask Martine the question nagging me. "Auntie Martine?" I always called her auntie when I wanted something from her. She knew this, but indulged me anyway. "Is it possible to ask Jean-Paul to attend the ballet with us?"

"I was wondering if you might speak of Jean-Paul. You know my child that you have made the boy nearly sick."

"What?!"

"Oh my...the poor man. He broods about the house for the full week now. How to comfort him eludes me. I thought that perhaps he fancies you, but how's an old woman to know these things?" she said, winking.

A waiter brought a refill of our espresso and some lemon cakes. I waited until he left before I responded.

"Oh, Auntie Martine, what are we to do? My mother's determined that I shall marry a man that I do not love."

"My sweet Cherie, you know that I have always been fond of you. You're like a daughter to me. Jean-Paul is like my son. Nothing would please me more than to see two of my favorite young ones being happy. Allow me to speak to your mother. I met Catherine before you were born."

"Martine! You're wonderful. How may I repay you?"

Martine laughed. "Your smile is my reward child."

"Merci."

"You know Jean-Paul drove me into town. He has the carriage and is waiting for me at Galeries de Zoologie. I shall go to speak with your mother. Perhaps you could keep Jean-Paul company until I return, non?"

"I would be happy to do this, Auntie Martine."

"Very well, after our dessert we will depart. I shall meet you and Jean-Paul at the park fountain in an hour. I love you my dear."

"I treasure you, Auntie."

We enjoyed the remainder of the lemon cake and our refill of espresso. Then Martine and I departed from our favorite café to our prospective engagements. The stroll to the Jardin des Plantes was one of my favorite strolls from this café. I enjoyed the walk whenever I had the time. The street leading to the park held my attention well with my favorite dress shop, a lovely fabric dealer and a chocolate importer that sold the best chocolates from Geneva, Amsterdam, Belgium and Paris. There were often samples offered and I enjoyed comparing how each country engaged the flavors of the bitter bean.

The crisp air brushed my checks and the sun peeked out from behind high clouds as I walked towards the nearby park. Yesterday's rain had left small puddles which froze overnight. I stepped carefully to avoid slippery ice. People strolled through the frozen gardens bundled in warm coats, hats and scarves. I wore my longest coat which nearly reached to my feet. My favorite knit blue scarf wrapped my neck snuggly.

I found Jean-Paul sitting on a wood and iron bench watching pigeons enjoy some seeds outside the Galeries de Zoologie. The birds pecked at small seeds that fell between cobble stones. My high heels clicked on the firm path. Jean-Paul turned and saw my approach.

"Bonjour, Monsieur."

He turned and smiled. "Bonjour, mademoiselle," he said with a nod and a blink, still smiling with his delicious lips. "Martine asked you to come here?"

"Fortunately she did. I wanted to see you," I said.

"I have thought about you very much Cherie."

"You did?"

"Oui, but I tried hard not to," he said.

"You tried not to think of me?"

"Of course, I'm in a terrible dilemma really."

"How so?"

"I'm leaving later this year for America."

"Are you certain?"

"It's my uncle's wish. I plan to satisfy his desire."

"I see."

"I wish to spend time with you before I leave, but it seems like that would be a waste and heartache for us both."

"How do you know this?" I asked.

42

"If you knew my heart, perhaps you would fall hopelessly for me. That could be terrible. I couldn't ask you to leave Paris or your family. It would not be right."

"What about what I want? Are you to be as my mother and decide what's best for me?"

"Non, Cherie, pardon me please. I simply could not ask of you such a sacrifice."

"Then do not ask, but allow me to make my own choices."

"With all due respect, I know what it's like to live without one's parents. I've lived without mine since age eight. There's a heartache and feeling of isolation that no other love can replace. Without knowing this loss you cannot imagine it. Protecting your relations with your parents is imperative to me. I cannot be the one to jeopardize what you have."

"I hope you will not presume to know my fate or make decisions for me."

"What would you suggest?" he asked.

"I suggest that you court me. If you are as loveable as you claim, make me fall in love with you. I will know what suits me best."

"Can you maintain your deep connection with your parents if your break your engagement? Family is of the highest importance," he replied.

"Does living a truthful, happy life matter?" I asked.

"I suppose it matters, but the happiness of love heals our heart."

"My parents will be delighted enough when they know that I'm happy. This shall please them, although they may resist at first. They love me and pray for my well-being."

"If your father will allow it, I will call on you."

"If he does not, then I shall hide it from him. For I must get to know you Jean-Paul."

"Are you confident this is in your best interest and that you can sway your parents?"

"I have great confidence." My confidence was not as high as I alluded to, but hope was growing within and determination was hope's companion. I sat on the bench sideways, facing Jean-Paul. The sun peeked out between clouds. His hair caught the sunlight;

reds and browns accentuated in the bright rays. His eyes stirred warmth in me as he gazed upon my face.

"I am reluctant to compete with your parents for your affections or with their proposed suitor. However, my heart speaks powerfully to me when I am with you. Your eyes are familiar, your smile touches me deeply. If I do not learn more about you, my heart may punish me forever."

We both smiled. Jean-Paul stood and invited me to walk the gardens. Although only evergreens provided any color this time of year, the paths were inviting and strolling beside Jean-Paul allowed me to look at something other than his handsome face. I found that staring at him produced a silly smile and blushing cheeks. As we glided along, we engaged many topics: ballet, art and family. "I've known your parents vaguely for years. But I've spent little time speaking with them. Tell me more, that I may win their approval."

A gust of wind blew directly at my face. I closed my eyes to shut out the breeze. We both laughed. It was cold, but being next to Jean-Paul gave me warmth enough to endure.

"Very well, my mother is traditional, could you tell? She wears her hair up and I've noticed that she averts her eyes from a man's gaze. She is beautiful, for her age, and when men see her eyes, they cannot look away. She holds her tea cup properly, dresses conservatively, and laughs only when it's appropriate. She's very loving and giving with family and friends. I learned to be giving from her. People don't see her warmth because of her tight smile, quiet manners and polite gestures. But they are deceived, her heart is enormous. She's very soft spoken, except with me. We are like sisters that fight. When she speaks with my father, its soft and respectful. She would never raise her voice to him or speak ill of him. She loves him of course, but I never see their passion, if it exists."

"Perhaps passion is deeply meaningful to them and they keep it private," Jean-Paul suggested.

"Possibly, yet I watch my mother perform her duties as if she were hired to do it. She enjoys completing her work, but I believe it is because she receives satisfaction from accomplishment. I don't know if she's truly happy. She doesn't do anything for herself. She gives all to my father and me. I don't want to be like her, although it's wonderful to look like her. My flowing hair and dark, brown eyes are just like hers. She hides this beauty from all of France. I want to be myself when I love a man, without losing my dreams and passions."

"That is an honorable goal."

"Merci," I said with a slight bow of my head. We turned right to enter another path and a small boy about three years old ran straight into Jean-Paul. He caught the boy and smiled down at him, but the boy ran on as if nothing had happened. Two black birds flirted in the sky and then darted away as quickly as they had appeared.

The wind tossed my hair in front of my face. I brushed it behind my ears before I continued. "My father has a quiet, tough exterior. Inside he is soft, sweet crème. He is stern with me on the rare occasion, when he deems it necessary. He doesn't allow many people to know his soft heart. My mother and I know it well. It's his tall, slender frame, gray hair and quiet manner that intimidate people. Also my father demands honesty and is impatient with deceit. Generally he's tolerant of me and spoils me. It was his idea to nickname me Cherie. You see my mother cannot have more children. She has already lost a child during pregnancy. Learning that she would never have more children was devastating, especially to my mother. That's why I'm cherished."

"I've no doubt that there are other reasons that you're treasured. How could a father resist that warm, sweet smile you have, or your unrelenting charm. I know how difficult it is for me."

"Are you trying to cause me to blush? Allow me to continue."

Jean-Paul gestured for me to continue, although he looked pleased with himself for distracting my focus. I felt my cheeks blush and I lowered my eyes to avoid his. The flushed feeling warmed my whole body and pushed away the cold.

A few children ran after the pigeons, as if they could catch one. The birds were quick to fly three to six feet away from the little ones and continue pecking at fallen seeds.

"My father reads all the time. If he is not at the University, then he is often reading near the fire. We speak of history and politics, occasionally. Mostly he just gives me advice about life or asks me about my studies. His wish for me is to be well educated. He sees knowledge as the value that improves life."

"That is a lot of information.. Your father's a complicated man."

"My father's not complicated. Like my mother, he values education, honesty, the Catholic Church and me. What could be simpler?" I said smiling.

Jean-Paul tilted his head to one side as if questioning me. His checks were red from the cool air and when the sun peeked from behind the clouds, his face seemed to glow. He returned a tight smile, loaded with a question. "Your father is quite religious?"

"Both of my parents are religious. Most of Paris is the same, non?"

"Oui, it's common." Jean-Paul paused briefly before he continued. "But I am not. After my parents died, I had a difficult time at church. I was already angry at God for taking my parents from me. Martine insisted that I attend church. As I grew up, I witnessed gross hypocrisy; clergymen taking advantage of the poor and the distraught, and priests casting judgment on others when their own behavior was deplorable. The Catholic Church is of no use to me. On holidays I attend to please my aunt."

Reflecting on Jean-Paul's words I realized that church was a welcome refuge to me. It was familiar and comforting. Attending church was what people did on Sundays. Jean-Paul's words worried me. How will I share this news with my parents? Perhaps this means Jean-Paul and I are not meant to be. "I would not share your sentiments with my parents," I said, "if you desire their approval."

"Very well, but does it reduce me in the eyes of Mademoiselle Cherie?"

I thought for one moment, still unsure of how this might impact me. Then I said the most honest thing I could, "I cannot say at this moment how your feelings might impact my future. Yet, how could I preach to you my need to follow my heart and deny the same to you?"

Jean-Paul smiled widely in appreciation.

The hour flew by. We both watched as Martine walked towards us, carrying herself as if she were heavier now than an hour ago. I felt certain that she had returned early. She gave us each a thoughtful look before she spoke. "I'm afraid that I haven't good news dear ones. Catherine was not receptive to my interfering with your betrothal on your behalf. She said there were many reasons why your parents chose this man for your husband. There was a deep knowing of the family and their values. She said that André loves you. She didn't seem closed to all other options, but she wishes to address this with you Cherie, and not with me."

Jean-Paul and I looked at each other. I tried to read his face, but all I saw was contemplation in his deep brown eyes. His gaze turned from me to Martine. "Then there's hope, I presume?" he asked.

"Winning my love is far more valuable to you than winning theirs" I injected. "Do you think that's possible?"

"If I cannot win the love of the woman whose smile melts my heart, then I shall be a lonely man. But you know that I value your parent's approval as well, for your sake."

It wasn't exactly the answer I was seeking, but my cheeks flushed anyway.

Martine watched us both intently, enjoying the romance blossoming between us.

Jean-Paul and Martine drove me home in their carriage and said good bye. As I walked through the front doorway, I wondered what my mother would have to say after her conversation with Martine.

"Bonjour, Cherie."

"Bonjour, Mother."

"Did you enjoy your visit with Martine and Jean-Paul?"

How did she know I saw Jean-Paul? "Of course, Mother."

"Come sit here Cherie," my mother said, gesturing to the parlor. "You know that I love you above everything, excepting your Father. I desire nothing but the best for you and your wellbeing. You know this, oui?"

"Mother, of course I know this. What are you implying?" I asked.

"Your father and I chose André for you for a very specific reason. André cares about you, and will make an excellent husband, provider and father to your children." I tried to interrupt, but my mother pointed her finger, directing me to allow her to finish. "And....more importantly, he will keep you with your family. André will live in Paris. You will raise your children in Paris. You will be respected, wealthy and provided for, as will your children."

"Mother, I don't love André."

"You mean to say that you're not in love with André. You love him. He's like family."

"Exactly, Mother. He's like a cousin to me. Becoming his wife repulses me. I must feel passion for my husband."

"I'm sorry to spoil your dream about love, daughter. But passion does not last. Lust and desire are temporary at best, in the most powerful relationships. Friendship lasts. Kindness, caring and family love is lasting. Young passion is exciting to be certain. It will fade, however, and then you don't have what it is that you really desire; stability, friendship, compassion and enduring love."

"Is that what you feel towards Father, enduring love?"

"Yes... enduring love is what I feel." She said slowly, as if to convince herself that this was correct. The wall clock chimed announcing it was two in the afternoon. Mother paused, listening to the clock as if she were lost in some distant memory. Then she gathered herself back to the present and continued. "This means that through the good days and the difficult days, I love your father. When he's distant, distracted, ill, grumpy, I love him. This is the love that will carry a woman through the challenges of being a wife. It's not as easy as it would seem, to care for a man and be his support emotionally and physically. Men are not always kind to us." She paused as she stared off into a corner of the room. Her eyes then came back to mine. "Yet if you're well provided for and have your family around you, you shall ride the good and the bad with a strong foundation. Your father and I know this. We have ensured it for you. We do not want you to get distracted by your young, whimsical feelings and destroy the future we have set in place for you. Your future is secured. Please trust that we know what's in your best interest."

I sat quietly before my mother taking in everything she had said. Obviously she realized that I preferred Jean-Paul. She had heard me say more than once that I did not want to marry André, yet she didn't waiver from her conviction about him. All the arguing in the world would not change her mind at this moment. I stood up, looked at her, and walked away in silence.

"Cherie? You're mistreating your mother. Sit with me and pour out your heart. Cherie!"

I didn't turn around to even look at her as I walked away. In my room I sat quietly, hurting, wondering and frustrated. What if my mother were wrong? What if Jean-Paul could make me gloriously happy for the rest of my life? Certainly stability is not more valuable than passion. How shall I know?

I devised a new scheme while sitting alone at my window staring aimlessly at the winter clouds. Jean-Paul would hear nothing of my mother's words. I would tell mother that I valued her opinion and would share nothing of my time with Jean-Paul. If I fell in love with Jean-Paul, then I would convince my father to allow me to marry him. Father could not resist my pleas.

One week later, Jean-Paul and Martine picked me up for the ballet. I wore a new solid blue, velvet full length gown that mother had purchased a few months ago. The dress draped nicely over my slim hips and the neck line plunged low to reveal some cleavage. Martine wore an elaborate gown of purple and gold with small red flowers. Jean-Paul looked strikingly handsome in his suit.

We sat in an upper balcony that Martine secured for this special occasion. Martine and Jean-Paul were in good spirits and I was seated between them. The crowd spoke softly in gentle whispers as we waited for the event to begin. Sitting next to Jean-Paul aroused me. The dimly lit room and perfumed air added to my excitement.

Once we were settled in, Martine asked. "Pray tell my child, what did your mother say to you regarding Jean-Paul?" Jean-Paul leaned in to hear my reply.

I was careful with my words. "She begged me to weigh my options carefully. She loves me dearly and wants only my lasting happiness."

"I can hear your mother saying this. It's no wonder that she wanted to address the matter with you directly. She had very sound advice. An intelligent woman indeed," Martine replied.

"Martine, I believe it's best for you not to address the matter with mother. If she feels that you have influence on me, towards Jean-Paul, she shall not be pleased."

"I concur. It is best that I not speak with her about it," Martine replied.

"It's important to follow your parent's wishes," Jean-Paul added. "Will your parents allow me to court you?"

I was presented with a great dilemma. If Jean-Paul knew her objection, he might walk away. I had to plant the seed of a small lie to encourage the man I desired. "My mother said, quite clearly, that my happiness is her desire. However, she didn't feel it was fair to André to spend a great deal of time with you while André is away. When he comes home in March, then she will view where my affections are towards André compared to you."

"How could you know your affections towards me if I have no opportunity to win them?"

"I offered her the same objection. She didn't present a solution. I suppose that will be up to you."

"That would seem like the respectful thing to do," Jean-Paul replied. "In honor of your mother I will grant this request."

"If what you desire most is my mother's respect above all else, then I know that a future with you would never be acceptable to me."

Martine moved away and decided to provide us with some privacy.

"I desire your affection, but not at the expense of losing your respect or the respect of your mother."

"I understand. Then you have no solution."

"With great respect for you Mademoiselle Bourguignon, might I ask if there's a way for me to spend time with you without asking for you at your home?"

"Of course, there is. I take our dog Lou Lou for a walk each day at noon. If you happen to go to the Jardin des Tuileries each day at noon, then there's no harm in walking together."

"I see Mademoiselle Bourguignon, and I suppose there's no harm in having a sip of coffee to ward off the chill as well?"

"Oui."

"Ahhh and I suppose that you enjoy chocolates?"

"Do you not notice that I'm a woman? Of course I love chocolates. You must be mad to think otherwise."

"Heavens, I shall not presume anything with you Cherie. You're quite independent and unlike any woman I have ever met. I would never postulate to know what you desire simply because you're a woman."

"Now that's a beautiful answer. Merci, chocolates are my favorite, dark ones."

"Good information for me. Would you like to instruct me on other details of how to court you, such as what I should wear, how I should speak and what other lies I should present to your parents?"

"Are you mocking me?" I asked.

"I am simply wondering how much of this courtship you should like to dictate? If you lead me to court you will I still impress you? Will you believe that I act of my own will? How will you know that I might think for myself without being given that opportunity?"

"You are mocking me! Well I can tell you that your words are not directed by me at this moment and you are not doing a good job of winning my affection," I replied.

"So then, I need further instruction on how to fall into favor with you?" Jean-Paul asked.

"Fine, as you wish, I shall leave it up to you to decide if you will pursue me. I didn't intend to instruct you on how you should behave. My intention was to be helpful. My mistake." I said and turned towards the stage. Although I had led him around to say what I wanted him to say, he discovered my manipulation and called me on it directly. How was I to get what I wanted if he was so astute?

Suddenly the candles dimmed and I sat embarrassed in the faint light between Jean-Paul and Martine. Much to my frustration, his scent perfumed the air and relaxed me as I tried to stay in my frustration. Some magnetic force made me want to have him touch me. I didn't show my weakness, however. If he had affections for me, he wasn't making them known, quite the opposite with his firm repartee.

I watched the dancers in silence without my usual smile and enjoyment. The first half of the performance was uncomfortable for me, yet Jean-Paul seemed relaxed and pleased with himself. My tension eased at intermission when he brought me a rose and glass of red wine. "Your mood may be buried in fog, but your smile is sunshine to me," he said handing me the rose.

I smiled, happy to receive his warm words.

Following the night at the ballet, Jean-Paul came to the park each day at noon, although he never promised to be there the next day, so each time was a surprise. He walked beside me with Lou Lou on long strolls through the park. Each week the weather warmed towards spring, as if our budding love warmed the earth. Several times a week he bought me cafe latte. On a few occasions we skipped the long walk and sat in the protection of a cafe to enjoy our tasty beverage. During January and February, Jean-Paul asked many questions while he studied my face.

Twice each week he surprised me with different kinds of chocolate, dark and rich. During the second week I asked him, "Why do you always smile the whole time I'm eating my chocolates?"

"Because…when you're eating your chocolate you always have some left over on your lips."

"All this time you're watching me with chocolate on my lips and you're not telling me?! Jean-Paul, you're rude." I slapped his shoulder with my right hand.

"But Cherie, it pleases me….because I keep thinking about kissing the chocolate off of your lips. I imagine that the little bit of chocolate was saved for me to enjoy from your skin to my tongue."

I blushed from embarrassment. Obviously I enjoyed the chocolates enough to not pay attention to how I ate them. Jean-

Paul was not generally so forward, but I had seen him each day for three weeks. Perhaps he was feeling more comfortable around me.

We continued this routine through early March. On March 4th, Jean-Paul admitted, "I feel quite fortunate to have this time with you while André does not. I've grown jealous of André and he has not even been near Paris."

"Oui, however, I just got word that André is coming for a break from school. He shall arrive in Paris mid-March."

Jean-Paul walked beside me in silence with his head down. He nodded his head a few times without a word. I didn't speak. After a few moments he turned towards me and then turned me towards him by guiding my arm. He looked into my eyes. "Cherie," he paused and seemed to be searching for his words, "in these past two months I have fallen in love with you. I can't imagine my life without seeing chocolate on your lips." He smiled and I returned a smile. "Yet I feel torn between my love for you and my duty to my family, as well as your duty to yours. If I chose to marry you, I would have to forgo my obligation to Jacques and Martine in order to keep you near your parents. This option feels like betraying my family. I have thought deeply about which choices I must make. Cherie, I could go to California….San Francisco, for two years, establish my uncle's trade connections and then come back to France for you. Would you wait for me?"

"Non, I would not wait here alone. If you leave me then it would be good-bye. I would come with you if you asked me. I want to see the great country of America. We could come back to France when you complete your work."

Jean-Paul was quiet again. His eyes darted about, right to left, up and down, as he frowned. After several minutes, he answered me. "You're an amazing young woman. Your bravery and sense of adventure surprise and delight me. However, I must not remove you from your homeland and family."

"I wish to be with you, wherever you may be in the world."

Jean-Paul took a step backwards, away from me and lowered his gaze from mine. "I will consider it. Family is important. I must speak with your father about such a proposal as well as asking for your hand."

"Jean-Paul, my parents have not seen André for some time. Neither have I, for that matter. I wish to tell André in person where my heart is. He deserves to hear it from me. Given my honesty, he should withdraw his interest out of respect for me. This gesture will make it simpler for my father to accept your request. Do you see the logic in this?"

"Oui, oui. Of course, I must wait until after André's visit. I understand. You will not fall for André while he's on holiday?"

"Jean-Paul, how sweet of you to be concerned. You needn't worry. André is an intelligent man, but he has never captured my affection. My heart is encircled in your passionate love."

We looked deeply into each other's gaze. My throat became tight and I swallowed hard. I took a deep breath and took in his masculine scent. His hand came to my face. His fingers climbed through my wind-tossed hair. He covered my ear and cheek with his palm as he stared at me. I wanted our lips to connect, to express our passion with our tongues, breath and sound. People surrounded us, moving about in different directions. Dogs and children walked with parents and owners. There was no privacy where we stood. Jean-Paul glanced around, I followed his gaze. There were tall bushes across the park, one hundred yards in the direction in which Jean-Paul looked. Yes, I thought. Please. I looked at him pleading, wanting his kiss above all other considerations. "Please?" I expressed.

"I will not attack you in the bushes as if you were some street girl here to satisfy my whims. You're too precious for such an idea. We must be patient. We will be together, in time."

Disappointment changed my smile to a pout. My heart dropped and my shoulders sank. I wanted to taste his lips and feel his hands on my hair while he whispered his love to me.

Yet his thoughtfulness made me desire him more. "Jean-Paul, could we go to your Uncle's flat?" I didn't explain myself or make an excuse. He knew the seriousness of my request. His aunt and uncle would be at the country house. We would be alone, with our desires tempting us. The consequences could be grave, to be certain. Jean-Paul thought quietly.

"It's not what's best, Cherie. We have much at stake. My goal is to win your family's approval, not destroy it. If we were found out…"

"Who would know?"

"Cherie, please. You are courageous to follow your desires. I love your drive and passion. It makes you who you are. However, we must consider the greater good. I want you for always, not just for this moment. I must not risk my end goal."

He was right and very strong for resisting. I wasn't as disciplined. I felt silly for asking. My face dropped again. Jean-Paul put his right index finger under my chin and lifted my head to see my eyes. He spoke as if he could read my mind. "My dear, do not be sad. I love you for wanting to be with me. I love your fervor. I cherish the day when I have you to myself. I love you."

A smile returned to my face. I heard what I really needed. I could wait. I just needed to convince André that he didn't want to marry me, and my plan would be in perfect order. I had no idea how badly my plan would fail.

    ***

Chapter Four: **When the Truth Hurts**

Paris, March, 1899

As André's visit approached, my stomach tightened into a knot. How to explain my feelings to him worried me. We were childhood friends, therefore I thought about leaning on our friendship and asking him to release me to my happiness. Should I tell him that I would make his life miserable if forced into this marriage? Nothing felt like the right choice of words as I practiced my speech. When the day arrived for his visit, I decided that I would just pour out my heart and tell him the truth.

André arrived at my home and we sat in the parlor. My parents were both in the dining room entertaining our neighbors, the Montes, and we were alone.

"Hello darling," André said smiling. "I've missed you so. It is lonely without your smile. If you only knew the nights I spent thinking of you."

"How are your studies?" I asked.

"I have realized that attorneys are some of the most intelligent men on the planet. You shall be happy to know that I'm in the upper five percent of my classmates; therefore you may conclude that I'm one of the smartest men in all of France. You may be proud to be sure. Boast to your parents if you like."

"My parents already adore you. They are well aware of your qualities."

"Thank you for saying that, my dear. You're kind."

"André, I wish to discuss a matter of grave importance."

"Of course, my sweet, pray tell, what is it you must share?"

"I'm not in love with you."

"You're not in love with me? Why are you stating this now? What's the point you wish to make?"

"I do not wish to marry you."

"Cherish, you're not serious. You must be confused. You have hardly been in my presence for three years. The distance has provoked a bit of doubt. My darling, I assure you that there is not a thing to doubt. We are betrothed and it's a good choice for us both."

"Forgive my directness, dearest André. We are betrothed because our parents intervened in our lives, deciding for us that we should have wealth above love, passion and free will."

"My sweet, you're naïve and know not of what you speak. The word passion is derived from the Latin; passo, which means suffering and submission. Is this what you seek more than a marriage to me? Additionally, do not undervalue wealth, for love will subside, therefore security is ultimately more valuable. Free will, at your tender age, is not recommended. Maturity lends itself to wise choices, through experience. That's why you must allow your parents to make this important decision for you."

"André, you're not listening to me. I do not love you."

"I know that you love me darling. We have been close friends for most of our lives."

"Oui, oui. However, I'm not in love with you. I do not desire you."

"Desire comes with time, precious. I love you enough for both of us."

"Are you in love with me?" I asked.

"Absolutely."

"What is my favorite dessert?"

"Mmmm…Sweet pastries, I believe," André replied.

"Non. What is my favorite activity?"

"Ah…Reading…non…walking in the park, or shopping."

"Non. How can you be in love with me if you don't know me, André?"

"Cherish, I'm in love with you because these things do not matter to me. You could love any dessert you wish, you may enjoy whatever activities you wish and I shall still be in love with you."

"Why do you call me Cherish? I don't like it."

"It is your given name. It is a beautiful name."

"Oh André! You frustrate me. You know that if I were to marry you I would be miserable and unhappy and make your life the same. This is not what we must do."

"I shall work tirelessly to win your affection and cause you to be happy."

"How shall you do that? You don't even know what makes me happy."

"Won't you share with me what makes you happy, darling?"

"Call me Cherie. That makes me happy."

"Then I shall call you Cherie darling. What else?"

"André, there's more that I need to tell you. I am keenly interested in another man."

André's face turned red as his lips pursed tightly. He took a deep breath and spoke slowly with a low, stiff voice. "Of what do you speak!? How could you know another man? Cherish, do you know the seriousness of what you speak? You're to be my wife. There is a commitment. You belong to me!"

"I'm trying to explain to you André that I don't belong to you. The commitment made to you was not by me. My parents made a commitment on my behalf. There is no law that states that I have no choice in this matter. My parents made a choice that affects the rest of my life, my happiness. There is nothing fair and right about this."

"I do not believe that I'm hearing you speak this way. What has happened to create this asinine change in you?"

"I grew up." I paused. "Before you is not the young girl wondering what love is, what marriage means and what I want. The woman who sits before you is committed to following her heart, doing what's best for her, not just what others want."

"You're too young to know what you want."

"You're incorrect. You do not understand what matters to me most."

"You're being unfair. You haven't told me what matters to you most. How can you judge if I shall understand or not?" he asked.

"Because, I know you André."

"And you suggest that I don't know you? Tell me what matters to you more than wealth, security, family and tradition?"

"The freedom to make my own choices and not live the same life as my mother. I desire adventure, experiencing new places, and expanding the limited horizons of my world."

"You're not making sense. This is a small tantrum and it shall pass. You need time to settle yourself. You may apologize when you feel better."

"Apologize for what fault?"

"For threatening me with another man and tempting me to jealousy. It's baffling to know your motive for this behavior. You know that I shall make you a great husband. I will provide well for you, be kind and keep your parents well pleased. You cannot be serious to tell me you do not want to marry a man of my stature. Another thing Cherish…it's inappropriate for you to speak to me about such things. It's not your place to threaten me. You will be forgiven if you withdraw what you have said and not speak of it again."

I sat in silence, shocked and angry. André was an old friend. I assumed he would care for my happiness above the wishes of our parents. He knew, on some level, that he wasn't really in love with me. What were his motives for the marriage if I didn't want him? I couldn't think of anything to say without screaming in frustration.

In silence, I thought of the boy I once played with, who used to make me laugh and chase me around the house for hours, the same young boy who would pull my hair just to hear me say ouch. I remembered the time when he found a frog and snuck up behind me to place the creature in the back of my blouse. Then he sat laughing as he watched me scream and cry. Perhaps I hated him forever after the scared amphibian left my clothing. When I cried to my mother she explained the nature of young boys. She promised that André would grow out of his mean behaviors and turn into a gentleman. Looking at him today, I question whether André would ever be a kind man.

André finally spoke. "I shall give you some time to consider what you've done and decide to apologize. I'm a patient man Cherie. I can wait. I am certain that we will spend our future together."

For a few moments I sat quietly. Then I said, "I wish to be alone André."

"Very well, we will meet again when you feel better. Perhaps you're simply angry with me for staying away. I shall be in Paris for two weeks. We can spend every day together and you shall be in love with me before I depart. Tomorrow I will call on you. Feel better darling. We shall have a sweeter conversation tomorrow."

André stood, leaned over and kissed my cheek, then walked to the front door without looking back at me. As I watched him, I felt a stinging pain in my heart, then a bitter resentment building. Suddenly I felt motivated to prove to all of them, my parents, André and his parents, that they couldn't control me. They will not decide my life for me. All of them were wrong to think that my life was their chess game.

Jean-Paul would make me feel better. Perhaps Auntie Martine knew what to do. How could I maintain my relationship with my parents and have what I wanted? My best strategies were not working for me. I went to my room and wrote a letter to Martine, explaining my urgent need to see her.

The next morning I walked to town to the courier office, asking for a rapid delivery. It could be days before Martine received the letter. Jean-Paul had decided not to meet me at the park while André was in Paris. I went to the park anyway, hoping he was there by some miracle. He wasn't anywhere to be seen.

Sitting on a bench in the park, I began to let the tears flow. With my face down, I sobbed holding my cheeks in my palms. Why had life become so complicated? My parents didn't understand me, and André didn't care what I wanted. There was the irony of liking the idea of marrying André at age eleven and being repulsed by it now. Why hadn't my parents betrothed me to Jean-Paul instead of André? My heart felt like it might burst from the pain of being alone and misunderstood. Gently a hand came down on my shoulder. I didn't want to look up through my swollen, tear-filled eyes. Embarrassment spread over me for my show of emotions in public. The hand didn't move. The shoes belonging to the person standing there were familiar. Looking up I saw Jean-Paul looking compassionately.

I stood quickly and embraced him right in the park. His arms surrounded me. Comfort spread over me. Taking in the sweetness of it, I needed this embrace more than food and water. "Jean-Paul, I'm happy to see you."

"Why are you sad, Cherie?"

"Oh, Jean-Paul, it's terrible."

"Pray tell."

"André..." I paused as if that was all there was to say. How could I explain what happened? "He was...simply selfish. He only thought of himself. He disregarded my request completely, as if my wishes meant nothing. He asked me to apologize for my inconsiderate treatment of him. Of him!"

"Cherie, he's a man. It's in a man's nature to fight for the woman he loves."

"He doesn't love me...romantically. He loves the idea of being married to me. He loves me as the friend with whom he grew up. He loves that I'm a woman and he desires to know my body. However, he knows nothing of who I have become. He does not know the essence of what makes me unique."

"He knows that he is a fool to let you go."

"You're not helping me feel better. If he will not back away from the betrothal then my father will resist your request for my hand. This is a quandary. Please say something to help me cope with this dilemma."

"My Cherie, please sit." Jean-Paul gestured to the bench and we sat together. "I wish I could change what is true. Alas I cannot. I see the impasse. We are in a more serious circumstance than we previously knew. You will never need to choose between your family and me. I could not live with myself if I were to be so selfish. I must step back and allow your life to unfold. My presence can only complicate your situation, causing you more distress."

"Jean-Paul, what are you saying? You're the only sanity that I find in Paris. Please do not suggest that André must fight for me because he loves me and you will not fight for me. This would destroy my world."

"My sweet, I love you enough to not want to cause you a day of pain. I love you enough to let you be with your family and not pull you apart from them."

"Do not give up Jean-Paul. My father is more reasonable than my mother. Allow me the opportunity to speak with him. Have more faith. Please!"

"Of course. This seems reasonable. Speak with your father and if he is amenable to speak with me, then I shall communicate my desires to him."

"Merci, merci. Shall we meet here in three days' time?"

"Absolutely, my cherished, my love goes with you." Jean-Paul stood and kissed my lips gently. He reached for my hand to help me stand. He gazed into my eyes and smiled. "It shall be a lonely three days for me. Your smile shall reside in my heart." He kissed my hand and turned away.

Sitting down again on the bench, I wondered what I could say to my father that would convince him to set me free of André. The truth hadn't worked with my mother or with André. Perhaps I should invent something. Nothing intelligent came to mind. The only idea that materialized was to use my father's deep love and compassion for me. I knew how to get my way with him. I could even manipulate him when I planned carefully. Being the only daughter had its advantages. Playing sick often gained his sympathy, as did tears, deep emotions and silence when timed correctly with a look of sadness and a pout. If I were calculated in my behavior, I would sway my father.

My father was dear to me. I didn't want to manipulate him or be cruel. But this matter was of grave consequence. If my father did not change his mind, once he knew my heart's desires, then I would have no choice but to follow my happiness without my parents' approval and face the consequences of that option. Hopefully I wouldn't have to make that choice.

The next morning I requested my father's attention. He agreed to go for a walk, to speak to me away from mother. We walked towards the Louvre at a slow pace. "What is it that you wish to address with me my precious?" my father asked.

"Father, my heart aches with great pain. I'm distraught and quite ill. My stomach hurts, my head hurts. Comfort eludes me."

"What is causing you such grief?"

"André is in Paris," I said with pain in my voice.

"Oui."

"He's the cause of my grief. When I haven't seen André, I'm most happy. Then when I spend a day in his presence I feel ill. The thought of marrying André destroys my happiness. After

63

André and I had our first kiss, I didn't ever want to kiss him again. I don't want to be his wife or bear him children. I told this to mother and she said that I was too young to know what I wanted."

My father and I walked side by side as he pondered my words.

"Do you understand what it is that you don't enjoy about André?"

"He's arrogant. He doesn't know my needs or wish to know them. I do not desire him. I do not have joy when I'm with him."

"Cherie, you understand that the matter is complex, non?"

"Oui. Father, this matter is to impact every day of my future. It's not natural for me to sit quietly and allow my happiness to slip from my grasp."

"Daughter, happiness is not a guarantee. If you're not to marry André, a very well suited husband, provider and deacon of the Catholic Church, then you have no assurance that happiness shall be found elsewhere. With André, your foundation for a good life is set. Finding a husband is no easy task."

"It shall not be difficult for me Father. I'm already loved by another."

"Of what do you speak child?"

"Jean-Paul Soule. He loves me."

"How is this known?"

"He has expressed it to me."

"If this is true, then you must come forward with this to André. If there have been any inappropriate activities for a betrothed woman, then André must decide if he is still willing to marry."

"André and I have spoken. He knows what has occurred. He doesn't believe it and wishes for me to apologize for saying it. I do not want my future to be decided by André. Jean-Paul is who I wish to marry."

"You wish to breech a promise of marriage, a commitment of faith and to God?"

"Father I was eleven. An eleven year old girl does not know whom she should marry."

"Cherie, do you realize how your behavior will be viewed in the eyes of the Church?"

"It's more important to me to smile at my children because I'm proud of their father, than to impress the clergy," I replied.

"Cherie, you know that I adore you. Your wellbeing and security are my priority as well as your standing with the Lord. I can't condone your behavior."

"I adore you as well. You're a wonderful father. Please don't leave me alone in this matter. I must be released from this promise."

My father stopped walking. He turned towards me and was silent for a few minutes. "There's a way to breech this commitment. It's not, however, an easy or uncomplicated matter. I shall not advise you to take this route. However, I will allow you to make the choice for yourself, without my counsel. The only thought I shall leave you with is this; you have to live with your decisions. All of us must. Sometimes we don't consider the final consequences of our decisions. Eventually we realize the consequences that were created by our actions."

"Father, I would rather live with the results of my decisions than the result of a decision others made for me."

"Very well child. Then I shall tell you everything that I know on the matter. The way to change the commitment is if you become engaged to another man. Bear in mind that it's not an appealing way to be seen by the Catholic Church or congregation. It does however breech the agreement. Following the engagement, you and your new betrothed shall need to discuss the matter with the Bishop. If both parties are in good standing in the Church, then the new engagement is usually accepted. If this occurs, and your betrothed can provide well for you in Paris, then Mother and I shall be well pleased."

My heart skipped two beats as my breathing stopped. Jean-Paul was not an active member, therefore not in good-standing, and he wouldn't change that. My teeth clenched together to hide the emotions I didn't want to show on my face. I swallowed hard and pretended that the situation was different. My face showed a smile while my heart nearly broke. "Then you support me Father?"

"I love you for your courage and for being who you are. What you have said has not made me happy. However, you have made up your mind. This old man is wise enough to know he cannot sway you from your stance, or love, or whatever is holding you firm."

"Thank you, Father."

"Did I help you daughter?"

"Oh you helped far more than you know. Would it be permissible for Jean-Paul to ask for my hand in marriage?"

"Oui, after he has the blessing from God's Church."

It was apparent that my father was not going to relent on the church issue. My hands began to shake so I stuffed them into my pockets. My eyes widened and my lips pressed firmly together. With all of the fortitude I could muster I responded, "Of course, Father. As you wish."

After my walk with my father, my spirits were laden with worry. The depression and fear of the past few weeks was still with me, now with new concerns. How will I share this news with Jean-Paul? Perhaps he might love me enough to reconsider his position with the Church. I didn't want to manipulate him. He had to love me and make his own choice if I were to have true love. If it were not his decision, then I didn't want him.

If only he would change his view of the Church, he could propose before André left to return to law school and the matter could be finalized while André was in Paris.

After sending a letter out, I waited at the park each day at noon. André asked me several times why I insisted on taking Lou Lou to the park alone each day. He begged that he might join me and I explained that it would not make me happy.

Three days after I sent the letter, Jean-Paul met me at the park. "Did you receive my letter?"

"What letter?"

"I sent you a letter. How did you know to come here?"

"Because my dear, the last time we spoke you asked me to meet you in three days' time. I recalled your request and I'm here."

"Oh yes. Please forgive me. Thank you for remembering."

"Have you spoken with your father?"

"Oui. My father delighted and surprised me. He said that I may get out of my commitment by making a new one."

"What new commitment must you make?"

"A commitment of marriage." Jean-Paul looked at me without understanding my meaning. I explained further, feeling a little embarrassed that I must tell the man I desire to ask for my hand. "If I'm engaged to another man, the first agreement will be broken. Of course it looks unpleasant to others, but that's of no consequence to me because I value happiness over status."

"So your Father suggested that you become engaged?"

"Oui."

"So I may ask him for your hand in marriage?"

"Oui, after we receive a blessing from the Church."

"The Catholic Church? Are you serious?"

"Oui."

"Cherie, the priest of our congregation considers me a fallen soul. He knows my objection to the ways of the Church. It is not likely that he will give a blessing to our union."

Jean-Paul and I sat quietly on the cold, stone bench. "Tell the priest that you have had a vision and a change of heart. Could you not convince him that you're a reformed, obedient member of the congregation?"

"You mean be untruthful to what I believe? It's one thing to tell a lie to a man that you do not respect who stands between you and your desires for a woman. It's another thing to turn against your own values and principles."

"You would not actually be abandoning what you believe, non?"

"Non, not abandoning what I believed, but I would be a hypocrite, like them; saying one thing with my lips while doing and believing something else. Playing their game will cost me my integrity. Then I'm acquiring you, but not worthy of you. There's no greater disappointment."

"Jean-Paul, if you love me you will compromise to be with me. If you believe in love you will do what it takes to have it."

"I must be true to myself before I can be true to you."

Light-headedness and nausea overcame me. I felt that I might fall off the bench.

"Jean-Paul? Hold me. There's too much heaviness," I said not knowing what I should do. Jean-Paul helped support my head on his shoulder as I leaned my body against his. "Jean-Paul, I need to rest. I am afraid. This stress is overwhelming. I need some privacy and reprieve from trying to satisfy everyone at once. I need to be in your arms."

"Cherie..." he said with such love and tenderness.

"Please, Jean-Paul. I might die without being in your arms. I'm most sincere."

"Very well, my cherished. We must be careful however. If others see us..."

"I don't care! My life is too vulnerable to the eyes of others. I must live my life as I please. They may all die."

Jean-Paul seemed to detect how distraught I felt. He gently put his arms over my shoulders and led me away from the park without a word. We walked unconcerned if others saw his touch upon me. Jean-Paul held me closely, making me feel loved. I knew right then that he put my welfare above the opinions and rules of society, so my heart let go and committed to Jean-Paul. Someone besides my father put my needs above anything else, which caused me to forever belong to him. My voice failed me, yet I wanted to say that my love could not be held by another as long as he existed. It felt as if something inside of Jean-Paul changed as well, as he led me away. Possibly I imagined the difference, yet it seemed to me that he claimed me in that moment, deciding that he was responsible for my wellbeing.

He held a key to the door and turned the lock and the door handle. He pushed the large door forward and waited for me to enter the flat. Crossing the threshold, I felt that I might collapse from the emotional burden. My head dropped, my eyes closed and my body immediately began to sink to the floor. Jean-Paul rushed forward, grabbing me under both arms to lend support. I managed to toss my head forward against his firm chest, but my legs would not support my full weight. Jean-Paul scooped me into his arms and brought me to the bedroom. He laid me down gently, and then pulled a soft comforter over my supine form.

"Rest here my sweet. I shall be in the next room."

"Non! Please stay. I'm scared. Don't leave me alone."

"As you wish." Jean-Paul climbed onto the bed beside me and lay close. I wiggled in next to him and placed my head on his left shoulder, closing my eyes and finding comfort in his loving touch. He wrapped his left arm around me. With his right hand he gently stroked my hair, running his fingers through my bangs and caressed my cheek…easing me into a deep rest. As sleep overcame me, I felt a sublime contentedness. I couldn't know at that moment the future pain I would endure from knowing such bliss.

***

Chapter Five: **New Explosions**

Paris, Late March, 1899

"Cherie? Cherie? Wake up my darling. Cherie?"

A satisfying sigh released from my body. Stretching, I noticed my left arm wrapped over Jean-Paul's chest as he gently wiggled my shoulder. "Mmmmm."

"Hello darling. Did you enjoy your afternoon nap? It's time for you to rise. You're expected at home. We must get you back."

Leaning on my right shoulder, I turned to face Jean-Paul and looked into his eyes. "Jean-Paul, I'm happiest here with you."

"I enjoy being here with you. I would like to enjoy this every day of my life." He looked deeply into my eyes with a kind and genuine smile.

"I would like that as well," I said begging him with my eyes to kiss me. He stared at me intensely.

Silently he watched my eyes. He touched my cheek with the back of his fingers, then he placed his palm behind my head, under my hair. I sensed it would happen before he moved. His face softened. His lips parted. I waited. I wanted. He leaned forward and pressed his mouth against mine as his hand supported my head. Without a thought, our bodies turned towards each other. My heart beat alongside his. His chest pressed against mine. The pleasure overtook me completely. Embracing the moment, I surrendered, without a thought outside of my connection with Jean-Paul. All that I was aware of in that moment was wrapped in the space that our two bodies occupied. Everything that I felt came from the touch of his lips and the warmth of his body.

The scent of him surrounded me, relaxing every muscle. At the same time I pulsed with the desire to get closer to him. An overwhelming feeling made me want to crawl inside of him, be engulfed in his strength, his touch, his heat, his taste and his affection. His shirt was keeping me from feeling his skin with my hand. His shirt opened and I slid my palm across his firm back and then the side of his body from ribs to hip. Jean-Paul lifted himself on top of me, placing his hips above mine. Another sigh released. Gratitude spread through. I desired this closeness above anything else. His heart pounded his lips moved from my mouth to my cheek, down my neck, to my collar bone. Jean-Paul pulled at my lapel, exposing my shoulder and drenching it with warm kisses.

My head naturally turned to expose the area and give him access. His kisses fell like large drops of rain onto the thirsty soil of my skin. My blouse limited his direct contact. He seemed to want more places to taste and caress with his lips. Gently he unbuttoned the top button of my blouse. Waves of excitement pushed through my body. He pulled my blouse off my shoulder, exposing more area to be devoured with lips and tongue. The kisses pleased my whole body. Desiring more, I moaned with pleasure and sighed.

Jean-Paul's lips found mine again. His passion intensified, pressing hard against my mouth, clasping his hands in mine, interlocking our fingers and stretching my arms above my head. His hip then pressed forward against mine. My body responded by pressing back and squeezing his hands with mine. My head tilted back, as I felt my hips open to receive him.

Suddenly, Jean-Paul stopped. He withdrew his lips and pulled his chest from mine. Looking into my confused eyes he said, "I'm quite sorry Cherie. Rest assured, I meant you no disrespect. My intention was only to kiss you before returning you to your home. It was not my intention to be swept away in the moment. Please forgive me."

"Jean-Paul, forgiveness is not possible, unless…unless…"

"Unless what my dear? Please tell."

"Unless you finish ravishing me, I shall never forgive you. If you stop now and leave me in this state of desiring you above air and water, I shall not forget it. Do not return me to the doom that I'm to face at home, without the satisfaction of knowing that I'm completely irresistible to you. Otherwise I shall hold the rejection against you."

"Are you certain that this is what you want?"

"Oui, most certain." I assured him.

"Your happiness I desire above my own," Jean-Paul answered.

"Then take me. Allow me to surrender my body and will to your desires. Nothing shall bring me more joy."

Jean-Paul stared long and deep into my eyes. His next kiss fell with certainty and determination. He took control of our movements. His hips began to move in a slow rhythm. He kissed my ears, cheeks and neck, then moved down to my chest. He unbuttoned my blouse to the waist and removed it gently. He kissed the top of my breasts, which protruded from beneath my corset. His lips returned to mine with purpose and focus.

He rolled me onto my side and unhooked my corset without looking. He lifted it from me and pulled it back to view my breasts. He looked at me and I felt beautiful. Jean-Paul brought his hands to my breasts and held them, squeezing and molding them into the shape of his grasp. His eyes watched as my nipples protruded between his fingers.

His gaze found mine. He looked to see my pleasure and approval. Smiling, I closed my eyes in satisfaction. He looked again at his hands massaging the softest place on my body. Slowly he lowered his mouth to my right breast. His tongue outlined my nipple before his lips closed in, enveloping the areola and sending fast rolling waves of tingling delight rippling from nipple to loins. The physical pleasure of his lips far exceeded any gratification I'd ever known. Each lick was euphoric, bursting with bliss and a desire for more.

Instinctively I lifted his shirt, pulling it up over his head and sending it flying across the room. The skin of his chest and stomach met mine. His warm skin against me gave me as much pleasure as his kisses.

My labia tingled with rapid sparks darting about. An insatiable hunger for his complete acceptance of my body gnawed at me. My hips thrust in rhythm with his while my hands pressed against his buttocks, pushing him closer, desiring more. I pulled at his trousers, indicating that I wanted them removed. Jean-Paul must have had the same thought, for he immediately removed my skirt and his trousers with ease. Undergarments shed quickly and we were skin to skin, bare against one another, exposed, vulnerable. Submitting fully, I silently begged for him to penetrate me as deeply and completely as possible.

Jean-Paul kissed me meaningfully, then he pulled back to see my eyes. He read my face; he saw my wanting and my approval of it. He kissed me again and allowed himself to penetrate my virgin labia. My back arched. My womb opened and received my lover, my love, my friend. Jean-Paul's hand held my buttocks and lifted my hips closer to his. Many wonderful sensations attacked me at once. Pleasure spread everywhere; my lips, breasts, loins, and buttocks. His hands caressed my ribs, hips and curves in such a way that it was obvious he enjoyed my body; which made me feel more beautiful.

His thrusts sent shooting euphoria rushing through me. I couldn't imagine missing this or being anywhere else. All of the excitement made me want more; never to stop. Muscles contracted beyond my control. Moans escaped my lips without restraint. My hands tightened and my fingers pulled aggressively at the skin on Jean-Paul's back. His thrusts became more rapid and firm. He grabbed my hands once again. Our fingers intertwined as he pinned my arms against the bed. He pressed himself deeper and deeper inside of me. My mind and body opened to the penetration, allowing him to fully probe my womb, my soul, my appetite. I hungered for all of it. My muscles tightened around Jean-Paul, holding him inside of me. The intensity climbed, higher and higher. My body wanted to explode from the force of it. Then something inside of me did explode, like a finale of fireworks. Jean-Paul's muscles tightened, along with mine. A magical air encircled us, wrapping us together into one. We bonded, as if knowing this shared bliss could never be taken away. Then, we both let go and slumped into a relaxed heap of bare skin and tossed limbs.

Jean-Paul lay motionless on top of me, holding me, hugging me. The moment couldn't be more perfect. Soft, gentle moans escaped from each of us. We laid still, recovering, resting in the bliss of it.

I could have stayed wet and naked beside him forever, never moving, and my life would have been complete. Alas, knowing he would send me home, I prepared my mind for the prying away. I didn't move a single muscle, as if holding still would preserve the enchanted embrace. The inevitable did come. His words melted my doubt and fears. "My heart belongs to you forever ma Cherie. It's with great pain that I give you back to your family and let you out of my arms until I may hold you again. Your scent shall satisfy my hunger and your beautiful nakedness shall never leave my mind."

Every muscle in my face created a big smile. No words could improve upon what he'd said. I kissed his cheek and hugged him tightly. Then I stood, smiling, fully naked before him, and dressed while he watched me. I wanted him to remember my skin and my breasts and desire to find a way for us to be together.

"You're truly beautiful my love."

"Mmmm," I murmured.

"Before we go darling, this is a most appropriate time to give you your gift."

"You have a gift for me?" I asked.

"Oui, it's a birthday gift, but I wanted to give it to you before your birthday dinner with your family. After making love to you, it feels like the perfect time to share the meaning of this present."

"Wonderful, let me see it!" I said, bouncing up and down.

Jean-Paul took my hand and led me from the bedroom into the dining room. Across the room, against the wall was a large object, covered with a sheet. Immediately I realized that it was probably a painting. My heart jumped and tightened while my breathing quickened. I did not own any significant art. There's no art that I would rather own than Jean-Paul's. That he would think to give me such a special gift thrilled me.

"Close your eyes," Jean-Paul instructed.

I obeyed. Jean-Paul let go of my hand and walked across the room to the covered object. He removed the cover and held the object above the dining room table. "You may open your eyes my love."

Before me was a painting of an incredible sunrise, surreal and magnificent. "Oh…Jean-Paul….oh my…oh my!! Amazing. This is for me?"

74

"It's exactly for you, and no one else. I wish no one else would ever see this piece."

"Oh Jean-Paul, I love it! Thank you. It's lovely."

"Look closely my sweet. Do you recognize it?"

My eyes studied the painting. It did look familiar. "We shared that sunrise."

"Yes, we did. Do you remember when?"

"Yes," I said smiling. Of course he would paint our first magical sunrise.

"How did you paint it so precisely?" I asked. "It has been months since we saw that sky."

"The morning and evening sky had become my study for months, in an effort to see the colors and patterns I remembered from that morning. The sky that dawn made a lasting impression. But it took months to paint what I remembered because I needed to see portions of the patterns and some of the colors again. My sweet, it's amazing how different the sky can be from day to day. There are many different colors and the lighting is never quite the same."

"You rose each day at sunrise to stare at the sky to paint my birthday present?"

"Why yes, darling. Now you have this memory in paint so you shall always remember how I feel towards you. If I'm ever without you, you and I shall see the same sun and the same moon. We shall be viewing it together."

"Jean-Paul, you're a wonderful man. I'm the most fortunate young lady in all of France. Thank you, for this treasure."

"To your parents, it will just be a painting of a sunrise that I gave you for your birthday. But to us, well, we know what it really is. Look very close in this area here," Jean-Paul said while pointing to the lower middle of the painting.

As I studied it, I leaned in closer. There was a small, black outline of two people. It would seem that they were turned to face the sunrise while arm in arm, but it was difficult to make them out and not noticeable without Jean-Paul's mention of it.

"That's us. But only we will know that too. This painting shall remain here until your birthday dinner, where I will present it to you as a gift. The meaning will be our little secret, just like our love making today will be."

Jean-Paul walked me home. He kissed my cheek at the doorstep and walked away. Quietly I entered my home and walked through the kitchen to the staircase. Before I could climb the stairs, I heard my mother's voice.

"Where were you this afternoon Cherie?" my mother asked.

"On my walk from Jardin des Tuileries to the Opera National, I stopped for coffee and looked in some boutiques. The time I spend alone is valuable to me, Mother."

"Were you alone?"

"Oui!" Did she have me followed? How does she always know?

"My ladies," my father interjected pleasantly. "Let us all enjoy our meal. All is well. We missed you Cherie."

"Thank you. I feel refreshed. The walk was good for my health."

"You missed André. He called on you. I told him you were at the park. He went looking for you. Did you see André?"

"Non," I said, hoping that André did not see me either.

"He has invited all of us to a dinner at his parent's home tomorrow evening. I accepted on your behalf," Mother said.

"Oh."

"We leave at six o'clock."

"Oh."

"We will bring wine and cheese. Would you please go to the market tomorrow and choose some excellent cheese?"

"Ahhh…oui."

After supper I tucked myself away in my room, trying not to fret too deeply about dinner with André tomorrow and my predicament. Jean-Paul loved me, which made me happy. But he wasn't willing to pretend to be a faithful member of a church he saw as unethical just to win my parents' approval. He would not obtain their acceptance falsely. It seemed ironic that André, an up and coming attorney learning ethics, found no fault with the Church, where an artist did. The hurdles to overcome seemed endless. My hope was that Jean-Paul could find a way for us to be together when my mind could not.

Lying on my bed, I remembered Jean-Paul's touch, his scent, and his eyes. Shivers rippled through my body from the excitement. When could I have it all again; the caressing, the vulnerability, and closeness? The fear of my parents' demands filled my head, nearly making me go mad trying to calculate my future.

The thought of sitting with my family and André's family for dinner tomorrow night caused a pain in my stomach. The thought of pretending all was well repulsed me. Many emotions would be with me that I could not share without upsetting two families. My complicated life was enough to make me cry. Tears began to form, then drip slowly into my hair. It isn't fair. How could I look André's parents in the eye and not scream that I love someone else? My belly and chest heaved with deep spasms while I sobbed. Tears flowed freely. Lying on my stomach, I buried my head into my pillow and released the pain as quietly as I could. Sleep overtook me as I lay on my wet pillow, fully clothed, ready to wake up to a new reality.

***

Chapter Six: **Over Sharing**

Paris, Mid-March, 1899

Mother walked into my room unannounced. "Cherie? Why are you not awake? Are you ill?"

My sleepy, salty eyes peered at my mother through swollen lids, as I lay in my wrinkled skirt that Jean-Paul had removed skillfully the day before. His scent was still on my clothes. "What time is it Mother?"

"It's eight fifteen. I wanted to send you to the market early, but you are…why did you sleep in your clothes? Your blouse is a mess."

"What Mother?"

"Please get clean and dressed. We shall go together. Are you feeling well?"

"I just awoke Mother. I don't know how I am feeling yet."

"Well come downstairs when you are dressed and I shall have a look at you."

Mother walked out and closed my door. I took a breath, disappointed that it was morning. Tonight I was expected at the home of André's parents. Dread shook me fully awake along with fear. Perhaps tonight was my opportunity to make my wishes known? However, I was not engaged to a parishioner in good standing. A lie could make matters worse. I needed liberation, not the bonds of convention that imprisoned me.

Lying in my bed, I wanted to avoid the inevitable requirements of facing this day. Then I realized that if mother and I did not return from the market quickly, I would miss the opportunity to see Jean-Paul at the park today. I sprang from my bed and freshened up. Bouncing down the stairs and over to mother, I said, "I feel wonderful mother. I am ready to go to the market. Please rest here at home. I shall get some fabulous cheese for the dinner. A long stroll, searching for the best Brie de meaux, Comte and Langre, is just what I needed. I shall not be too long, or perhaps I shall enjoy the walk and find a bouquet to bring as well."

"That is kind of you darling. I have decided that we shall go together. It allows us a chance to talk."

"Very well mother. Shall we go?"

"I am enjoying my coffee. Relax yourself child. Would you like coffee?"

"Non, I am looking forward to the market."

"Wonderful. Does that mean that you are looking forward to dinner this evening?"

I chose my response carefully. "Actually, mother, I find walking around Paris refreshing. The market is a wonderful place to walk."

"I feel the same. Let's go."

Mother and I walked casually, enjoying the fresh air as Paris approached the first day of spring. Green buds tipped the tree branches while the grass grew brighter and squirrels chased one another. The sounds of people surrounded us as many ventured from their shelters.

It wasn't long before mother's motive was obvious. "What did you and your father discuss on your walk?"

Carefully I formed my reply, not knowing what father shared with her. She should hear as much of the truth as possible to prepare her for what was to come.

"Father and I spoke about the same things that I shared with you. I explained that I would make a miserable, depressed wife for André because I didn't want to be with him. Father answered my question of whether it was possible to marry another man."

"What did he tell you?"

"He said that if I became engaged to another man who was in good standing within the Church, then my agreement with André would be breached."

Mother was quiet for a moment. "Is this your intention?"

"It's my desire to be engaged to another."

"When had you proposed to share this with André?"

"I have shared it with André, before I spoke with Father. André did not accept my words. He thought perhaps I was simply upset and emotional. He expected that my feelings should pass."

"I must warn you, Cherie, that at your age such feelings do swing in different directions. You really could not be sure if André could make you a happy woman until you give him the opportunity. If you pass up this perfect arrangement you may regret your decision when you come to your senses." My mother's voice was firm and serious. She was, however, much more passive than the last time we spoke. "Tonight is an important dinner. Do not embarrass our family. The most you should share is that you are not ready to wed. Perhaps that will ease the discomfort if you do become engaged to another. You have your eyes on Monsieur Soule?"

"Oui, Mother. My heart is captivated by him."

"Young love is dangerous fire. You may get burned."

"He's a wonderful man. You have known him most of his life."

"He was a quiet boy. I assume he attends church regularly with Martine and Jacques?"

"I would have to assume that he does." I said it--a lie. Lying could cause me serious problems. Webs of falsehoods could entangle me and limit my options. Frugality must be used with my untruths.

"Is he a deacon?"

"I am uncertain."

"Martine spoke briefly of Monsieur Soule living abroad, in America. Did you hear of this?"

"He spoke of it. He explained that it would be a temporary arrangement. He desires to live in Paris."

"I see. Martine didn't mention it to be temporary." Mother paused again, as if collecting her thoughts. Silently I walked beside her with shallow breaths in fear of more reprimand. "You always have been a determined and stubborn daughter. There is no surprise that you resist the choice your father and I have carefully made for you. You may not know what is best for you. However, I also realize that you have some choices in your life. You may choose to be happy or you can choose to be miserable. If you are planning to be displeased with André, then I might be inclined to support your decision not to marry him. It's difficult to think of the family gathering tonight with your head-strong resistance ever-present. Many young girls in Paris are blessed if they have one suitor willing to marry them, with or without an arrangement. You are most fortunate to have two suitors who are each of fine families, have a means to provide and are members of the Church. Be grateful for what God has bestowed upon you. Choose wisely. Youth is temporary."

"Mother, I am grateful to God for you and Father. Of course you love me and desire my wellbeing. Your efforts to secure my future are appreciated."

"Are you certain that you appreciate it? It's kind of you to say so, nonetheless."

"Mother I feel light and gay that you understand the importance of this to me. Thank you for this walk. May I continue to walk and meet you back at home when I have appreciated the gifts of Paris?"

"Are you done with me this quickly?"

"Not at all mother. Would you allow me to dream in my head as I search the trees for buds and lose my cares in the coming spring air?"

"Oh, to the days of youth. Enjoy your walk. Dinner tonight shall be challenging. Please be careful with your words Cherie. My friendship with Monsieur and Madam Monet is valuable to me."

"Of course, Mother. I will be on my best behavior tonight."

Mother walked away toward home. When she was out of sight, I quickly turned towards the park to look for Jean-Paul. It was nearing noon and I hoped that he would come find me for an update. Our usual bench was empty. I waited. Soon I heard the church bells announce the arrival of the noon hour. I tingled with delight as I anticipated seeing him. As I waited I reflected on my conversation with mother. It had gone remarkably well, much to my surprise. Her insistence during our conversation at the beginning of the month was far different from today. What changed her mind? Did she know something that I did not? Had father influenced her, or perhaps Martine? Either way things were looking more in my favor. I was excited to tell Jean-Paul the progress. We had only the issue of the Church to overcome now.

81

Thirty minutes passed. Maybe he decided not to come today. Perhaps he was upset about our rendezvous yesterday. I wasn't certain how long I should wait, but I continued, hoping, excited, expecting. An hour passed, and still no sign of Jean-Paul. Another thirty minutes ticked on by and I sat alone. It was time that I should head home. Tomorrow I could update him on how tonight's dinner went as well. Feeling optimistic, I buried the disappointment in some small place in my heart.

**

When we arrived at the home of the Monet's, everyone was cheerful, full of smiles. André was especially pleasant, grinning the whole evening. Once we sat down for the elaborate meal that their cook had prepared, Madam Monet began with the topic I dreaded. "Cherie, when will you begin making your selections and plans for the wedding?"

Before I could find words to respond, André jumped into the conversation. "Mother, please withhold any questions of matrimony this night. In good time the details and date can be discussed between Cherie and me. For now let us have respect for the bride to be. The last thing to inspire a bride is pressure."

Everyone sat at the table in silence. I was shocked at André's words. The family stayed quiet. I couldn't imagine André's motive? Whatever it was, I was grateful that we might avoid the subject completely. My mother smiled awkwardly, possibly relieved or frustrated. My father didn't seem to care one way or another, but Madam Monet seemed very upset by the request. She obviously wanted to discuss the matter. She looked quite displeased, as she searched for an acceptable response. Her mouth hung open with barely detectable sounds escaping as she nearly started several sentences that she decided not to say.

Finally she spoke. "I find your comment rude. I want to hear from the bride."

"Mother!" André paused. "The matter is closed for tonight."

André continued to smile as if everything in the world were perfect. Whatever he was up to, I knew that he had some intention he did not share. Somehow he felt that things were going his way, although why he felt that way eluded me.

Painted with Love

The rest of the dinner was tense, but without event. After evening dessert, we said our departing pleasantries as if everything was as it has always been. I fought myself several times to share my emotions. I held my tongue at each temptation, not certain if holding the truth was a wise decision.

The next morning all I could think of was speaking with Jean-Paul. All morning I was restless waiting for the noon hour when I could walk Lou Lou. Unable to prevent myself from rushing the day, I left a few minutes early. Scanning the park, I looked for signs of Jean-Paul. He usually arrived before me. Today was different. I sat on our bench and waited impatiently. Lou Lou wanted to walk. He sat looking at me, wondering why we were sitting. Obviously he wanted to relieve his bladder, but I was certain that Jean-Paul would be here any minute. My heart became heavier with each passing moment. I wonder where he could be. Did our love making turn him away? Did he find me unattractive to him? He said such reassuring words to me. What has happened?

If I didn't know why he didn't come, I might go mad. I hired a carriage and asked the driver to take me to the home of Jacques and Martine. The driver was certain I was joking when he realized the length of the journey. I reassured him, and promised he would be paid for his time. Of course, I could only hope that Aunt Martine was at home and would pay my fare.

As I traveled, every possible scenario entered my head. Perhaps he was ill. Perhaps he was injured. Maybe he changed his mind. Maybe my parents spoke with him. What could it be? I needed to relax before I made myself crazy.

Thankfully Martine was home and met me at the front door. She was obviously distraught. She quickly paid the carriage man and asked him to wait.

She shuffled me inside and asked, "What do you know?" she asked.

"Pardon me, Auntie. What do you mean?"

"Do you know anything about his whereabouts?"

"Jean-Paul is not here?"

"Non! He's been missing for two nights. Jacques and I assumed he was staying at our flat in Paris." My cheeks blushed

83

when she mentioned it, but she seemed too upset to notice. "That's where he was staying for a few nights per week. But Jacques stayed there last night and Jean-Paul was not there. Then we received a delivery today. Here it is. It hurts too much to read it to you."

Her face was solemn as she slid the envelope from her hand into mine. From her expression I could tell that the letter contained something terrible. She nodded, encouraging me to read. The letter began, "March 22nd, 1898. I spoke with Monsieur Soule at the pier this morning. He asked me to deliver a message to this address, stating that he has departed for America and will not be returning. He will not be in contact with you for some time. His wish is for time alone to grieve." It was signed, "With Regards, A Stranger."

"You see? You know now why I'm worried?"

My dear Auntie and I stared at each other. I shook my head in small, rapid jerks. "Non. Non! This is not true. Someone is playing a trick. Non. Jean-Paul would not do this. Something is amiss."

"It's true. I feel it. He's injured also, or maybe dead. This note is to stop the police from looking. Jean-Paul would not leave us without saying good-bye or taking his personal items. All of his belongings are here. He did not depart for America!" Martine insisted.

"I fear for him. Someone is interfering. Who would do something to Jean-Paul? He is the nicest man. No one would want to hurt him. He has harmed no man!" I said, realizing as the words left my lips that they weren't true.

"His heart is pure. I know this boy well," Martine replied.

"Do you know anyone who has something against Jean-Paul?" I asked.

"Of course not. The only man who may not like him now is your André." Martine's words drove a piercing arrow through my heart.

"André?" She was right. He was the only man who could feel ill towards Jean-Paul. "Oui, it's true. But he doesn't know Jean-Paul. André is boastful and arrogant, but I don't think he's capable of criminal behavior."

"Arrogance can lead a man astray when he is in love with a woman. Jealousy can do even more harm, especially if he saw you with Jean-Paul."

Her words seized my heart in a tight grip of pain. "When was the last time you saw him?" I asked her.

"He left Wednesday to meet you in the park. He never returned."

Today was Friday. The dinner was Thursday. André was up to something at dinner. Jean-Paul went missing after we went to Jacques's flat. Was it possible that André saw us together? Did he see us at the park? Could André have done something to Jean-Paul? "Auntie, I think it may have been André. Jean-Paul and I spent the afternoon together. Maybe André saw us."

We stared at one another, perplexed, apprehensive, and afraid. My brain couldn't decide what to do. Then it came to me like a whisper in my ear. "Auntie, maybe André sent him away on a boat to be rid of him. Let us go to the pier and find out if they have a record of Jean-Paul departing. It will have an arrival date and place. Can we go now please?"

"Ahhh, oui. Let us go."

Martine sent the driver away that brought me to her home. She explained to me that she didn't want him to know where we were going, in case we needed to keep our plans secret for future safety. Then she called for her driver. "Take us to the pier straight away," she said urgently.

Martine and I held hands in the carriage. We barely spoke, both fearing what might have happened.

We walked together arm in arm to the ticket booth at the pier. Martine spoke. "Excuse me please monsieur. Would you please check on a passenger to see if he made it on board a boat yesterday?"

"The name please," the gentleman asked.

"Jean-Paul Soule," Martine stated proudly.

The man ran his finger down page after page of names with signatures next to them. He flipped the pages slowly, but scanned quickly. "I checked all of the registries. He did not depart yesterday. Did you want to check another date?"

"Oui. Check Wednesday please," I asked.

He scanned more pages. Finally his index finger found something. "Here he is. Jean-Paul Soule."

"May I look?" Martine asked. He turned the book around to allow Martine and I to read the name and signature. "That's definitely not his signature. There must be a mistake of some kind."

The man looked at the page. He looked above and below Jean-Paul's name, using his finger to guide his old eyes. "Are you a relative?"

"I raised this boy."

"I see." He paused, studying the name above Jean-Paul's. "Oh yes, I remember these two."

"Two?" You mean that Jean-Paul was not traveling alone?" My heart fell into my stomach. Who was with Jean-Paul? He had not let me know he was leaving and then he left Paris with someone else? Who?

"Oh he definitely was not alone. Poor fellow. Did you see him after his fall?"

"What fall?"

"The gentleman he was with said he had fallen down the stairs carrying his baggage as he was about to travel to the boat. He had broken his nose, which blackened both of his eyes. He said the poor man's jaw was broken too, and some ribs. Your nephew couldn't talk without assistance. The nice monsieur with him said he would see him to the ship in Le Havre to ensure that Jean-Paul did not miss his voyage to America."

"When is he scheduled to arrive in America, and at which port?" I interjected.

"I must search a separate book for that information. We sell the tickets here. I can tell you shortly if he purchased the final destination ticket here." He pulled out another book and looked at Wednesday's sales. He didn't find what he was looking for, so he searched another book, tracing the page quickly. "Ah, here it is. He is scheduled to arrive in New York on April 18th."

"April 18th? Why should it take four weeks?"

"He chose to take the cargo voyage, which stops in Spain and then in Canada before reaching the United States. It's a less

86

expensive fare. Not very pleasant accommodations I am afraid. But that's what his friend paid for."

"You mean that Jean-Paul did not pay his own fare?" Martine asked.

"Non, the monsieur with your nephew paid the fare. He wanted to help the poor man out."

"What's the name of this KIND man?" Martine asked as nicely as she could.

"Oui, let's look. He turned back to the first book where the page was still open. It says Monsieur Charles Batton. Do you know of him?"

"I do not," Martine said. She looked over at me and I shook my head no. "You have been most kind and helpful. How much does it cost for a ticket to New York on the best accommodations that you have?"

"Three hundred francs. Did you want to purchase one now?"

"Not yet. Merci."

Martine and I walked away from the ticket office and stood on the pier away from her driver and all ears. She said softly to me what I already knew. "Cherie, Jean-Paul is in danger. Someone has forced him to board this ship under duress and has harmed him. We don't know who, although André may have the most obvious motive. If he is capable of such subterfuge, then we can't be certain of what else he is may do. He could harm you if you do not cooperate with him…"

"I will never cooperate. He cannot get away with…"

"Cherie, Cherie. Please remain calm. We must take the upper hand here and protect you. If André did this, then you must be away from him. We need a careful plan. My first thought is to take you from your home where you can stay with me for a few days, but if André finds out that you are at my home he may suspect that we know something. It is best if you go home and appear like nothing is out of the ordinary. I will make arrangements for your needs in America including housing and contacts. Once everything is arranged, then I will tell your parents that you are staying at my home. You will pack your things and I will take you to the boat. Your parents shall hear everything from me, once you are safe. You can meet Jean-Paul at the ship in New York when he arrives and get him to a doctor."

Martine looked at my face and noticed the distraught look forming and the tears pooling. "Be strong, Cherie. I too want to cry. That's my son out there injured and alone. He loves you and you love him. We must be brave for Jean-Paul. You cannot allow anyone to know what you suspect. There's great danger in this right now. Please, no emotions." With my eyes closed, I drew in a few deep breaths. Could things get any worse? I didn't want to tempt fate with that question. I changed my thoughts to the tasks before me.

"I will take you home. You must pretend that all is well when you see your mother and father. They will also not believe that André would resort to action so vile. It's best that I have more certainty that André was involved before I speak with them. Once you make it to America and find Jean-Paul, you may have the details I need. You must be kind to André for now. It is in your best interest."

I nodded my head in agreement.

"Once you're safely away from Paris, I will share with your parents what has happened."

Anger was beginning to form in my head. How dare André injure Jean-Paul! Then I realized that if André had followed us and watched us enter the flat for several hours, he may have felt justified in killing Jean-Paul. I wanted to scream. I wished I could kick André until he was hurt and bleeding. My whole body started to shake with rage. He's evil!

We rode to my home in Martine's carriage. Martine walked me inside and began the acting. She kissed my mother as if everything was normal. Then she added, "It's always good to see you dear Catherine. Thank you for sharing your daughter with me. I'm afraid she's a bit distraught with the news that I have shared. Jean-Paul has already departed for America to work for Jacques. He left quite suddenly. It would seem that the situation was difficult for him and departing was easier. It's unclear, for he left without explanation. Be gentle with Cherie. Her heart is tender at this time. Well, I wish I could stay and enjoy your kind company, but I have an appointment I must not miss in town. Please Catherine, let's meet again soon. I miss your company."

My mother face showed a look of confusion and surprise. Martine had spoken quickly without an opportunity for mother to offer an invitation for tea or a word at all. She didn't seem to know how to respond to Martine's unfriendly, rushed visit.

Martine turned to me. "It was lovely to see you Cherie. Be strong child. We must meet together more often. I enjoy your company. Please accompany me to the ballet soon. Au' revoir." Martine turned and walked away.

Mother put her arm over my shoulder as we watched Martine walk out the front door. "Are you feeling all right my dear?"

"Eventually I will be. Right now I'm hurt and confused. I shall freshen up and see you at supper."

My legs reluctantly carried me up the stairs to my room. With the door shut, I collapsed in a heap on my bed, lost in a whirlwind of disbelief, determination and longing to see the man I loved.

A feeling of abhorrence welled up in my being.

Jean-Paul was alone on a cargo ship, bruised, broken and possibly threatened by André to never return to Paris. Tears rolled down my cheeks. I must get to him, without letting André or my parents know of my plan. Crossing the ocean scared me; being at sea away from land for an extended period. I could not swim and the thought of such a vast expanse of water was stressful. Traveling across the Atlantic would challenge my adventurous spirit. Yet the thought of living in a new land with Jean-Paul excited me. That was the kind of adventure I longed for.

On my back, facing the ceiling, I wiped the tears from my cheeks with my hands. Dinner would be soon and I would have to look at my parents and pretend nothing was amiss. Overcome by complexity and deep emotion, I had to wonder if I would ever enjoy simplicity again.

With courage and a shield of armor to hide and protect my emotions, I prepared my mind for this journey. Getting to Jean-Paul would change my life's path forever. Nothing else mattered to me. Finding Jean-Paul appeared to be the only option worth considering.

    ***

Chapter Seven: **Two Lies Balance the Scale**

Paris, March 21, 1899

In the days following the dinner with André's family, I felt as if the devil stalked me while he laughed at my fake smiles, the little lies I told and my attempt to pretend everything was normal. André wouldn't leave me alone either. He was at my side at every opportunity. The three of us could never find much to talk about, André, me and the devil. The tempter of evil found that amusing too. The mocking felt endless.

Eight days after I learned of Jean-Paul's odd departure, André asked if I would dine with him that evening. Reluctantly, I agreed. Every time I saw André I was sick to my stomach. Dinner would be brutal. Yet I wanted to see some proof from him, some truth that would answer how he could take it upon himself to destroy my happiness when I asked for it honestly. Why did he feel that I didn't deserve to be content?

We dined at la Fermette Marbeuf. André dressed in a fine, black suit. He looked handsome; a villain in sheep's clothing. The conversation seemed strained, and I wondered if he noticed. Being his wife and dining with him night after night felt mortifying. Being a lonely old maid appealed to me more than enduring every dinner across the table from André.

"You look radiant my sweet," André told me. "You grow more beautiful with each passing day."

"Merci," I replied.

"How do I look this evening? Do you like my new jacket and trousers?"

"You look…well-dressed." I sensed immediately that he searched for more. "You look intelligent and wealthy," I added.

"Thank you. Does that have appeal to you, my sweet?"

"What lady does not want intelligence and wealth?"

"Ah, well said, my love." André paused and smiled, looking pleased with himself. "While I'm looking dashingly irresistible, would you like to take this opportunity to apologize for your hurtful words upon my arrival?"

"I would like to apologize. André, I'm sorry for hurting you. Inside of you is a wonderful person whom I've loved since my early youth. You're my friend, above anything else. It was not my intention to cause you pain. Your happiness is my wish. Hopefully my actions shall not prevent you from a good life."

"There now. Do you not feel much better? Don't worry about mistakes you shall make in the future, for there are bound to be many. Your apology is always welcome."

He obviously heard what he wanted to, instead of my sincere apology for breaking his heart. "Very well, André. Thank you for accepting my apology. Truly I meant you no harm."

The waiter came and took our order. He brought the wine that André had requested. André and I were silent until the waiter left.

Then André spoke. "I appreciate your apology darling and I shall accept it right after God does. You know of course that this matter must be cleared with the Church prior to our marriage. Like God, I'm a forgiving man. So, I shall forgive you after this is addressed in confession, which is necessary prior to marriage. You could address any other immoralities at that time and walk forward with a clean soul and body for your husband."

The way André spoke about confession, I could feel that he knew things that he didn't share. My stomach turned in summersaults and my heart sank as I imagined him following Jean-Paul and me. It would be best to bring everything out in the open, honestly talking with one another, as I remember doing when we were children. Too much was at stake this time. André would only be hurt and infuriated by my confession. He knew that Jean-Paul and I had been alone, but the details did not need to be expressed. Words could not explain to André how my body and soul pined for Jean-Paul with an aching greater than I have ever known. Telling him that our bodies became one being sharing the same space would not be understood by this man who had never felt that sensation. Nor would he care.

"Of course, André. I will go to confession before I'm wed."

"I know you will, darling. It's required. I encourage you to share all discretions, including your relations with Monsieur Soule, in order to be clean entering the marriage."

"Oui. I shall." What did he know?

"There's another matter Cherish…I mean Cherie. Your parents, my parents and I spoke over the past week. We all agreed that it's best that you and I marry as soon as possible."

"Excuse me? What do you mean? Why would we rush our wedding?"

"Because darling, I'm far away from Paris for two more years. Focusing on school work would be impossible if I'm to worry about suitors who may try to steal my fiance away from me. When you're my wife, you can accompany me to Aix-Marseille and make me meals, rub my shoulders and keep me happy and focused. You may travel home to see your family and I shall know that you are mine."

I stared at André. It didn't matter what he wanted, because within a week's time I would board a boat out of Paris. Yet it baffled me that my parents and André felt responsible for decisions regarding my life.

"When do you think it would be best to wed?" I sputtered.

"The priest said he could do a ceremony, to legalize our union before God, prior to me returning to school. Then during my summer school break, your parents have agreed to host a large celebration with a ceremony in our honor."

"My mother has agreed to this? Does she not worry about the appearance of such a wedding?"

"Your parents agreed that since Jean-Paul has left you, and you're in this distraught state, and considering your past behavior, marriage is a wise solution."

"I do not appreciate other people taking liberty with my life."

"Get used to it, darling. That's how life is. Women submit to their husbands. It is stated in the Bible. Surely you know this. You mustn't be so naive about things."

Our dinner arrived. My plate of filet mignon and sweet potatoes looked and smelled well prepared, but my stomach tightened and I didn't want to eat a bite. With my fork I pushed food around on my plate, pretending to consume it.

It was pointless to argue so I dug for information. "How were you aware that Jean-Paul left Paris?"

"I believe I heard the news from your father."

"Did my father share the strange way in which Jean-Paul left?"

"Not in detail. He stated that the man left abruptly."

"Do you find it strange?"

"Non, not under the circumstances. This Jean-Paul obviously felt guilty for interfering with a woman promised to another man. All men know the seriousness of such behavior...and the consequences."

The tone and confidence in André's voice gave me further confirmation of his involvement. This was a dangerous subject and I opted to change the topic. "Where are you expecting that we shall live? Not in the male dormitory, as you do. Are we to get a flat?"

"Yes, darling. I shall return to school after we are wed and will have a house for us in a month or two. You may live with your parents until I find the proper place for us to dwell. Until then I shall miss your soft skin and warm kisses that I shall enjoy on our wedding day."

Silently I sulked, not responding to André. I drank my wine and asked for more. I wanted to leave Paris tonight and not wait for Martine to make all of the arrangements she was fussing about.

During the rest of the meal André talked about moving back to Paris after he graduated and becoming the best attorney in France. Politely I nodded, happy that we were off the subject of marriage. The rest of dinner was spent with André trying to convince me how great life would be when he graduated, while I tried to prevent myself from vomiting. The wine seemed to help. By the end of the dinner my speech and judgment were influenced by the alcohol.

André and I rode to my home in an open carriage. When we arrived at my door, he held my hand firmly while we sat unmoved on the bench seat. "We shall be wed in ten days my sweet. Now is an appropriate time to have a celebratory kiss." With the effects of the wine swimming in my head, I braced myself and shut my eyes, allowing André to bring his selfish lips to mine. As his lips touched me, a strange thought occurred to me. I was selfish also. André and I both wanted to have what made us happy. The difference was that he had to force me into marriage to get his way and I had to leave him stranded to get mine. In either case, one of us would hurt the other. It didn't seem fair that each of our happiness would only come at the cost of the other.

The kiss was uneventful to me, causing neither repulsing nor pleasing. Only sorrow for our plight rose up. André seemed quite content with the kiss, gauging from his grin. He leaped from the carriage and spun around to the other side to help me out. He walked me to my door and held my hand in his. Raising my hand to his lips and said, "I am thrilled that we shall be together. I've imagined you as my wife since I was a young boy. Holding you and touching your soft skin has been my wish for years. Soon it will be real." He kissed my hand with his wet lips. "Dream sweet things, Cherish. Soon, I will be dreaming beside you." He turned and jumped into the carriage like a young boy. It reminded me of when he was twelve and he used to try to impress me by jumping and running. The memory was an odd contrast to how I felt today.

Inside the house, I managed to climb the stairs and enter my bedroom without being noticed. The elixir at dinner pushed me into a fast, hard sleep. Morning came too soon with a pounding sensation. I rubbed my aching head with both hands, noticing how my scalp hurt as well as with everything inside of it. As reality came into focus, I remembered some of the conversation from dinner. Ten days!!! Ten days!! Ahhh, I must get out of Paris!

Before I dressed or washed my face, I wrote a letter to Martine. "I must see you immediately. Very urgent! Cherie." Then I dressed quickly and ran down the stairs. "Good morning, Mother. It's a lovely day for a walk. I shall return in a short while."

"Where are you going?"

"For a brief walk!" I ran out the front door without another word to deliver the letter to the mail service. I returned home to find Martine's driver sitting in front of the house.

When I entered, Mother and Auntie sat in the parlor talking. They turned to look at me. "What's the matter Cherie?" Martine asked. "You look as if you have seen a ghost."

"I was just thinking about you, Auntie, and here you are. What a surprise and a delight all at once." The devil laughed at my expert way of deceiving my mother.

"You are a vision as well. Your mother just explained to me about your new wedding plans. Congratulations my dear."

"Merci." More laughter teased me. Does my mother not hear the mocking?

"Catherine and I were just discussing if I might take you to the ballet tonight and keep you for a day or two, if you would like to come? We could address your wedding plans. Events are my specialty."

"That sounds lovely. Do you have any objections, Mother?"

"When could we do some wedding planning Cherie?" Mother said.

"Might I suggest this Catherine?" Martine said before I could reply. "If I could have Cherie for two days, I could organize all of the decisions she must make and then you can take her to the dress shop to finalize all of the details. I will also help you plan for this summer's event. It's my pleasure to assist."

"Since the ceremony is just immediate family, there's not much to do yet. You may go Cherie, if you would like."

"Pack some of your favorite dresses darling. My tailor shall stop by and make you some new ones as a wedding present," Martine suggested. "Your mother and I have more to talk about. Could you please pack, darling, and be ready to depart when I am through visiting?"

"Certainly." As I walked to my room, relief washed through my whole body. Martine's timing could not have been better. Desperately I needed to leave Paris and the devastating situation that I was in. Leaving my family unexpectedly was terrifying and cruel. I felt horrible for the hurt I would cause my mother and father. Yet I couldn't be André's wife just to please my parents. I

96

loved them very much, but not enough to be miserable with an arrogant, violent man that I didn't love. Perhaps my parents would forgive me and I could rejoin them in Paris after André married another woman. My options were limited. Afraid and desperate, I packed everything that fit into my luggage bag. After leaving my bag at the front door, I casually entered the parlor.

"I'm ready any time that you are Auntie."

"Merci, my dear. We should be on our way. There's much to do and there is the ballet to get ready for."

"Perhaps I shall come to the ballet with you," Mother interjected.

"Now Catherine, we know that you shall not enjoy the ballet as we do. Let us all go out for lunch after I've had Cherie for a couple of days. We will discuss the summer reception. It will be lovely. Let us depart Cherie. Au revoir, Catherine."

"Au revoir, Mother." I kissed my mother on both cheeks. Pain squeezed my heart knowing that I was walking away from my mother for an unknown period of time without a proper good-bye. How could she ever forgive me? My father was not at home to receive my farewell kiss. I swallowed hard, hoping that Mother didn't see the distress in my eyes. "I love you, Mother."

"Au revoir, Cherie. I love you as well. I shall see you in two days, oui?" Mother emphasized her question, demanding that we respond.

"Two days, Catherine. Three at most. She's in good hands. May God bless you until we see you again."

Martine and I climbed into her carriage as her driver loaded my luggage. Mother stood at the door, as if she didn't trust our departure. She may have felt something amiss in her heart, perhaps not have known why.

We rode away while waving sweetly to Mother. Then I spoke quietly to Martine, avoiding her driver's ear. "Auntie, you have no idea how desperate I was. I was going mad. André took me to dinner last night and talked about confession and apologies and that I would make mistakes but he would always welcome my apologies. He was…"

"Cherie…please, relax your mind. Many details were addressed which delayed me. You knew that I would come, oui?"

"Oui," I replied.

"Now let me tell you all that happened, for there is much to tell. I went to the pier to buy a voucher for you to travel to America. The man at the window remembered me. One of the crew members returned back to Paris with a letter he received from a passenger who was traveling on the boat between Paris and the ship at Le Havre. He offered the note to the ticket master, who presented it to me. It's of such a serious nature. I hesitate to show it to you."

"Martine, let me see the letter. Is it from Jean-Paul? What is it?" I asked.

"Are you certain you want to know this? Perhaps you should know what happened; but it's quite upsetting."

"Oui, please allow me to see it," I begged.

Martine pulled a letter from her pocketbook. Slowly she handed it to me, watching my face as I took the paper. Unfolding it, I carefully read:

Dear Monsieur Jean-Paul Soule,

It is with deep regret that I write to you, under the circumstances. You see, I'm aware of your time alone with mademoiselle Bourguignon on March 20 from 1:00 PM until 5:00 PM. I saw you and Mademoiselle enter 322 Rue Street, alone, and exit, arm in arm four hours later. Knowing this information hurts my heart, of course, as I'm engaged to marry the lovely mademoiselle when I graduate from law school.

Your broken ribs and swollen face are the work of close friends of mine. You may not remember your encounter with them, but if they see you again in Paris, they will finish the work they began.

You're on your way far from Paris. I thoughtfully chose the longest, least expensive route to America for you. By the time your vessel reaches your new country, and you attempt to get back to Paris without any money in your hands, I will have already convinced sweet Cherie to follow through with her commitment to marry me, prior to my graduation.

Don't worry about paying me back for the cost of the voyage. It was a parting gift. Also, I have the solution for keeping

Cherie and your family from looking for you. Don't count on any help from them.

Here is a parting thought: if you attempt to contact Mademoiselle Cherie, then I will share the events of your encounter with her family and the Church, humiliating her and allowing her to be punished accordingly to pay the price for the sins of you both.

There is not a man or judge in Paris who would hold my action against me, under the circumstances. Your actions, however, are unforgivable!

Without Regret,

André Monet

I held the letter in front of me for a long moment. My mind raced with thoughts; André watching us, how distraught I was that day, and André's friends finding Jean-Paul and beating him for loving me. Now Martine knew that Jean-Paul and I had been alone, at her home in Paris. Several emotions flooded me at once; it was difficult to land on one. I closed my eyes, unsure of what to say or do.

"Are you all right, Cherie?"

"It's my fault. I begged him to take me to your flat. I was distraught and wanted him to hold me. We were at an impasse. I just…"

"Shhh…don't blame this on you. Love is not your fault."

"But I didn't need to beg him. He was only…"

"Shhh! Blame will not change what has happened. You must focus on your future. Upon seeing this letter, it was obvious that you must not marry André. He may take you to be his wife, but he will never forgive what has happened between you and Jean-Paul. Nothing you ever do would make him love you fully now."

"I could never marry him, regardless. I have to be…"

"Cherie. You have no need to convince me of anything. I have a plan. This is what we are going to tell your parents. While you were staying at my home, you asked to borrow some money for a gift you saw for André. While I was napping, you left with my driver and the money to Paris. Instead of shopping, you departed on the first available boat to Le Havre and then America. You left me a note apologizing for taking the money and stating that you cannot marry André. You included this letter," she said reaching for the letter I was still holding, "that you had obtained a few days earlier when you inquired at the pier regarding Jean-Paul. I will state that I had nothing to do with your disappearance, while I am leading them to conclusions and towards understanding. Is this clear to you?" she said quietly.

"Oui, it's a good idea."

"I have thought about this quite a lot, especially after I obtained this letter. I fear for Jean-Paul. His injuries could be serious," she said.

"Let's not dwell on such thoughts. We must focus on following your strategy. When do I leave Paris?" I asked.

"Tomorrow."

"I will write the letter when we reach your home."

"Let's have lunch first. I invited Marion to join us but she is lying down upstairs. She suddenly has a stomach ache and says that won't be able to visit with you before you go. That's unfortunate because I have a nice meal planned with lots of goodies." She paused, then added, "It's difficult for me to let you go. I shall miss you greatly."

I looked into Martine's eyes, which were forming tears and becoming red. My eyes copied hers. Soon we were arm in arm, quietly acknowledging the gravity of my departure. There was a chance that I would never see her or my family again. We sat silently holding hands for the rest of the carriage ride.

Her staff had made an elaborate lunch with fresh pastries, jams, fruit, tea, coffee, quiche, and fresh lemonade. There was far more food than we could eat. After lunch Martine insisted on a visit to her sun room. When I entered the room it looked like Christmas. There were wrapped presents stacked high on a center table.

"What is this?" I asked.

"I won't be able to give you a proper wedding reception and gifts. Therefore I am giving you my blessings now. Please, open them."

I sat in a chair she had placed at the table. I noticed after I sat down that there were larger presents underneath the table. Under bows and decorative fabric wrap was a traveling trunk, blankets, new clothes, a sewing basket, a mirror and brush, a beautiful new night gown, a rolling pin for pastries, powdered chocolate, two soft pillows and silver spoons and coins. "Silver is more valuable in America than francs; at least that's what I am told."

"Auntie, I cannot…"

"You have no choice. You would not deny me the pleasure of giving to you and Jean-Paul now would you?"

I didn't know what to say. I stood up and reached over to hug my dear friend. I felt overwhelmed with love and appreciation. Tears pooled in my eyes. "Merci."

"Merci, to you."

"Moi?" I asked.

"Oui, your smile and company have warmed my heart for many years."

We were silent again. Holding back floods of tears.

Finally Martine spoke. "Let us pack your beautiful trunk with your new things. Then you can write your letter before supper. After supper I want you to relax in a hot bath and retire early. You have a big day tomorrow."

"You are the best, Auntie." Martine smiled and called for my luggage bag to be delivered to the door outside of the sun room. She didn't allow her staff to see what we were packing. The two of us laughed and spoke while we carefully folded her gifts into my new trunk. "Martine, I am sorry that I used your flat to be alone with Jean-Paul."

"I can forgive the transgression."

"Pardon me?"

"I understand wanting to be held. I understand passion and young love. Perhaps this is God's way of forcing action to occur. Your parents were not listening to your pleas. Something huge had to happen to correct this error. I do wish that Jean-Paul is not hurt badly. I am not angry. Do not give the matter another thought."

"Merci, Martine. I wish my mother were as understanding as you." Martine just smiled.

When my trunk was packed, I went upstairs to my usual guest room. There I found paper and pen waiting. I wrote the letter that Martine would show to my parents. I poured out my heart to express my love to them and asked them to forgive my unannounced departure.

I showed the letter to Martine, and she approved. We enjoyed a spectacular dinner, with wine and dessert. After dinner a bath was waiting for me, hot and bubbly. I soaked in the tub and tried to imagine what I would say when I saw Jean-Paul. I tried to remember what he smelled like and what his hand felt like on my face.

The water began to cool. After a long soak, I wrapped myself in a robe left sitting for me. I walked to her room where she was reading a book. "How are you feeling?" she asked.

"Warm and happy for the moment," I replied.

"Wonderful. I shall see you in the morning before you depart. Pleasant dreams darling."

"Good night."

I climbed into the fluffy, soft bed and pulled the covers under my chin. Thoughts swarmed my head. I tried to relax and drift off to sleep, but slumber didn't come easily. Eventually, I slipped into the world of dreams, but they were far from pleasant. The night was restless and I woke several times. I dreamt that I was looking for Jean-Paul. I looked in many strange places that I didn't recognize. I was on a ship, then in a hotel, then a museum and a restaurant. I couldn't find him. Then, when I thought I'd finally located him, I walked up to him and it was André. He was smiling an evil grin. He grabbed me and trapped me in a cage. I woke up suddenly. I sat up in my bed, sweating.

I began to wonder if André had followed me today. What if he followed me to the pier tomorrow and stopped me from departing. Lying down, I imagined all of the ways that I could disguise myself. I wondered if he might find me on the carriage ride from Martine's home into Paris. What if my parents told him that I was staying with the Aunt of Jean-Paul? He might worry that she knew something. I lie on my back unable to fall asleep. My muscles tightened as I feared getting away safely. Eventually I drifted off, holding a pillow to my chest with my fists closed tightly. I dreamed once again. This time I was on a great ship traveling on a sea that never ended. André stood on the only shore, laughing.

Painted with Love

***

Chapter Eight: **Into the Unknown**

Paris, Late March 1899

I woke from my night of wicked dreams, terrified of the coming day. If André had visited my home and found my whereabouts he may suspect something. He may try to follow me to see what I was doing. He had no reason to think that I knew something. Yet visiting Jean-Paul's family may be the hint that he needed.

I walked downstairs to the dining room where Martine sat at the table waiting for me.

"Bonjour, how did you sleep child?"

"Good morning Auntie. Sleep eluded me except for bad dreams. André may know that I'm here and come looking for me."

"You may be right. My intuition tells me to take some necessary precautions," Martine said. Marion walked into the room, took a biscuit from the table and walked out without greeting either of us. Martine and I gave each other a look of surprise and then she continued. "We must sneak you out of here without anyone knowing that you have left. Here is my plan. My staff will be told that you have gone for a long walk. Meanwhile, we shall hide you in a trunk and send you to Paris in a wagon with my driver. He will be instructed to deliver the boxes, with you in one and your belongings in the other, to my nephew's dress shop where you can safely exit the trunk. From there you will be taken to the pier by another driver. In case André is waiting at the pier, you shall be dressed in my servants clothing and wearing a reddish wig under your bonnet. You must board the boat wearing this attire. This is the only way to protect you."

"Thank you, Martine. You are wonderful." No one was nearby as we spoke, but I hoped that none of her staff overheard our plan. If someone could manipulate a person to spill the beans, it was the up-and-coming lawyer, André.

"I am not certain that my plan is foolproof," she continued. André could still interfere. We must be very diligent. If he finds out you have left Paris he could try to board a boat and bring you back. Your ticket is purchased under the name Margareta Sonnet. Here is false identification for you. At least he won't know by looking for your name. Your letter to your parents will remain with me until you are safe in America and have a place to stay in New York. I shall say that my housekeeper found it under the bed when cleaning."

I sat at the dining room table in silence. Things were getting more complicated. Already I was running from my home, searching an ocean and new country for a beaten up lover who didn't know I was coming. Now I risked being followed or captured. The excitement was far more than I wished. I hadn't desired to be chased and scared. The price was high, but worth the rewards of pressing my flesh against Jean-Paul, the rush of tingling, and looking deeply into his eyes to hang on his every word.

The boat from Paris to Le Havre was scheduled to leave at 2:45 p.m. Martine and I decided to have me leave first thing that morning to give us plenty of time to execute her plan. She found me the clothing and wig. Wearing the dress, apron and bonnet belonging to her house maid, I felt like a mocking impostor in an outfit that I would never be made to wear. The thought of walking onto a boat dressed as a servant embarrassed me. My first class ticket would certainly seem inappropriate and cause strange looks. Once I departed from Le Havre by ship, I could don my own clothing. Even if André, or someone he sent, managed to find me on a vessel at Le Havre, they couldn't turn the ship around to take me back to Paris.

"I feel terrible placing you in a trunk darling. It's a long bumpy ride into town. The bottom is lined with blankets. I pray that you survive well. It's a good thing that you are petite."

"It's not your fault Auntie. My appreciation for your help is beyond what I can express. There's no one else for me to turn to."

"I would do anything to protect you...and Jean-Paul of course." We smiled at each other, knowing that we may spend the rest of our lives apart. "Let's see if you fit in here."

I climbed into the open trunk lined with blankets, scooting around from one cramped position to another to find the most comfortable way. "Could I have a small pillow, Auntie?"

"Oh, oui, I know of the perfect pillow."

Auntie left the room and returned with a small engraved pillow. "This is the pillow I made for Jean-Paul when he came to live with us. My mother taught me needle point. It's a bit worn, but this is the perfect pillow for you to take. Perhaps you can even smell Jean-Paul's scent on it." She smiled, handing me the small cushion.

"Thank you, Auntie. I shall treasure it."

I placed the pillow behind my head and nestled in the trunk with my feet and buttocks resting on the bottom and my head against one short end leaning on Jean-Paul's pillow. My back was curved into a half moon and would soon become tired from this position, but it felt like the most comfortable way to begin the journey. "Let us see if we can close the lid." Auntie brought the lid slowly over my head and rested it gently on the box. "It shall appear latched from the outside, yet you will have the only true latch on the inside that I had my workman fashion to allow yourself an exit if need be. How does it feel?"

"It's dark," I said loudly. "I shall be fine for a while, but certainly not days," I said smiling.

Martine lifted the lid. "I made you some food for the journey." She handed me a sack, placing it in my folded lap.

"Merci, you're kind. You think of everything."

"We must get you on your way. Cherie, I shall miss you with all of my heart. I shall pray endlessly for the safety of you and Jean-Paul. Jean-Paul knows our friends, Claude and Ester Batton, in New York. He will most likely find them immediately, if you miss him at the disembarking of his ship. They will meet you at the dock in New York. If you do not find them, here is their address in New York. You must go to them immediately, for your safety. They shall help you locate Jean-Paul. You arrive five days before his cargo ship is scheduled. You may go to the pier with Monsieur and Madam Batton.

Today when you reach my nephew's shop, give him this note and money. He will arrange for a discreet ride to the pier," Martine said handing me an envelope addressed to Pierre.

"Merci, again. When all is well with the business, I will return to Paris so you may hold my children." My heart was bursting with love for her.

"Let us focus on today. We shall see each other again one day, if it be God's will. It is more important that you are safe and happy.

"Martine, why are you doing all of this for me?"

"I love you, Cherie, but I'm doing this for Jean-Paul more than for you. Since the day he came to live with me as a little boy, I saw the spark of hope go out of his eyes. He was content as he could make himself, but he lacked an excitement or love for life. When I saw how mesmerized he was by you, I watched him carefully. I saw the spark come back in his eyes. I loved my sister dearly. I know that she would want to have her boy live a happy life. The most I could do now to honor my sister is to help Jean-Paul be happy."

My heart felt gratitude as tears flowed down my cheeks. Before I could say a word Martine spoke again.

"It's time to close and lock the lid now. Locking will happen automatically, but only you can unlock it. It's time to load the wagon."

My eyes engaged Martine's for one last moment with love and appreciation as she lowered the lid on my hiding place. My world went dark and small. Moments later, I heard muffled voices. Martine spoke to someone. "You're the only one I trust. You're not to tell a soul about this. If you're approached by any person, even the police, you're to lie about what you're transporting. Do not open this box unless Mademoiselle Bourguignon's life's at stake. The box is locked and can only be opened from the outside by breaking the lock or from the inside by mademoiselle. Deliver both of these trunks to his address. Then leave. The contents will be cared for from there. Do you understand your assignment?"

"Oui, Madam."

A fear gripped me as I realized that if her plan went badly, I would look like a runaway servant with false identification. Could I trust her driver to not be bribed to sell me off, pretending there was a robbery. Something inside of me felt worried there were important details that I didn't anticipate.

Another person entered the room. Martine spoke again. "I have valuable breakables in these two boxes. They must be delivered safely to Paris. Both of you must protect my belongings from any would-be thieves. Carry them gently. Guard them with force if you must." My hiding box was lifted by two strong men and carried down the stairs, outside and loaded into a wagon. I held my hand over my mouth to avoid making a sound as I tilted and jostled in the small container.

Within moments we were rolling our way towards Paris along the dirt road. I braced myself for the hour ride of bouncing along. I felt much safer in the box than riding comfortably in a carriage. If only I could sleep in the darkness, but the excitement of my voyage, the fear of discovery, the guilt of leaving my parents all played a loud chatter in my head that didn't allow for rest.

As my mind wondered about my new life ahead, our wagon slowed and then stopped. I thought maybe one of the drivers needed to relieve his bladder. Then I heard a voice that made the hair on the back of my neck stand up.

"Merci, for stopping. Could you please direct me to the home of Jacques Soule?"

"Do you have business with Monsieur Soule?"

"Indeed. I'm a friend of the family."

"Monsieur Soule is not at his country home this day. He's away for a few days I regret." I cringed as I heard the exchange of words. The driver was giving André too much information.

"Are you from his staff?"

"Oui."

"What are you transporting?" I scrunched down into my little box as if I could further hide from André's grasp.

"We are transporting belongings of Madam Soule to a shop to be sold."

"What kind of belongings?"

"We were not shown the contents of the boxes that we are to deliver."

"Please show me the contents. I'm on a quest for many items." Could André suspect me to be hiding in a box, or did he want to spend his time looking though trunks?

"The items are promised to a shop keeper. They are presently locked."

"I would like to see them!"

"You may ride up the road and ask Madam Soule for the key."

"Have you seen Mademoiselle Bourguignon at the home?"

"Oui, Monsieur. Mademoiselle was seen at breakfast this morning. You shall find the estate at the end of this road."

"Merci, I shall go see Madam Soule. Then I shall ask Madam for the key and see what she has for sale. I'm sure that I can find you on your way to Paris when I return. My horse is fast."

"Oui, Monsieur."

"Au revoir," André replied.

His horse's hooves galloped off behind us. I tried to calculate in my mind how long it would take André to ride to the house, find out that I'm not there and ride back to search the trunks. My hiding place began to feel made of glass. Suddenly I couldn't get enough air. Did I breathe in all of the oxygen? Am I going to suffocate? Will André find me dead in this box? What am I to do? The wagon moved forward for about five minutes. Then it stopped again. I listened and waited, wondering in fear.

"Mademoiselle, open the lid please."

The voice may have been the driver's voice, but I couldn't be certain. I didn't respond.

"What are you doing? Do you think that is some kind of magic box? Do you think there's a genie inside who can open it for you? It's locked Oubear," another voice said.

"Mademoiselle, the horseman is far from sight. Please open the lid."

"I will open the lid, but why are you doing this?"

"What was that?" the other man asked the driver. "Is there really a genie in the box?"

"Shhh! It's safe mademoiselle."

"I pressed reluctantly on the lock on the inside of the lid. Nothing happened. Fresh air and light motivated me. Again it didn't work. "It's not working. It won't release."

"Try again mademoiselle."

Again and again I pushed. "I need air. I'm out of air."

"Hurry up, Oubear. The genie is running out of air. She might die."

"There are holes for air in the lid and sides. You can't see them, but they are there. Breathe slowly. We can get you out."

"Why do you want me to come out?"

"The Monsieur shall return soon and he will search the trunks. We must put you elsewhere."

"Where?"

"I have an idea. We must first get you out."

Lying on my back, I placed my feet directly above me. Perhaps I could push the lid open. With my feet against the domed ceiling, I pushed as hard as I could. Nothing happened. Maybe Martine did lock me in here to have me thrown me in to the Seine River.

Out of frustration I banged against the side of the trunk with my hands. My left hand hit a clasp I had not noticed before. It felt like the one on my right side. I pressed both clasps at the same time and the lid came loose. With my feet I pushed the lid open and saw daylight and smelled fresh air. A huge sigh of relief came over me.

"Are you a genie?" asked a man I didn't recognize.

"Do I look like a genie to you?"

"You're not dressed like a genie. You look like our house staff, but I've never seen you before."

"Be quiet," Oubear said. "We must act quickly. Get up," he shouted at the other man. "Come mademoiselle," he said reaching for my hand. He helped me out of the trunk and on to the front of the wagon.

"This won't do. He shall see me..." My objection was interrupted.

"Quiet please." He lifted the seat upon which they had sat. Under the seat was a space for tools to fix the wagon. He moved some of the tools to the side. The larger ones he removed. "Quickly, lie down. We need the blankets to fill the trunk. You will have to lie on the wood." I climbed into my new hiding place still holding the letter I was to give Martine's nephew, Pierre.

"I must seal this lid shut, to ensure he cannot open it. Do not fear mademoiselle. I shall open it up when you're safe."

I heard a hammer pound one, two then three nails into the wood seat, sealing me into a coffin like space, to hide from the man who said he loved me.

Then I heard the two men at the back of the wagon. "Help me move things into the empty trunk. They must seem full of items for sale," Oubear said.

"Did you steal this girl?"

"Of course I did not steal her?"

"She's hiding in a trunk. She's a servant. We must report this or we will get punished for…"

"Be quiet. You don't know what's happening."

"Tell me what's happening then."

"Madam Soule asked me to take her niece safely to Pierre's shop. He will then get her out of Paris. The man on the horse is a bad man and he is engaged to marry the girl. Her parents don't believe that he is a bad man."

"If we are caught then…"

"Madam Soule would explain everything. She didn't want anyone else to know in order to protect this girl."

"Let us get this delivery completed and settle my nervous stomach," said the other man.

My new container was hard, rough and dark. If only I'd thought to grab the pillow from the trunk. When we moved, my head bounced against the bottom of the small space. The box smelled of oil and dirt. My white blouse and apron would look terrible when I emerged. The darkness of the small space was suffocating. Again I felt that there wasn't enough air. My stomach tightened. My breathing was shallow. I closed my eyes wishing for all of it to be over.

I feared the moment when André would catch back up to us and search the wagon. When we finally stopped, I listened carefully for André. Instead of André, I heard the driver talking to me. "Mademoiselle, we must go inside and speak with Pierre. Wait here for a moment. Then we will open the seat."

"Excuse me. You must know that André is very cleaver. He may have followed us here and he may be watching this minute. He may see you take me out of the seat."

"I'm going to speak with Pierre about taking the wagon to the alley. It will appear that we are loading the trunks into the back space. In the alley we can hide you well. Please wait."

Quietly I wondered if André spied the wagon at that very moment. What were the two drivers saying to Pierre and would this plan keep me safe? André could follow me to the dock. He could board the boat to Le Havre, find me, threatening me, and taking me back to Paris. He could report my activity to my bishop and force a marriage. The worst case scenario waltzed an evil dance in my head. I began to hate André, my childhood playmate, for causing me to hide and run as if I were a delinquent.

Several minutes passed before I heard the men again. A new voice was present. Perhaps it was the voice of Pierre.

"These are all the boxes?"

"Oui."

"Take them to the back of the shop please. You may unload them there."

"Merci."

The wagon moved again, hopefully to a safe location. Before we stopped, I heard tools prying the wood, working on loosening the lid.

"Quickly, Mademoiselle. When the lid opens, please move as fast as you can. Go straight inside."

The lid of my mobile coffin lifted and bright light hit me boldly. With my sore muscles, I climbed out while looking for danger and seeking reassurance that I wasn't being watched. Pierre helped me step out of the wagon and quickly directed me through a doorway. Inside I took my first deep breath in over an hour. With my back to a wall, I observed my surroundings: a small storage room, poorly lit, yet apparently safe.

My clothes were soiled and wrinkled. Boarding the ship as a servant with dirty clothing and a first class ticket would cause suspicion. Pierre walked up to me and I quickly said, "Thank you for your assistance today. I need more of your help before we depart. This attire does not suit me."

"I would have to agree," he said.

"I want to purchase one of your finest dresses. This money should cover it," I said handing him the envelope from Martine. "If not, then ask Martine for the difference." Quickly he opened the envelope and read. Smoothly he slipped the letter into his jacket pocket.

"I'm happy to assist with a new garment," he said smiling with a slight bow of his head.

"I need a proper dress for traveling first class."

Pierre's dress shop was full of some of the finest apparel in Paris. Martine had brought me here once or twice before. The dresses were suited for elaborate gatherings and wealthy wives. None of his dresses suited my daily attire.

"This is the most appropriate design for you." He held up a dress the queen of England may have chosen. With large padded shoulders and bottom, the gold dress was covered with semi-precious stones, pearls and beads. I touched the thick fabric, dreaming of an occasion to wear such a gown.

"Pierre, this is perfect."

"I like it for your frame, unless you like something else more. But we must hurry."

"This is the best disguise, and it fits the occasion. A woman must look her best when she's slipping away quietly and chasing her love," I explained.

"I agree," he replied.

Behind a dressing screen at the back of the store, I slipped the magnificent garment over my head with the help of Pierre's assistant, Elyse. Noticing the weight of the fabric and adorning beads, stones and pearls, I felt as if my fairy godmother was waving a magic wand over my head. Transformed in the moment, it was as if my life would never be the same. The sleeves caressed my arms with their smooth silk lining. The weight of the dress hung balanced on my shoulders and hips. Elyse assisted me in fastening the back buttons. This garment was designed for royalty and the very rich. For the first time in my life, I imagined myself as one of the women who would wear such attire. New sensations swarmed through me like swirling colors of light. I saw myself at fancy gatherings, the opera, auctions, and government parties. It wasn't where I would typically desire to be, but to have occasion to wear this dress made me smile as wide as ever.

"Pierre, there's a blonde wig in the window. May I have it, please?" I asked.

The same shop helper assisted me in slipping the yellow hair over mine, pushing and tucking my thick locks behind the fake ones. It seemed an endless task to hide what was naturally mine. Eventually I covered all of my own hair. In the mirror I saw a woman with the blonde mane and golden gown. Not even I would recognize myself if I walked past me on the street. If André was looking for me, he wouldn't spot me in this dress, not unless he came face to face with me. The dress and wig was a much more pleasant hiding place than the trunk or wagon storage.

"You look like a queen. This dress suits you well mademoiselle," Elyse told me.

"Merci," I replied. "Do you have lip color and rouge?" I asked.

"Oui." After I covered my face with color, I said to Pierre, "I'm ready. Thank you again Pierre. May I express one more concern? André saw my luggage today. It's new. I would like to stay separate from my luggage."

"Very well Mademoiselle. One of my men will carry your luggage and I shall accompany you to appear that you're not alone. The pier is very busy. With your disguise and your arm in mine, you shall not be discovered, even if your luggage is. André doesn't know that it's your belongings, non?"

"Non. He only knows that it came from Martine's home where I'm staying."

"I see."

"May I see those shoes please?" I asked. "They shall add to my height and change my gait." I took the expensive heals and traded them for my own shoes. I admired them in the mirror.

"Lovely. Let's depart," I said as Pierre turned and opened the front door for me.

I climbed into the most beautiful carriage I'd ever seen. The interior was lined with fine velvet. Rich fabric draped the windows, thick carpet lie under our feet. If the dress wasn't enough, now I was certain that my fairy godmother was nearby. Of course the wealthy would get used to such fine accommodations. A nice lifestyle was my upbringing; but this was beyond what most Parisians ever saw.

We rode steadily and calmly to the pier, while nothing inside me was calm. My heart raced in fear of seeing André, anticipation of getting closer to Jean-Paul and for the excitement of this brief fairytale adventure. When the carriage stopped at the dock, my heart nearly stopped as well.

    ***

Chapter Nine: **A Long Way to Go**

Paris, Late March, 1899

I pulled the velvet drape of the carriage window aside to look out into the crowd. Scanning the many people, I looked to ensure a safe exit. Suddenly my heart was in my throat. At the ticket counter, I spotted André.

He was talking with the ticket master and looking through the many pages with the list of passengers. He must have looked for my name. How did he know that I would come here? André knew that I thought Jean-Paul left me without saying good-bye. Why would he expect that I should leave Paris? The only possibility was if someone told him. Perhaps one of Martine's staff knew about my conversations with Martine. Maybe someone had seen the letter Martine obtained from André to Jean-Paul. André could have paid someone to spy for him. Why else would he look for me here? Only Martine and Marion know my plans.

Sitting across from me in the carriage, Pierre saw the terror on my face and responded. "Cherie, this dress does not make you into a woman of great importance. You already are that woman. You're every bit as valuable and beautiful as the women who purchase similar dresses." He paused briefly to watch for my understanding. "Your only job today is to wear it well. Wear this dress like you know who you are, know your worth and what you want."

"But André is here. He knows something. He's looking for me. Someone told him I would be here."

"Do you know what you want Cherie?" Pierre asked.

"Oui. I must be true to my dreams, to be free to make my own decisions, love whom I please, and make my own mistakes. My husband will have integrity and conviction. André would force his will upon me. I would rather die than be with such a man."

"Are you certain that this is what you want?"

"Oui, I'm certain."

"Then exit this carriage and walk across the platform like a woman who knows what she wants! Exude your conviction to the world around you. Can you do that?"

"Oui, merci," I said with a firm nod of my head.

Pierre opened the carriage door and stepped out. He held his hand out to assist me in exiting the carriage. I lifted my head high, brought my shoulders back, took in a deep breath and stepped gracefully out of the beautiful chariot. Immediately eyes were upon me. No doubt people were wondering who this important couple was. My hand gently slipped under Pierre's elbow, resting it on his forearm. The driver retrieved my luggage and walked a considerable ways behind us.

My gait faltered. My confidence waned. "Cherie, you must keep your focus. You deserve to have what you want. You must go and get it."

"I shall!"

"Not even your own Mother should recognize you today. Be the confident woman that you are."

Walking in my new shoes required my full attention. Deliberately, slowly, I made my way forward. Besides concentrating on my gait, I thought of moving towards Jean-Paul and becoming his happy wife. Nothing would stop me now!

I focused on my steps, shoulders, head and facial expression. With the grace of a queen, I walked toward the boat. From the corner of my eye, I saw André turn and look at me, not to see if it were me under the garb, but to admire and possibly ponder how to meet the important couple walking by. Had Pierre not been at my side, André may have had the audacity to approach such a woman for his own business advantage.

Pierre walked with me to the first class seating on the boat. He helped me settle in comfortably, acting as if I was of great importance and deserved special care. The area was closed off from the rest of the boat. It was lined with fine linen, upholstered with red, velvet, spacious seats. There were tables available and a toilet we didn't have to share with the other passengers. Most of the seats were already filled with people that seemed particularly interested in who I was. Pierre leaned in closely and spoke in my ear, "Remember your fictitious name when they call to verify your pass."

"Merci, mon Pierre," I said more loudly. "I shall be well. Thank you for seeing to my every need." I enjoyed playing up the role of a person of prominence.

"It's difficult for me to leave your side darling." Pierre now spoke loud enough that the passengers could hear. They watched me intently. If André found me on the boat and tried to harass me, the first class travelers seated around me would protect me for the mere fact that I was a wealthy, important married woman of stature. "I'm certain that the Senator and his wife shall treat you well in New York darling, but I look forward to your safe return. Enjoy the wedding. Journey well."

"Merci," I replied.

Pierre turned to leave the boat, walking like the prince of Spain. As he exited, all eyes fell on me. I offered the room a coy smile, and played it off like it was nothing.

The boat was about to depart. With every passing moment I felt more confident. Soon I would be away from the grasp of André.

A steward entered the first class seating and made an announcement. "Des Madam and Des Monsieur, we have a slight delay in departure. Please relax and we shall be on our way shortly."

A man sitting near me stopped the steward from walking away. "Good sir, what's the cause of the delay?"

"There may be a young run-a-way girl on board. She's a servant's daughter. The master of the house is looking for her on the ship. He has been given ten minutes to search the boat."

My throat tightened. If André looked into my face, surely he would recognize me. I could find the rest room or perhaps engage in deep conversation. What was I to do? I spoke up, with a calm, clear voice that didn't match my insides. "Certainly he does not need to disturb us here does he? Obviously there are no children of servants in this area. Please assure him of such and tell him not to interrupt our day," I said like a woman who knew what she wanted.

"Yes, of course, Madam," the steward said as he walked out of first class.

Again the passengers looked at me, well pleased with my request. Ten minutes turned into fifteen and then twenty. My hands began to sweat. My face turned flush. The woman beside me asked if I were feeling well. I replied, "I'm simply not looking forward to the journey across the sea. The thought of being on the ocean upsets me."

She smiled politely, as if pondering my thought. Then it hit me all at once. André was searching the boat for a runaway servant. André would not have called me a servant on his own accord. Someone was feeding him information. He knew that I was coming here. That's why he insisted on searching the boat.

We still had not departed. Perhaps he was using his lawyer skill to argue his case. He wasn't giving up. I rose from my seat to go to the washroom.

In the small washroom space I tried to breathe calmly and decide who was helping André. Martine had only told her driver. He was the one who insisted that I get out of the trunk and under the seat. The driver didn't know that I'd changed my clothing at Pierre's because he had left. Yet why did he move me and nail the lid shut if he wasn't trying to help me. Perhaps in Martine's note to Pierre she offered to pay for the dress that I was now wearing. Some tiny gnawing in my stomach told me that there was someone close to me that was helping André. Could it be Martine? Marion knew I was leaving, but what motive would she have to tell André? Who else would know? If the driver told André, then he would have knowledge of Martine's involvement. What about the second driver? Martine didn't confide in him. Perhaps André found them on their return? *Who is betraying me?*

The boat moved and I used the walls in the small room for support. The movement was subtle, but enough for me to know we were leaving port. Cautiously, I exited the washroom to find out if André had left the boat.

Returning to my seat, I looked at the woman next to me with an inquisitive look. She explained, "Oh the young man was allowed to peer his head in this room but was not allowed to speak to any of us. He only looked for a moment, and then he left. We are on our way to Le Havre."

"Is that man a passenger to Le Havre?" I asked.

"I'm not sure. He didn't say."

"How rude of that man to delay us," I added.

"It's rude for a servant's daughter to flee," she stated.

"We do not know. Perhaps her master was not decent to her?"

"That could be true. He seemed like a good gentleman."

I didn't respond. It was likely that my comment would reveal emotions that I felt towards André.

During the ride down the Seine River, guests chatted and wanted to know who each person was and if they were continuing from Le Havre. Eventually all eyes turned to me and I was asked, "Mademoiselle, are you traveling from Le Havre to America?"

"Oui."

"What are your plans in America?"

I shared the first story that popped in my head. "My sister is to marry the son of a Senator in New York. She asked me to attend the wedding as her maid of honor." Everyone enjoyed my story and wanted to know more.

"How did she meet the Senator?" asked the woman next to me.

"How long will you stay?" asked another gentleman.

"Have you met the family?"

"Are your parents going to attend the ceremony?" Questions flew at me from every direction.

"It is kind of you to ask. However, I am very tired and would like to rest." Fortunately they respected my request to be silent.

I sat back and closed my eyes, reflecting on all that had occurred today. It had already been a long and difficult day, and it was only 3:30 in the afternoon. André could still be on board and someone was keeping him abreast of my plans. Out of exhaustion from the stress, I drifted off to sleep.

I awoke when people began to move about to gather their belongings. My neck stiffened from its angle while sleeping in the chair. I stretched, but the encumbered gown limited me to minor movements. All passengers exited the boat. Many of us climbed into carriages waiting at the pier. Others walked the mile to the big ship, docked where the ocean met the land.

When we reached the giant liner, I swallowed hard. The Deutschland arrived in Le Havre from Germany and would be my home for the next seven days, while I escaped my doom. Only André intimidated me more than climbing aboard a boat to venture out away from the safety of solid ground. Perhaps if I could swim, I wouldn't feel as afraid.

Staring at the large structure, I asked myself, *How does it float? How does water hold a heavy object at its surface?* People filed into the opening at a steady stream. Watching them, I wondered if I might panic at some point on the trip, begin crying and screaming while passengers threatened to throw me overboard just for some peace and quiet. Forcing the thought out of my mind, I confidently walked towards the ship. My new life was about to begin.

My cabin was first class, small, but well-appointed with complementary wine. A tiny window looked out to the vast sea. Already feeling confined, I set my handbag on the small bed, picked up the key to my room, and headed to the deck for fresh air.

On the outside deck there was much activity. A German man played a lively tune on a harmonica. Small girls spun around to the music, twirling like pinwheels while their skirts floated in the air. Women strolled about the deck and men sat in chairs under the partially cloudy sky. I looked around carefully, but saw no sign of André. The exuberant atmosphere caused me a brief moment of delight.

Mixed feelings fought for space in my heart as the great ship floated away from the country I adored. The land shrank away from my view. Excitement about my adventure across the Atlantic Ocean to start a new life with Jean-Paul contrasted sharply with the pain of leaving my homeland. I couldn't feel entirely happy or sad. Emotions tossed like ocean waves inside me as the giant vessel carried me from one shore to another.

The faces of my fellow passengers also sulked into the gloom that surrounded them. Fog, rain and gray water stretched as far as we could see. Was leaving Europe causing the quiet, distraught looks, or was it because of the dreadful weather that approached.

We ventured toward the dark clouds at a slow and steady pace, rolling on waves of liquid. Soon the swells grew larger, rain fell upon the deck and passengers resolved to take refuge in the small spaces below, filing single file into the one person doorway leading to the hull.

Before the last passengers were safely below, the rain increased and the ship tossed forward and back. The vessel rose and fell on angry waves. Strong winds kept us sealed below in the dim cabins. My stomach turned upside down as the waves tossed people and belongings around in the stale air.

Late on the first day I heard a knock on my cabin door. Cautiously, I opened it. A young woman stood before me, pleasant and serious. "Mademoiselle, we are searching the ship for Cherish Bourguignon. Is that you?"

"Non," I said. "Why are you searching for a passenger?"

"The captain asked us to find her. As I understand it, her attorney must deliver some important papers to her. He claims she is on the ship, although there are no records of her." I was glad the woman volunteered so much information. Immediately I knew it was André. I couldn't imagine a reason I would be delivered legal paper aboard a ship or anyone but André trying to contact me that way. Missing a crucial notice seemed far less risky than disclosing myself to André.

"Oh," I replied swallowing hard. "If I meet her I shall mention it."

I had assumed that I wouldn't need the wig, but I kept it handy just in case. Now I realized that André had access to my specific travel plans, except my fake name. Someone was definitely feeding him the details, but who would Martine tell? She couldn't possibly be telling André what I was doing, could she? If it was Martine, then she would give him my traveling identity as well. It had to be someone close to her who missed this one detail.

"Ask her to see a member of the ship staff if you speak with her. Apparently the matter is of grave importance. Sorry to have troubled you," she replied.

Grave importance to André, I thought. "It's not a problem."

"Are you well?" she asked.

"Oui, a little sick to my stomach, but otherwise I am well."

"We have medical facilities one level below this floor at the end of the long hall if you need any assistance."

"Is it....common for ships to have medical quarters?"

"Illness is a frequent problem among the many voyages across the sea. There are rodents that always make it aboard every vessel. Disease is inevitable. We help as many passengers as we can on each voyage. Please don't hesitate to seek assistance if you need it."

"Merci."

I closed the door and leaned on it with my back, as if I were holding the heavy door in place against André. How was I to avoid him on a ship for a full week? I had several new dresses and a wig, but if he saw my face, my disguise would be useless. For several hours I stewed about my plight while my stomach got tighter. I decided that I needed a friend who would be my partner in hiding. I wanted to find an unsuspecting woman to help me be stealthy.

I went to bed without a solution or new confidant. I slept well, feeling safe in my locked cabin. I woke late. A small amount of light leaked in through my tiny, round portal. My first stop was the bathroom. This risk of exposure had to be taken. First class did not provide us adequate amounts of toilets, which meant there was a long line to wait in. Possibly people from other areas stole turns to use our toilets, but it was difficult to know who belonged, and everyone seemed to tolerate the lines. Eventually it was my turn and I held my breath to avoid the stench.

Painted with Love

Quickly I returned to my room, realizing I had six more days of this to endure. The ship still rocked back and forth with rains pounding the deck. On my bed I laid wondering how I should pass the time. Then I heard a knock. I didn't know if I should answer it. Maybe André stood on the other side.

Nervously, I opened the door. A well-dressed young woman stood at the door. "Bonjour, Mademoiselle. My name is Elisabeth Chopra. I stood behind you in the line for the toilet this morning. May I visit with you? I am traveling alone. You are traveling alone, oui?"

"Oui."

"A friend would help with the boredom. Do you mind?" It was impossible to know if this woman was really seeking a friendship, or was a possible spy. I knew I couldn't divulge much.

After my surprise wore off, I answered. "Bonjour, My name is Margareta Sonnet. Pleased to make your acquaintance. Having a friend for this miserable journey would be lovely. Would you like to come in?"

"Oui, this tiny room offers some peace. The dining room is full of people who speak of the ocean swallowing the ship or the storm getting us lost at sea. People can be too dramatic. Boats have crossed this sea for four hundred years. It's far more fun to speak of the adventures we shall have in America."

I liked Elisabeth from the moment she introduced herself. She helped distract my mind from constantly thinking of Jean-Paul. We sat in the small space and shared our stories.

Her dark brown eyes stared into mine. She watched me with grave intensity. Her smile seemed a bit too kind and her body just slightly too close. I felt thrown and confused by her overtly friendly gestures, although I responded with warmth and invitation. Something was different about Elisabeth. My mind worked to decide if I could trust this beautiful woman.

"Tell me, what brought you on this difficult journey?" she asked.

I thought of Jean-Paul on his three week voyage in third class or worse. In his weakened state, I wondered how he would fare under the difficult conditions. A sting of hatred for André

124

shook me. Then the anger turned towards me, as I realized that I begged Jean-Paul to take me to the flat where we were watched. The suffering he experienced was my doing.

"Oh, um," I waited, wanting to know that I could confide in her. If I didn't tell her all of the details then my story was probably safe. To begin with I would share a little and then more if I could trust her. "You see my love has already departed for America to set up a business. I am traveling there to join him. We are to be married. He's also an artist. He paints beautifully."

"He paints? How charming. Has he done well as a painter? Will I have heard of him?"

"Non, he's not well known in Paris. He will be, someday."

"Why were you not married in Paris? Won't your family miss your ceremony?"

"My parents are not excited about this marriage. But we will either return to Paris to be wed or they can travel to America. My love is not planning on staying in America. He will establish the business and return to France after a couple of years." I didn't want to give her the real story, just in case she told the wrong person. "And what about you? Will you return to Paris someday?"

"Non, I shall never return," she said in a serious tone. She paused briefly and then changed the subject. Her story could be more interesting than mine, or perhaps similar.

"Where are you going to live in the vast land of America?" she asked.

"California, in the San Francisco area. What about you? Have you decided?"

"I have no plans yet. I am ready for a new place, that's all." She looked off into the empty space of the cabin, dreaming, remembering something.

"What brings you to leave our great country?"

"My goodness, that's a greater question than you know. Where to begin? Can I trust you Margareta?"

"Oui, you most certainly may. I promise."

"Then you shall get an ear full." She paused and swallowed. Then she took a deep breath and began. "I am running away from my family and they do not know my whereabouts. My family is furious with me. They consider me a rebellious child, an unruly girl and a sinner. If it were a few hundred years ago my family would have had me burned at the stake for disgracing them. My best option was to flee."

"My goodness, Elisabeth, dare I ask why they feel this strongly towards you?"

"Dare only if you are brave enough to hear it."

I nodded my head, a bit hesitantly with wide eyes and much curiosity.

Elisabeth continued. "My parents call me unchaste. They found out that I have been intimate with a boy...or two. As if God shall disown me. It doesn't matter that my father has touched this body for his own pleasure, but that a boy my age has enjoyed me, means I am sinful, and worthy of hell. Well, I am a strong-minded girl. I don't need my family's judgment or morals to guide me. I will make a new life for myself in a new country with friends who do not judge me."

"Do you have anyone to help you in America?" I asked in amazement.

"Non."

The thought of traveling to a new land without a person to greet me at the disembarking of the ship scared me. Suddenly I felt concern for this girl who would find herself alone in a foreign place, if this story she told was true. It was possible that André had sent her to me to learn of my plans once I exited the ship.

Although I didn't know if I could trust her, I realized in some ways she was like me. Our families wanted to decide what was best for us. We had to flee our families if we wanted to make our own choices. We were alone on this ship, and we both had been intimate prior to marriage. We came from religious upbringing and decided to make choices against that dogma. Yet I had a man traveling to America who loved me and would protect me. She was alone. It hurt to think of how that must feel. People may take advantage of her. How would she find a job? Why did families put morals above loving their children? Would a loving God really do such a thing? Would a loving God want this beautiful girl to go into New York City alone?

We visited for hours. She agreed to bring my lunch to me after I told her that a man on the ship had frightened me the first day with his strong advances and I preferred to eat in my room rather than the dining room. She didn't like the dining room either and didn't mind bringing our meals to the cabin to eat with me. We laughed and shared stories. For moments at a time, life seemed easy and painless. It was great to have a friend with whom to share the ride.

The sea tossed our floating home for four days without reprieve. I considered myself to be a durable woman, yet I had never experienced the difficulty of this discomfort. The food served aboard the ship was poor quality. The only meat available was chicken bones with a small amount of overcooked flesh, along with a watery, onion soup. I consumed the meals only because of hunger. The cabins lacked fresh air. Many passengers became sea sick, while the stale air filled with a stench of vomit and urine, making it next to impossible to not become ill. There were not enough restrooms aboard the ship, and they didn't seem to ever empty.

Each day I lay in my cabin bed wondering how Jean-Paul survived these conditions with possibly broken ribs and swollen eyes. Sadness for his plight and discomfort, along with guilt for bringing it upon him, plagued me.

Each day I visited with Elisabeth, learning more about her siblings, parents, dreams and the boy she loved. She left him when she left her family, knowing they would never accept him, or her. She never thought to ask him to come with her.

On day five of the journey, the boat floated smoothly. Stewards came through the ship announcing that the sun was out and passengers were free to walk about the deck. "Elisabeth begged me to come on deck and see the sun with her. Reluctantly I put on my wig and followed her for some fresh air.

I noticed that people were slowly leaving their cabins they had grown to appreciate for the safety they provided from the weather and to despise for the confinement and stench it forced upon them. My eyes squinted against the bright sunshine not seen for days. Other's faces held a protective look against the new air and light, but then softened to one of relief and then joy.

On deck people showed their enthusiasm for their new start coming soon. Travelers began to communicate with one another, asking about their plans, sharing their own dreams. Comradery was high as people felt a brother and sisterhood with their fellow, captive boatmen.

Elisabeth danced to the harmonica and asked me to join her. I declined and tried to remain anonymous. Unfortunately my wig was beautiful and drew the attention of many men. I kept my face covered with the large locks.

When the music wasn't playing, Elisabeth and I stared off at the sea and made our wishes to the sun and waves. In a few days I would never see her again. That thought made me sad, but I also knew that we were different. She was looking for a different adventure than I. Her ideas intimidated me, and I didn't want to see how her unplanned future turned out. Even if she was André's spy, I would never forget her.

Chapter Ten: Reality is Perception

Nairobi, Kenya: Kenyatta National Hospital, November, 2005

I blinked my eyes open to overwhelming brightness. Nothing came into focus. Shades of white and gray shadows surrounded me. Blurred objects moved about the room.

"Her eyes are open! Nurse, she opened her eyes!" a man's voice said loudly.

A new shadow appeared closer to me, and she spoke with a strong accent I hadn't heard before. "She be seeing. De pupil es responding. I will git de doctor."

"Dee, can you hear me?" someone said. "Dee, it's Brian. Can you say something? Anything? Make a sound. Nod your head. Dee?"

Brian? I wanted to say, *Do I know you?* My mouth didn't obey me. "Auhet." A sound came out of me, but it wasn't a word. "Ahnn." Another sound escaped. *What's the matter with my mouth?*

"Dee! That's fantastic. Wow. You had me worried. This is amazing."

What's amazing? I can't form a word. I can't see where I am. I can't remember why I'm lying here without vision. I have no idea who is speaking to me. Where is Cherie? This must be a dream! God I'm sleepy. I'm incredibly sleepy.

"Dee, wait! Don't sleep. Dee. The doctor's coming. He needs to check on you. Please don't sleep. Wait just a few minutes. Please."

"Uh wheet. Ahuu!"

"Everything's all right, Dee. Your jaw was broken. It's still healing. Your mouth is stiff from when it was sown shut. See if you can wiggle your jaw. Can you see me?" A shadow formed above me, hovering over my bed. "I'm here for you, Dee."

I blinked my eyes and squinted. But I couldn't make out any features. *What the hell?* "Ahhhhuuh!!"

"It's okay, Dee. The doctor said that when you woke up you could have trouble with speech and motor skills. Don't worry. You just woke up from…from…an eight week coma. There's no easy way to say this. You were in an auto accident. You had several injuries, including a head injury. You're now in the Kenyatta National Hospital in Nairobi. There are excellent doctors here who have performed…"

"Am I hearing you complimenting our good staff, young Brian?" A man with an Indian accent, interrupted the man speaking to me and a new shadow approached my bed.

"Doctor, we have great news. Look at Dee. She's awake. She made sounds too. This is great, right? Just like you said. She will get better now, right?"

"Be taking some breaths, Brian. It is good to be breathing and relax when beside Miss Dee. Keep her knowing that all is well. Yes, this is all bery good. We expect her to be awaking as the swelling is subsiding. More improvement should be happening with de time. Let me examine our good patient and see de progress she's making now. Look at the light in front of you Miss Dee, please."

A small bright light appeared directly above my head. The intensity irritated my eyes, causing me to blink several times. "Excellent response," replied the doctor. "Squeeze my finger if you can Miss Dee."

A finger slipped in against my palm. With focus, I pictured closing my hand, but I couldn't tell if it was actually making the motion that I visualized. Then I felt my fingers close around the finger against my palm. I tried to smile but I couldn't tell if my mouth moved.

"You will feel some tapping Miss Dee. Not to worry. I'm just testing you reflexes." I felt tapping on my elbows and knees. Then I felt fingers pressing under my chin and at my neck. "Her progress is most wonderful. You can be smiling now for certain, young Brian. Your friend is getting much better now."

"Oh, thank God. Thank you, doctor. Thank you."

"Mostly it is God and Miss Dee that did the miracle. I'm just the servant. She will still want to rest much. Please let this lady take the sleep so often. You will do this, yes?"

"Of course, doctor. Whatever you say."

"I will see you later, Miss Dee. Don't be fearing no things. You're healing bery fast going forward."

The doctor walked away and I tried to piece things together in my mind. This couldn't be real. It didn't feel real. I couldn't move, speak, see or remember. It was definitely like a dream. It had to be a bad dream. Soon I would wake up in a ship leaving Paris, or…or I would wake up in Seattle, Washington. Wait…if I woke up from this dream where would I be, Kenya, Seattle, Paris or on the ocean? Nothing made sense, or felt clear. I just felt tired, extremely tired.

The nurse woman spoke again. "Miss Dee, de doctor tells me to gives you de bath while yous es awake. He is saying that de stimulation is good pour the body to wake up to. You could be tired Miss Dee, but first you must have de bath. You must be going, young Brian. I will tells you when you can come see her."

Two women undressed me in my bed and used warm water and towels to wash my skin from head to toe. Without seeing them, I lay naked before them and they could see all of me. It felt uncomfortable to not see the women who were intimately caring for me.

Most of the warm towels felt nice against my skin. Some areas they touched were very tender or the skin felt hypersensitive, as if I'd been burned there. Flinching was a challenge because my muscles wouldn't obey me. Sounds escaped my lips, and the nurses tried to understand. "Does dat hurt Dee?"

"Aaann."

"Maybe dis hurts. Be careful dere."

They dried my body, dressed me in a fresh hospital gown and changed the sheets right underneath me by leaning me to one side and then the other. The bath was very medicinal, and didn't feel like a dream. But it didn't feel normal, nor did I. Pain surfaced all over my body. It seemed suddenly cold and as if involuntary shivering could begin at any moment. Weakness,

131

discomfort, confusion and frustration overwhelmed me all at the same time. *Wake up, wake, up, wake, up. I want to wake up!!!! This can't be real.*

The nurse invited Brian back into the room. He stood over me. "How do you feel now Dee? Was the bath okay?"

"Ah ouu…wha wha." My mouth just would not express the words I wanted to say.

"You're going to be good as new, Dee. The doctor said that after an injury like yours, it will take time to walk, talk and be functional again. Just keep trying. It will be easy to get frustrated, but this is all a part of recovering. Would you like me to tell you what happened?"

I wanted to turn my head towards him or nod my head, but could do neither, so I blinked my eyes twice. It was all I could think of.

"Okay, I think that was a yes. The doctor said that you may not remember much, so I will start at the beginning. You and I live in Seattle, Washington. You have three daughters, and two son-in-laws. You and I are friends, but moving towards being more than friends. We met two years ago. I invited you to come to Kenya with me to take some pictures. I'm here to talk to different Masai tribes about allowing education for their young people. You came to photograph the Masai people and traditions, such as circumcision, to help the world understand the problems that the Masai face in Kenya and the surrounding countries. Are you following me so far, Dee?" he asked.

I blinked again.

"Oh good, you and I were in a van traveling towards Mt. Kilimanjaro for pictures. You were standing up in the van when we were hit from behind and then hit head-on by a delivery truck. Our van tipped over and slammed into the ground. You're very lucky to have survived the crash from where you stood. You wouldn't have made it if it weren't for Leboo."

My whole body jerked. Goosebumps formed all over. *That name, Leboo. Yes, I knew it. That name makes me smile. It's a boy right? Was Leboo a little boy who smiled a lot?*

Brian continued unaware of my reaction to the boy's name. "Leboo grabbed you. He got your head into the van before we tumbled. Your head might have been chopped off otherwise Dee. Sorry. Maybe you didn't need to know that. The driver and I were wearing seat belts. We survived better than you and Laboo. When I finally got to you, Leboo was wrapped around you, even though he was unconscious. You both were thrown against the side of the van when it tumbled over and hit the ground. The window busted and you each had cuts and abrasions covered in dirt and head injuries. You broke your arm and Jaw. Leboo broke his shoulder socket and color bone. His neck is injured, but not broken. Your hip is bruised and you have a puncture to your leg. We don't think you have any paralysis from the head injury, because the doc says your reflexes are good. You have swelling in the back of your head and you need to have brain surgery, but they won't do it until you are awake and will consent to the risky surgery. Hopefully you're ready to hear all of this. For eight weeks I sat here wondering how I would tell you all of this. I guess it's best to just tell you everything."

I began to cry. Tears pooled in my eyes. I felt sad for Leboo. He saved my life, again, and it cost him greatly. Perhaps I cried for me too. I couldn't move my body, speak or see. I tried not to panic, but all of it felt unfair. *How would I survive this life if I didn't get better?*

"Um, here, let me get you a handkerchief for those tears. Relax. It will be okay. You will get better. It's okay to cry Dee. I've sat here with you since they released me from the hospital. I always knew that you would wake up. You're strong Dee; exceptionally strong." Brian grabbed my hand and held it. It felt strange to be so intimate, but it helped me not feel alone. I wanted to squeeze his hand as a return gesture. All I could do was lie still. I couldn't even turn my head.

Brian wiped my eyes. Then he spoke in monotone. "You look much better today. Your face has better color. It felt like you were away somewhere while you slept. You look different now." He paused. "The doctor told me to talk to you while you slept. He said that a familiar voice and touch could be helpful in waking up a patient. I said many things while you were sleeping. I mean, I had a lot of time here, sitting in this quiet space. Mostly I was talking to try to wake you up. I held your hand a lot, and stroked

133

your head. I told you that I want to be with you. You need to give me a second chance, Dee. Um, we can talk about that later. You probably didn't even hear what I said. Forget about it." He paused again. "I love you, Dee." Brian's voice was matter of fact.

For a moment, I was relieved that I couldn't move or respond. I didn't know how I was supposed to answer Brian. I didn't know what kind of relationship I had with Brian previous to now, but I didn't feel emotions for him at that moment. As I lay immobile, I felt grateful that he was beside me and relieved to hear a voice of someone who knew me. A sense of safety came with him watching over me. Perhaps I used to love Brian; I didn't know. Why did his words cause me to feel afraid and defensive? If I could have spoken right then, I'm sure the wrong words would have blurted out. The silence was my friend.

My life was coming to me in tiny, quick flashes. I saw my daughters, son-in-laws, house and the street where I walked down to the lake. It didn't feel all connected and it seemed a distance away, as if I was watching a movie trailer. I took a deep breath and closed my eyes.

Paris rushed into my mind. I saw my home in Paris, my mother and father. I felt André presence like a coiled snake around my neck. Jean-Paul's eyes were the clearest image I could visualize. Comfort wrapped me up as I focused on those beautiful eyes.

"Time to check yous blood pressure," another voice said. My arm was lifted and wrapped with a cool, vinyl cuff. She started to pump it with air and it tightened. While she held my arm, a sick feel rushed over my body, beginning at my center and spreading out to each limb. Muscles tightened in my face spontaneously and I thought I might cry. A sharp pain started in my head, mild at first, then gradually it got worse. Suddenly I was in terrible pain. "Nnnnnnnn!!!!"

"What's wrong Dee?"

My body started to shake, in a full body spasm. The shaking became more violent. Suddenly I was choking.

"Nurse!!! Help her. Something's wrong. Hurry!"

A steel object was forced into my mouth. My body kept shaking. Brian was shouting. Others were calling for a doctor.

My mind retreated to some dark corner where sound doesn't exist and light is absent. Body sensations faded, replaced by calmness. And then....there was nothing.

Chapter Eleven: New Perspective

Atlantic Ocean, Late March, 1899

Elisabeth walked away, leaving me alone with my thoughts. Fears of André finding me consumed my mind. I couldn't be certain if he was on board or not, spying in silence to learn my plans. Although I'd not seen him present, he may have been among the hundreds of people onboard. If his informant knew all of my plans, André could be following me straight to Jean-Paul. There was no way to be certain, and I couldn't relax until I knew I was safe from his reach.

André had not materialized, so I ventured more often to the deck for air and sun. Early on the sixth day of my journey, I stood at the balcony and stared beyond the ship at the vast sea. A flat, one dimensional horizon met my gaze without variation. Boats, whales and floating debris were absent. Nothing broke the monotony of the solid spread of water reaching to the edge of the horizon.

Halfway through the morning, as I stood staring mindlessly, Elisabeth bounced over to me with bubbly enthusiasm. "One more day, one more day, one more day!" she announced.

"One and a half," I replied. "We don't arrive until late afternoon. We have the rest of today and most of tomorrow."

"You're far too downcast about this. Don't you see the pleasure in it? Tomorrow we shall be in our new country. Tomorrow we are home. Why count the hours? It's a special day!" Elisabeth bounced around more, jumping the way I did when I was exuberant. "Why do you look so…worried?"

"I'm happy. God will provide. All will be well."

"You didn't convince yourself. You certainly didn't convince me," she replied.

"There are many unknowns for me Elisabeth. I…don't know what to expect."

"Neither do I. That's part of the fun you see? You said that you have people who will meet you when the boat arrives, yes?"

"Apparently, Martine said that she arranged for that."

"Well, you have much more than I have."

I didn't respond. I felt silly. Elisabeth didn't know where she would stay tomorrow night. She didn't have a lover to look for when she arrived. Yet she was excited, while I was scared.

"You worry too much Margareta" It felt more odd than ever to have this girl I knew so well not know my real name. I wanted to tell her the truth. "You will be just fine," she continued. "You were brave enough to leave your family to follow your dreams. You certainly have the courage to make the life that you want. We both do. We are sisters of determination." I smiled a sincere thankful smile. "I need to go now," she said. "You are depressing me. Here I thought I had a great life ahead of me and you are bringing me down."

"Elisabeth, please. I am sorry to dump my issues on you. Especially when my worries are not as…"

"Stop speaking Margareta. That's why I must end this charming conversation. Let's not compare my life to yours. My life is what it is. I won't apologize for it, nor will I condemn it. It's all that I have. I am only willing to appreciate every moment of it, short or long. My opportunities will be created by me. How I live is now my responsibility. I shall savor the gravy of every morsel, and when my supper is finished, I shall know that it was well enjoyed."

She walked off with a wave. I felt badly and turned to stare at the stretch of sea to the west.

The seventh day took forever to pass as I waited for signs of land. It was apparent when Lady Liberty came into view of the boat. People rushed to the starboard side to see her raised torch to welcome us. I squeezed into the crowd to see for myself what I had only heard about. It seemed obvious that if André was on board he was not going to approach me, so I enjoyed the exciting moment of seeing her welcoming torch as we approached. She was small, off in the distance, growing larger in graduated increments. People smiled with their eyes glued to the frozen figure. Exciting noises and whispers escaped at once.

As we floated towards shore, she drew us towards her strength and beauty. For a few minutes I felt alone on the large vessel, my eyes fixed on the great Statue of Liberty, letting her bring me to her bosom and wrap me in her safe haven. Her outreach of hope became my comfort, along with a crowd of people I didn't know. We united in her welcome. People looked at one another with large grins, as if they had won a great prize. Many coming to cross this new country sought freedom, like I did. And freedom was a gift I would celebrate.

When we neared the pier, people were less friendly as they pushed around the boat ready to escape its confinement. An announcement was made that first-class passengers were to disembark first and go to the first building which was customs. The announcement caused me to smile, only because I didn't want to be mixed in with the rush of people who wanted off. Fortunately, Martine had taken care of my immigration papers during her week of preparation. How could I ever doubt her motives? Then it was announced that second-class passengers would disembark next and that third-class passengers would be taken by ferry to Ellis Island for inspection.

Customs was simple. There were lines for different languages. A man looked at my papers, asked me several questions in French, which I apparently answered correctly, and let me pass through out to the crowded pier of New York. The pier was chaos as people shouted names and looked for loved ones. Immediately I felt worried that I would not find the man and woman that Martine had described. There were vast numbers of people at the pier selling goods or services, such as hats, carriage rides, hotel stays or train passes.

The air smelled different than it had ever smelled before, much different than Le Havre which smelled of sea, tides and fresh clean oxygen. New York smelled much more industrious, as if man was constructing something new at all hours of the day. Burning coal and hot steam engines were hard at work. The city smelled alive and exciting, but certainly not like home. Suddenly my home land felt a million miles away and I feared that I might live and die among strangers. Monsieur and Madam Batton approached me in all of the confusion. "Are you Mademoiselle Bourguignon?"

"Oui! You found me. Thank you for coming. I am pleased to meet you!" I said smiling with relief.

As I started to walk toward the luggage area with the Batton's, Elisabeth ran up to us. "Margareta," she called loudly, "Please wait." She spoke firmly and calmly, "Don't look around, look only at me. A man will pay me a lot of money to find out the address where you will be staying. He told me to say I would write to you. He will pay me as soon as I deliver the address to him. It must be the man who tried to make advances on you the first day on the boat. You were wise to hide from him. Please," she said looking at Monsieur Batton, "Do you have a fake address for me to give him?" Monsieur took the envelope from Elisabeth's hand and wrote out an address.

"Give him this. It's the address of the chief of police. He's a friend of mine."

"Thank you!" Elisabeth replied. She hugged and kissed me and waved as if we had a pleasant exchange.

"Elisabeth," I said as she turned to leave, "You cannot trust this man. Don't give him other information that's true, even if he sweet talks you. He's not safe. I can feel it."

She ran off skipping. I didn't allow my eyes to follow her and possibly find André watching me. He must have silently followed me onto the ship, trying to learn of my plans and possibly learn Jean-Paul's whereabouts. It was possible that he followed me to get to Jean-Paul and finish what he started.

Monsieur Batton looked at me for an explanation. "I will explain when we are safe in your home. It's best that we are sure we are not followed," I said, trying to not sound frightened.

Together we walked to the large baggage area and waited for my belongings, including my new trunk and gifts from Martine. I glanced around casually, looking for André's watchful eyes. I didn't see him; apparently he was better at hiding than I was. It took a long time to unload all the passengers' luggage and even longer to find my own. Monsieur paid two men to bring my trunks to a carriage. We all boarded a beautiful carriage with a driver.

Chapter Twelve: Reuniting with Disappointment

New York City, April 1899

We rode to their apartment building in downtown New York City taking several quiet side streets along the way to be sure no one was watching us.

An elevator took us to the fourth floor. Their flat was beautifully appointed, but with an influence I didn't recognize. The furniture was simple, with clean lines. The fabric had simple patterns, although rich and of excellent quality. I assumed it all was from American designers. It didn't feel like a French home, although that's what I expected it to look like from the way they had greeted me and spoke.

Madam Batton gave me a tour of the apartment. "Here is where you will sleep. You may put your things in the bureau and freshen up. There is clean water in the basin," Madam Batton said. She walked away and left me alone. I sat on the bed and rested my weary body. I let my thoughts go, as my head swam with worries, wondering, and anxiety. After a fifteen minute rest, I quieted my worries and joined them in the dining room.

"Have some warm soup and bread Mademoiselle. You must keep up your strength," Madam said.

"Merci." I sat at the table and tasted the warm dish. "Mmm, delicious."

"You have learned a few English words. I will be happy to assist you with pronunciation and teach you some important phrases if you would like me to," Madam offered.

'Merci, that would be wonderful."

"We know that you must be quite tired Mademoiselle. Rest well. Tomorrow we can show you some of New York City. We checked on the schedule of Monsieur Soule's arrival. He arrives the day after tomorrow. You arrived here with perfect timing."

"Merci, for everything you are doing. Please call me Cherie."

I slept hard that night, free of the confines of the ship and the soft wave motions. I dreamt only one dream that I recalled. I saw Jean-Paul, but I couldn't get to him. He was far off. He couldn't see me and I couldn't close the gap on the distance between us. I watched helplessly as people took him somewhere. I couldn't even follow him or scream to get his attention.

The sun lit the bedroom through the window when I woke. I turned towards the light and saw the ball of fire rising above the horizon of buildings and streets. The brilliance seemed to be promising me something, as it lit up my face and hair. It felt like a promise of hope for a better existence than the one I left. I allowed it to fill me up to my core as the sun's warmth inspired each centimeter of my being. I resolved to myself to walk forward with courage and conviction. Then I committed to follow my resolve, in return for this daily encouragement.

Stepping out to the streets of New York should have stirred the winds of euphoria within me. Instead of excitement, isolation whipped up and down my spine. The city felt unfriendly, empty and without meaning. I couldn't decide why. I looked around at the faces walking by on the streets. I saw the sky and surrounding structures. This country, my new home, was lacking something I needed. What more could I ask of a place? Suddenly I realized what was absent; a familiar face, one in particular. I was alone in an amazing metropolis. Although it could meet my needs on most levels, this city didn't have my lover within her arms and New York was a harsh place for me to be alone.

New York City had similarities to Paris, and other European countries. The influence was strong, but mixed. One area of the city had buildings that resembled Paris. Another area had buildings that looked more like Great Britain. Although I had not traveled throughout Europe, I'd seen many paintings and drawings of other cities. New York took parts of all of them and mixed them together. Buildings were tall, in many parts of the city, taller than the average buildings in Paris. The most memorable part of the day was Central Park. In the middle of the city was a giant park with a lake, bridges, trees, animals, ponds and rock formations. It was larger than any park in Paris. The Batton's took me by carriage through the grounds, but it was far too large to see it all. There were two museums, but we didn't take the time to see them. The more of the city they showed to me, the more the day became a blur. I swirled in a haze of busy streets, unfamiliar languages, new smells and different architecture. The food was different, even the coffee tasted unfamiliar. I tired of our tour and wanted to go to their home and wait for the time to pass. I tried to be polite and enjoy their hospitality. I made an effort to be interested in New York. I wanted to be interested. But I could only think of Jean-Paul. The distraction kept me from enjoying this new place.

I let the day slowly drift into the next, looking only for the hour when I would move towards my lover. The boat was due to arrive at one thirty in the afternoon. The morning pushed forward like a dense fog that refused to move. I noticed that my breath surged in and out in quick, short bursts at times. I couldn't quiet the anxious pressure gently squeezing my heart. Sometimes my buttocks muscles twitched from the thought of my lover's touch on my thighs. My labia tingled for ten minutes, then again for thirty, until it was nearly constant. Whole body-shivers occasionally grabbed me when his naked body flashed in my mind. My fingers stayed in constant motions, as if they danced to some music without rhythm. There was a satisfaction that awaited me; the taste of him, the feel of his skin on my tongue and the scent of him upon which my being floated as I breathed it in. Every part of my body desired the pleasure I craved, not just the sexual, but the intimacy, the comfort of my lover's caring eyes, the kind words whispered and the safety of two.

Madam prepared an appetizing lunch at 11:30. I sat at the table, hoping that my body would accept food when it focused on other hungers. I bit into a warm croissant, the first one I enjoyed since leaving Paris. My lips and teeth closed around flaky, buttered bread that filled my taste buds with a familiar indulgence. All of my sensations heightened as my body seemed to want to glean a climax from this physical stimulation. I closed my eyes and chewed slowly, appreciating every detail of the complex pastry. My mouth reveled in it, and my stomach accepted it, as if it were the prelude to something forth-coming. Every bite of lunch seemed to build towards a wanting that didn't end.

We packed some food for Jean-Paul, and departed a little early for the freight harbor. Our carriage could only take us to the streets edge, which meant we had to walk about a half a mile toward the docks. Other roads approached the docks, but they were marked for delivery wagons. I looked around at the cargo ships unloading freight with large cranes next to long warehouses. The ship we searched for was called Belle Eue; Pretty Water. Martine had bribed the ticket master to tell her the name of the ship Jean-Paul had boarded. We asked around but no one seemed to know where Pretty Water would unload. They directed us to seek out the dock foreman, but no one knew his location. We walked from dock to dock while curious faces traced our steps with their eyes. I looked out across the bay. There were more cargo ships unloading far from where we stood. It was all confusing.

I saw ships drifting like swans on the water, barely moving. I saw tug boats pulling at large barges. Where is Jean-Paul? I asked myself. I scanned the harbor, as if I could see him behind the armor of a ship's hull. I willed myself to know where he was. At the edge of the harbor a smaller boat came into view. It looked to be half the size of the larger craft. It moved a bit more quickly and caught my attention. There was friendliness about this boat, like a familiar face. As the boat approached, excitement grew inside of me. I felt a desire to run towards the boat, but I didn't know where it would land. "I think that might be the right boat. It just....feels right," I said to Monsieur and Madam.

"That small boat, over there?" Monsieur asked pointing.

"Oui, that one. It makes me feel...tingly."

"Tingly?" he asked.

"Oui, happy all over."

The three of us watched the boat approach. We looked for the name on the boat, but it was too far away. More excitement built inside of me. I wanted to jump up and down. I was wiggling with no way to stop.

The boat approached a dock across the water. Panic attacked my chest as I saw too many obstacles between me and the boat. Before I could say a word, Monsieur had all of us directed back to the carriage. I didn't say a thing. I was headed toward Jean-Paul. Something told me he was there. Monsieur directed the driver to the other side of the harbor. Maneuvering around the water's edge proved to be difficult. Delivery wagons waited on both sides of the road and traffic stopped as one lane waited for another to pass. I thought I might explode from frustration. I wanted to jump from the carriage and run.

Finally we approached the boat and I saw the name painted on the front side, Bella Eue. I released a huge sigh and looked around the dock to see if he had debarked yet. There was no sign of passengers. Monsieur found a dock man from the boat and asked about travelers.

"Yes. We have fifteen men aboard. They will all be required to take a ferry to Ellis Island for inspection."

"When will they disembark?" I interrupted.

"Uh, I don't know. Soon I guess. We have to unload this cargo and reload. We are leaving as soon as it's done. I need to get back to work now."

Monsieur directed us to the warehouse wall and out of the way. "Now we wait," he said patiently.

About fifteen minutes later, I watched intently as passengers climbed off a plank onto the dock, led by a crew member. Jean-Paul was nowhere in sight. The crewman asked everyone to stand together, instructing them to wait for a ferry to take them to Ellis Island. The passengers looked weary and dirty. Where was Jean-Paul? I sent my distraught look over to Monsieur. He shrugged his shoulders. The steward was about to walk back on to the boat. I couldn't hold myself back. I walked up to him and asked, "Are there more passengers? I am looking for Jean-Paul Soule."

"Hum? Oh you mean John? He's the only guy left. You must mean him."

"Perhaps. Where might I find him?"

"They will bring him up. The men are working on a way to get him out right now. All the guys here liked him and gave him special treatment. He's going to a hospital. If we dump him at Ellis in his condition, well, they will probably send him straight home. We all enjoyed his story about the woman he loved and lawyer guy who she's going to marry. Hey, are you that girl. I can't remember her name." I assumed he was confused about the way the story ended.

"My name is Cherie."

"That's the one. Yeah, he really loves you. What a great guy."

I didn't really want to ask the next logical question. I wasn't sure that I wanted to know what was wrong with Jean-Paul. With tears beginning to form in my eyes I asked as he was about to turn away, "Why's Jean-Paul going to the hospital?"

"Oh right. You probably want to know that. Well, we don't know what's wrong with him. He came on board pretty beat up. He has a few broken ribs. Who knows, maybe there was some internal bleeding. He's been vomiting blood and having other problems. He just needs to get to a hospital. He didn't mention that you would meet him here. Did he know you were coming?"

"No. He doesn't know. When can I see him?"

"Hold on. I will see if they are ready to move him. The boys have been taking care of him as best they could you know. They made a little board to carry him out of the boat."

"Oh God, I hope he's okay."

"He made it this far. The trip was hell. Oh pardon my language mam. I'm sorry. He's one tough guy. He said that thinking about you kept him alive. I can see why. You're awfully pretty mam. I hope John don't take offense to me saying so."

My head dropped into my hands and more tears leaked from my eyes.

"I will go see about John mam. Don't you worry about it. He'll get fixed up, good as new."

The man walked away and I stood unable to move. Monsieur and Madam were standing behind me. I hadn't noticed until the steward walked away. Madam placed her hand on my shoulder. Then she wrapped the same arm around me, hugging me from the side.

Ten minutes later men emerged carrying a make shift cot with a man lying down. I walked quickly toward the injured man. When I approached the cot, the men carrying Jean-Paul stood still. I looked down and gasped. I covered my mouth and probably scared Jean-Paul as he might have wondered what frightened me. A gray gaunt face resembling Jean-Paul met my gaze. I recognized the eyes immediately. The way he saw me with his eyes made me feel beautiful and complete. No gaze had ever made me feel more alive. He managed a weak smile. I bent down to hug him but before I could reach him a voice stated firmly, "Don't get too close, for your own safety. We don't know what's wrong with John. He's terribly sick. He's lost maybe fifteen pounds. He might be contagious. It's better to be safe. Jean-Paul didn't say anything. I waited to hear his voice, to have him say he was happy to see me. I wanted him to tell me that everything was going to be all right, that he would marry me and we would be overwhelmingly happy. "Jean-Paul?"

His voice was soft in response, "Why are you here? How…did you find me? Cherie, you should not have come."

He closed his eyes momentarily and swallowed hard. I had no idea how to respond. *Does he not want me to be in America, or does he not want me to see him like this?* I wondered. What was he really asking me? "We can talk later; when you feel better," I replied. I looked at the men carrying Jean-Paul. "What hospital are you taking him to?"

"St. Vincent. I'm not sure when he will be delivered, maybe an hour."

"We shall take him from here to the hospital. Can he sit?" Monsieur asked.

"We better take him in. He doesn't have papers or money. The captain said he was willing to vouch for the guy. You know…political stuff. Just go to St. Vincent and he'll be there later.

I just stared in disbelief at Jean-Paul. I couldn't imagine leaving him right now. I wanted him to embrace me. If he could just hold me, everything would fall into place. How could everything be well if he could not feel my love and warmth against him?

For the next few hours I sat in a daze waiting for Jean-Paul to be released, and waiting to talk to his doctor, while nurses, tears, IV fluids, vomiting, fear and wondering overwhelmed me and hospital smell attacked my senses. When the doctor finally came in to tell us his diagnosis, I felt almost numb from the roller coaster of emotions that had flooded my body all day.

"Jean-Paul has suffered from broken ribs and trauma to some internal organs as well as trauma to some muscles with severe contusions. Fortunately for Jean-Paul, he is young and strong. It appears that the organ trauma created some internal bleeding. His body is working to eliminate the blood from the abdominal cavity. Compromised circulation has caused the gray tone in his skin. The vomiting of blood appears to be due to prolonged lack of food. Jean-Paul said that he was kicked in the abdomen several times and has found it uncomfortable to eat. His medical emergency at this time is severe dehydration and lack of nutrients. We are rehydrating him with intravenous fluids. This will help him regain his strength. I am going to release him into your care after his fluid level is satisfied. He needs to be fed light meals that are easy on the stomach. I suggest broth for a few days, soup and cooked squash or rice. When he can hold these foods down then he can have other food. If he does not eat and drink he will become ill again and will need to come back. This young man is lucky to have survived three weeks in this condition."

"Thank you doctor," Monsieur said. "We appreciate your help."

Several hours later, we had Jean-Paul at the home of Monsieur and Madam. Monsieur helped him into a bed in a room next to the room I occupied. Madam brought a chair into the room for me to sit on and asked that I leave the door open. They left the room and Jean-Paul and I were alone. I was the guest in the home of very generous people whom I barely knew. I understood their rules and convictions about intimacy prior to marriage. Yet I felt an overwhelming desire to lie beside Jean-

Paul to lend him strength to push through this trial. I didn't know if either of them had knowledge of why André became jealous and caused these injuries to Jean-Paul. If they had knowledge, they did not speak it aloud. Their requests, however, for proper behavior were communicated clearly. I sat on a chair beside Jean-Paul and held his hand.

Jean-Paul looked at me and said, "I feel silly needing all of this care."

"I want to care for you. It gives me pleasure to do something for you," I replied.

"How did you find me? I am surprised to see you here. How did you get here?"

"The letter that André wrote to you made it back to Martine. She arranged everything for me to come here, stay at this home, and find you. She's amazing."

"Why did she do all of it?"

"Because she loves and adores you. She knows that André is a man who would hurt you. Your loving aunt wants what's best for you, and for me. She agrees that we belong together."

"André was just protecting what he felt he deserved, which was to marry you. Many men would have done the same. He had an oath to rely on."

"I don't agree. There are far more respectable ways for a man to handle the situation. His was ghastly and barbaric. I know that you would not do such a thing. Besides, he knows how I felt, and that was never considered. I suspect that you would at least consider how I felt. Oui?"

"I can't say what I would do if I was betrothed to you and you wanted to breach the oath."

"Jean-Paul, André doesn't love me. He loves the idea of marrying me and touching me. He doesn't even understand me."

"André probably does love you in the way that a man loves a woman." Jean-Paul paused briefly. "A man falls in loves with a woman because of how she makes him feel. Men feel inspired to be the best man they can be and excited to be near a woman they love. They can lift more weight, fight with more strength and even paint better when inspired by a woman they

149

love. Many men don't understand that true love will consider what's most important for the woman as well."

"I don't understand this kind of love. I don't feel loved unless I am understood by a man on a deeper level than others understand me. I like it when you look at my face and can tell that something's wrong when no one else can. I love how you appreciate my smile and laughter when others don't notice. When you look into my eyes, I can tell you really see me, not just a pretty face, but me, a woman who cries, pouts, gets sick and wants more than most people. You feel who I am deep down, what I care about and what I am willing to give up in order to follow my heart. I feel safe around you, knowing that you know who I am and what I need. I also love that you are not trying to change me or ask me to be something that I am not. You love me exactly the way I am."

"It's true. I do love who you are. But I also love you enough to consider what is best for you."

"You are what is best for me," I said with a smile.

Jean-Paul didn't smile. He looked at me quite seriously as he spoke. "Cherie, I had a lot of time to think on the boat while I was sick and in isolation," Jean-Paul said soberly. "I thought about everything that happened. I sent that note from André back to Paris to ensure my loved one would not worry about me or think that I abandon everyone. I didn't send it to cause you to risk your safety by traveling here alone."

"Jean-Paul you don't understand. In ten day they would force me to..."

"Let me finish Cherie, please. My duty was to come to America, to assist my family. I would do anything for my family as they have sacrificed much for me. Your family has sacrificed much for you as well Cherie. Your parents love you, their only child. They have done the best that they know in providing for you. It would be wrong to abandon them. I cannot take you from your family and feel good inside."

"Jean-Paul? How can you even think these thoughts? Your words hurt me deeply. You are the one and only person on this earth who I want to be with. You are the only person who cares at all about what I want. If you abandon me, then I shall have no one. I won't return to my parents unwed. They have betrayed me by forcing an ill man upon me. They have each other, and that will have to be enough for them, considering what they have done to me, their only daughter!! If you cannot feel good in your heart about being my husband, companion, lover, provider, confidant and best friend, then I would rather drown in the sea. I want nothing more than your love. If you won't give it, then be gone from me. But know this, I am not returning to Paris to be forced into a wicked matrimony with a lustful, greedy, self-absorbed, pompous bastard. How could you even think to say these words to me? How could you tell me in one breath that you love me and then..." I looked away and began to cry. I quickly left the room unable to say one more word.

I walked downstairs and put on my jacket and shoes. I walked out the front door and didn't say a word to anyone. Tears filled my eyes and flowed freely down my cheeks. I couldn't see the faces of the people I passed on the street that I walked upon. I didn't know where I was going or if I ever wanted to come back. How could I feel loved in one breath and abandoned in the next? It was as if the world spun upside down on me in an instant; the unimaginable happened in a flash.

Seeing Jean-Paul was nothing like what I expected. I imagined that all my fears would melt away when I saw him and he held me in his arms. Why would he tell me that my family was more important than us being together or more important than my happiness? Why would he even think of risking me being forced to marry André, the man who hurt him? I could not imagine what made him say such things. We were not communicating like two people in love. If I didn't find a way back into Jean-Paul's heart, then I had nothing.

I found myself turning a corner and walking on a different street. I didn't notice the street sign, if there was one, but I noticed that people were gathered up ahead. There were two cafés mid-block, nearly side by side. I walked to the first one, wiped my tears away, and went inside. I quickly sat at the only empty table and turned my head from the crowded room. I could see out the window onto the street where people stood and talked as if this were a natural meeting place. I wondered about their conversation. Some of them arm in arm or face to face. Did they speak of families back home or obligations to loved ones?

A young waitress came to my table to take my order. I wanted a coffee, but in my haste I left without my pocketbook. "Hello. I am waiting for someone. May I wait to order until they arrive please?"

"Yes," she said turning and walking away.

"Thank you," I said loud enough so she could hear me.

I stared out the window and wondered why life was complicated. It didn't seem as if love should be confusing. When I was with Jean-Paul it didn't matter to me what we were doing, I was happy. When he spoke, I felt how sweet and sincere he was. I knew of his good heart from his words. He did kind things for me that André would not do. He asked if he could carry anything I had in my hands, he went far out of his way to see me, and he touched my hair and face as if he were looking at an angel. His strong legs, rich skin, broad shoulders and lean stomach drew me towards him like a magnet. I had to counter the force to pry myself away.

Our conversations were real and connected. He wanted to know what I was thinking. My opinions mattered to him. He said I fascinated him. What man would give up the woman he loves to keep her with her parents? Are my parents going to provide for me and make love to me for the rest of my life? NO! What is he thinking? Where was the man who couldn't live without me?

The waitress looked over at me several times. I was afraid that any moment she would tell me that the tables were for paying customers only. I thought of how I might escape unnoticed, perhaps when her back was turned I could sneak out and wander the streets a bit longer. Eventually I may have to go back, to scream at Jean-Paul or to talk some sense into him. I looked at the door and planned my departure. As I stood, Monsieur walked in through the front door. He scanned the room and his eyes met mine.

"There you are," he said to me. I didn't respond other than with embarrassment on my face. "We were worried."

"Oh, I am sorry. I didn't mean to..." I began to cry.

"It will be all right mademoiselle. You will see. Give Jean-Paul some time. He's ill and possibly he was delusional while he was on the boat."

"You know what he said to me?"

"Non."

"He said that he must not take me from my family."

"Jean-Paul is a man of honor. He feels that he must do the right thing, for everyone, even when it's difficult."

"Doesn't he understand that I can't return to Paris? I can't marry André. I can't. I won't. Why won't he just acknowledge that we belong together? My family made their decision."

"You need to have this conversation with Jean-Paul," Monsieur said.

"I don't know if I could keep my composure. I am too upset to speak rationally right now."

"You will feel more settled in a few hours. Decide what he must know and only share the most essential part. Speak from your heart."

The waitress approached the table. "May I take your order now please?"

I looked at Monsieur and said, "I would like a coffee," looking for his approval.

"Two coffees and two strudels, please." I smiled. I wasn't ready to return to the house. I hoped that Jean-Paul was worried about me and thinking about how he hurt me.

"Monsieur, why do men and women see things differently?"

"It's part of the allure, the differences."

"Are you certain? Jean-Paul has confused me. We both know that the connection that we share is unique and difficult to define. We feel comfortable with each other, relaxed, yet excited. We are interested in what the other person is thinking and how each other is feeling. When we are together we don't act selfish. We act like we are Siamese twins and what one twin needs affects us both. We have a rich, powerful relationship. Why would he consider giving me up to make my parents happy? That doesn't feel like love."

"Mademoiselle, you must ask Jean-Paul your question. He's a man of honor. He will do what he feels is right, even if it's not what he wants. He's a good man," he said.

"I understand that I must ask him. I was hoping for some perspective. I would like to understand why he would be willing to give up what we have in order to honor my parents, who didn't love me enough to honor me? Why do they deserve more honor than I do? That's my question to Jean-Paul."

"Then return to the house and ask him."

"I will. I am not ready to ask him yet. He can wait and wonder if I will ever speak to him again."

Monsieur smiled at my dramatic behavior. "Your passion is infectious."

"Do you think Jean-Paul can catch it?"

"I hope so." He smiled a sincere smile. I tried to smile back, but all I could wonder was if I had already made the biggest mistake of my life.

Chapter Thirteen: The Power of Two

New York City, April, 1899

When Monsieur Batton and I arrived back at his home, I felt too angry to approach Jean-Paul. I didn't say hello as I walked past his room. Madam announced that dinner would be served in thirty minutes. I politely declined.

"Mademoiselle, your feelings need to be spoken. You and Monsieur Soule need to communicate about your differences. Every relationship requires communication. If you two cannot communicate now, you will grow apart over time. I suggest you speak to him before dinner, so we can all enjoy a relaxed meal, please?" *Perhaps Jean-Paul and I don't have a relationship,* I thought silently.

It was difficult to hear Madam's words. My pride and heart were in such pain that I wanted to feel better before I spoke to him. Yet, I knew she was correct. The longer I waited, the worse I felt. I walked to the doorway of Jean-Paul's room and he immediately smiled.

"Come in, please Cherie," he invited.

"Jean-Paul, I feel very confused and hurt. I feel like there's nowhere for me to turn. There's no one who I can trust, who understands how to protect me from disaster, except for Martine. I ran toward you thinking that you would be the one person who would keep me safe and who would understand how important it is for us to be together."

"Cherie, please sit down." Reluctantly, I walked the few steps towards the chair beside his bed. I slowly sat, feeling nervous and unsure. "Thank you. I have more to say. You didn't allow me to finish speaking to you before you stomped out. You're very cute when you stomp and speak your mind. I enjoy your forceful tongue."

"What is it that you didn't have the opportunity to say?" I asked.

155

"Oh, we are going to jump right into this discussion are we?"

"Madam wants us to be cordial by dinner. You have thirty minutes to make me feel cordial."

"Well that is a lot of pressure. I don't know that I can turn your fury around in half an hour. I will try, however. You must allow me to finish my thought before you rebut or stomp out."

"I shall give you that much consideration."

"Cherie, your parents are important to me because I don't have mine. It's easy to take your parents for granted when you have them. Do you know what I would give to have my mother meet you? If my father could see our children...I will never see their loving faces again. I have no choice in that matter. You still have a choice. I can't let you dismiss your family from your life. I have lived eighteen years without my parents. I don't want you to have to live without yours. Your children deserve to know their grandparents. How would you feel if your mother was on her death bed right now? Would you want to see her? Your parents love you. You're pushing them away because they made a decision to guarantee you a safe future. They don't deserve to be abandoned for giving you everything they had to offer."

"How would you feel towards your parents if they tried to kill me? Would you feel the same devotion?"

"Your parents didn't try to kill me."

"No, they just tried to force me to marry the man who nearly killed you."

"Your parents don't know that." I didn't respond. My rebuttal didn't have much strength. Jean-Paul continued. "As far as they knew, they were protecting you from the harsh realities of life. If you really thought it through, I don't think that you would make the choice to walk away from your family. Your mother and father would not consider abandoning you, no matter what you did."

Still I couldn't reply. Words would not flow, which was an unusual problem for me. My heart fought to defend my actions to leave Paris, as much as it felt overwhelmed with love for Jean-Paul for caring about my family. While André didn't care about what I wanted, Jean-Paul cared about my family more than himself. He saw a bigger picture.

"I don't want you to wake up one day full of regret. I don't want to be the man who idly allowed you to give this part of your life away. I don't want to wake up and decide that I compromised too much for you or for me. We still have the matter of the church in order to have permission for your hand. There are hurdles ahead. We must return to Paris and face our fate."

"I cannot stew another moment of my life without knowing if you plan to marry me or not. You speak of it and yet avoid it in the same sentence. Be frank with me. What is your intention?"

"For three weeks I have thought about getting back to Paris to dual with André for you and ask your parents' permission for your hand. Now you are here and suddenly I must devise a new strategy."

"Your plan would have failed. My family was forcing me to marry André before you returned. My options were to marry André or run away."

"I see. André's letter was correct when he said you would be married before I could return."

"Did you doubt his words?"

"Darling, would you please give me a couple of days to heal from starvation and develop my new pathway forward. It's my intention to win you with honor and the approval of your family. Allow me to pursue this path that I might be worthy of your love."

"Very well, I have faith in you and will be more patient," I replied.

"Shall we dine?" Jean-Paul suggested.

"Certainly."

"I'm surprised that I won your heart back in less than half an hour. It's amazing what can happen when I can finish my sentences." Jean-Paul looked at me and smiled.

Madam saw us walk into the dining room and asked, "Did you two love doves resolve your differences?"

"We are moving in the right direction," Jean-Paul said.

"Good. I want to have peace around here," Madam added in a friendly, but firm tone.

The four of us sat down to a pleasant meal. We talked and laughed as if Jean-Paul was not recovering from near death, as if I hadn't run away from my family and fiancé, as if our future were solid and plans certain.

The next two days Jean-Paul recovered without complaint and grew stronger with each sip of broth or soft egg and toast. On the third morning after his return, he spoke to me in a determined tone. "Cherie, I have a New York site I would like for us to see today, while we have the opportunity."

"That sounds lovely. What is it?"

"You shall have to wait until we are close. Please dress warmly, including a hat."

Jean-Paul and I rode in a carriage through the city. After a twenty minute ride we approached Central Park. "I might know where you're taking me," I said.

"Perhaps," Jean-Paul replied, "but I challenge you to state where in this enormous park I'm taking you."

I smiled with anticipation, although Jean-Paul tried to look serious.

After more traveling through the spring tree buds, cobblestone paths, past creeks and bridges, we finally stopped. The air was cool and the sky was dotted with clouds. Moments of sunrays warmed me followed by shadows of coolness. "This, my dear, is the Reservoir, the largest body of water in Central Park." The lake was beautiful, surrounded by many deciduous trees, some of which were beginning to bloom. Pink and white blossoms dotted the opposing side of the lake.

"This is magical. I love how still the water is. It reflects the trees and sky."

Jean-Paul led me around the path surrounding the lake. "You give me the peace that I also find in nature."

"Thank you. It's surely one of the most beautiful places I have been," I replied. We stared out together noticing the ducks and other birds. We walked to a bench close to the water. Jean-Paul led me by the hand to the bench. Before he directed me to sit, he turned my body toward his, his hands held my cheek, his gaze fixated on mine and he drew me towards him. His kiss released days of stress and fear. The heat and passion of his embrace made me tingle from head to toe. For a moment I thought he might tear my clothes from my body and ravish me with his desire. He pressed his full body against me and kissed me harder, pressing his lips firmly into mine. His body flinched, and I knew that his ribs hurt, although he didn't complain. His hand moved behind my head and held me to him. He released my lips and showered my neck with kisses, pulling at my clothing and running his hands over my body.

A few moments later he pulled himself back and looked at me. "Oh, what you cause to move inside me. It's dangerous." I didn't reply but secretly I smiled.

Jean-Paul directed me to sit beside him. His face winced ever so slightly as his left arm wrapped around his waist, protecting his wrapped ribs and bruised back. He paused, then spoke again, "Although this is a spectacular sight, I have never seen anything as lovely or mesmerizing as you."

"Oh, thank you." I wanted to comfort his pain, but I knew he had something else on his mind, so I listened quietly.

"I want nothing more than to spend every day with you and grow old gazing into your spectacular eyes. Your eyes have captured my soul," he said with a serious face.

I smiled and looked back intently. He reached for my right hand to hold in his. He lowered himself from the bench to his right knee without taking his eyes off of mine. I gulped.

"Cherish Bourguignon, I love you with every part of my being. You complete me and warm my heart. You enhance my life. I want to hold you for eternity. Would you do me the honor of becoming my wife? Will you marry me?" At the same moment he presented a black velvet box with a significant diamond solitaire ring. I hadn't even notice that he had let go of my hand to present the ring.

Tears began to flow down my face as I started to nod. "Oh, Jean-Paul, you make me the happiest woman in the world. Yes, of course I shall be your wife. I shall love you forever. I will care for you..." I reached to hug Jean-Paul and he raised himself to embrace me.

Jean-Paul pulled back to see my face. He looked at me with another serious expression. "It's my life-long goal to make you the happiest woman in the world."

I smiled in response. "And it's my life-long goal that you're the most satisfied man."

"I became the most satisfied when you accepted my proposal."

We sat together for a long while on the bench, staring at the water and talking. My feet didn't touch the ground, for I floated on the clouds high above the motionless lake.

"We will leave immediately for Paris and be wed as quickly as possible," he said smiling. "I will send word to our families."

I smiled with much reluctance. André had not showed up in New York. Perhaps he waited for us in Paris. I expressed my concern. "If you send word that we are coming back to France, André will likely learn of it and try to harm you."

"If André comes after me I shall fight him."

"And what if he sends a small army for you?"

"I've thought about that. There's the opportunity of marrying outside of Paris, perhaps in Le Havre and then departing afterwards. We could have a seaside reception. I will find us a solution my love."

"Thank you, Jean-Paul. I trust that you will."

"I will see that your parents attend our ceremony," he assured me.

"While you're contemplating our forthcoming wedding, could you please tell me what happened the day you left for America?" I asked.

"Yes, if you must know. After I took you home, I walked back towards my uncle's flat. I walked through the park, where we always meet, and as I neared the edge of the park I had a strange feeling, as if I was being watched. Then four men surrounded me, one from each direction. André came at me from the front. The other four men held me while André took one punch deep into my gut. He said, 'You've taken something that belongs to me.' He stuffed something in my coat pocket. As he

160

turned to walk away, he waved his right hand and said, 'Finish him men. You know what to do.'

"At that moment I thought perhaps he wanted them to kill me. I struggled as best as I could. I kicked and fought, but two men held me while another took swings. When I finally fell to the ground they started kicking me in my back, head and stomach. I thought that perhaps this is where I might die, in our park, being kicked to death. I thought of you in that moment and how amazing it was to touch you hours earlier. One man finally yelled for the other two to stop. He said, 'That's enough. We have to be able to get him on the boat.' Then I assumed that they were going to finish me in the water, to avoid leaving a dead body in the park.

"With firm grips the men carried me to a carriage and took me straight to the pier. One man bought two tickets, one for me and one for him to Le Havre. He also purchased a ticket for me from Le Havre to America. I was standing right beside him when he purchased it. He told the ticket master that I had fallen and he was my brother. In that moment, I thought that perhaps they might let me live. On the boat to Le Havre, I read the note that André stuffed in my pocket. I had one chance to get that note out of my hands and back to Paris to let someone know where I was. My escort went to the restroom. I put all the money I had in my pocket into the hand of a young steward and asked him to make certain that Jacques or Martine Soule received the note. He promised he would. He walked away before the bully returned.

"When we reached the coast of France, André's man loaded me onto the cargo ship and asked a crew member to make sure I didn't get off the boat. I could not have run twenty feet in my condition. There was no escaping for me. I was happy to be alive, but leaving you in Paris felt like my limbs were ripped from my body."

I didn't say a word during Jean-Paul's story. I didn't even make a sound. Every emotion swept through me; anger, shame, guilt, compassion, empathy, and gratitude. More than any emotion I wanted Jean-Paul to know that I saw him as a victor for withstanding the trauma both physically and emotionally. He was my hero for making it through the boat ride in his condition and for not allowing André's fury to turn him into a vengeful man.

"Jean-Paul, there are men of valor, men of bravery, integrity and strength. There are men of honor, courage and self-control. There are men who would die for the people they love and men who would stand in honor of the ones they love. You have every quality of all of these men. If I thought that I have loved you before now, then I must love you even more today, for my heart has opened to you ten times above what it was before. I could not ask for a better man with which to walk this life. I trust you implicitly my love. My heart is yours. I shall do anything you ask of me. I surrender my safe keeping into your capable arms."

"Cherie, please understand that a great deal of my courage comes from the smile on your face, the love in your heart and the thought of holding you. Nothing inspires a man more than a woman's devoted love. You give me too much credit."

"Not true my love. I've known of men in love before. You have more integrity than ten of them put together. I expect that you could never disappoint me."

"Oh I shall disappoint you to be certain darling. It's the job of all men to infuriate their women. We've all made an oath together. Each man has promised to anger his wife on a regular basis. This is to protect the whole of mankind. You see, if a few men are flawless while the majority cannot be, then most men would be rejected by women for not being perfect. This would jeopardize the human race. We made a commitment to all be alike, in order that all men stand a chance with a woman to procreate. We have agreed to have no perfect men on the earth…simply to protect humanity from extinction." Jean-Paul tried to look serious at me, but he failed to hide his faint smile.

"Jean-Paul!" I thought to rebuke him, but changed my response into witty repartee. "I do not approve of this oath you have made. Take it back immediately. I expect perfection and I shall absolutely have it. After all, I am an intelligent, capable woman, am I not? Do I not deserve something equal in return? Hmmm?"

Jean-Paul looked at me a bit baffled for a moment, until he realized that I was playing along. He continued the game.

"You speak the truth my sweet angel. You deserve perfection. Therefore, I retract the oath that I have made with mankind. I shall be the faultless husband to my impeccable wife, even if it puts humanity in peril, for I have no choice but to sacrifice humanity to give my lovely partner all she desires and deserves."

"Why thank you darling. That wasn't difficult now was it?"

"Anything I do for you my dear, I do with ease."

After a few days of gaining strength and exploring New York City, Jean-Paul explained to me his plan to wed. "I shall send a telegraph to Jacques and Martine with these details. We shall arrive in Le Havre unannounced. No one shall know the date. We will make arrangements to wed at a Catholic church. When the arrangements are set, I will ask Jacques and Martine to escort your parents to the church where they may witness us being married. After your long absence, I suspect that they will be delighted to know you're safe and enjoying your decision to include them in your life. I shall ask Jacques and Martine to carefully set the stage."

"Darling your plan is beautiful. I must share with you one small detail of which you were not aware. Someone within Jacques's home has become an informant to André."

"Are you certain?"

"There could be no other way. Martine told me on the day that I was departing that I was to wear servant's clothing to not be recognized. She said that she told no one else. Yet André knew that I was to leave Paris, both the time and the date. He searched my boat leaving Paris for a runaway servant. Fortunately, I had changed clothing prior to boarding the boat. He also knew the ship I took to New York and a search was conducted on that vessel. He was on board, or one of his men was, because someone was inquiring after me. He could only have known if someone had shared that information. If you wire Jacques and Martine, it's possible that André will be notified by the same person. He may find out the details of our wedding and interfere."

Jean-Paul pondered my information quietly for several minutes. I watched his face as he searched his mind for a safe alternative. "I will send the telegram to my cousin, Marion, explaining the situation. She will get the information to Jacques discreetly. Jacques would do anything to protect me, and you as well. He will make sure that we are safe. I won't tell them the location. We will have a carriage meet Jacques, Martine and your parents at a designated location and the driver shall take them to the church we specify. Do you feel better now?"

"We don't know if Marion was the one who told André." I asked.

"That's not likely. Besides, she will honor my request. We are very close. I will ask her not to share our plans with anyone except Martine."

"You have thought of everything. When shall we depart for France?"

"I will make some arrangements and we shall leave tomorrow. I want to wed as soon as possible, so I may hold you and ravish you day and night."

"My love, I understand the integrity that burns within you. I respect your fortitude to do what you feel is moral. I don't want to ask you to compromise your convictions. However, in regards to intimacy, I must ask, why would you feel committed to saving our love-making until marriage? Would that conviction not be the ideals of the Church or conventional wisdom? If you were to listen to the whisperings of your own heart, what would your heart say to you about sharing your whole self with the woman you already love? Do we need a legal stamp on our passion to make it real?"

"Ma petite Cherie, I withhold all of my advances on you at this time to protect your prestige. You deserve for everyone to respect the qualities you have that make you a woman worth waiting for. I also want you to know that I am willing to wait because you are worth every sacrifice I must make to have you as my wife. I would slay dragons, fight André, and wait for years if it were required. You are a woman of great quality and exquisite beauty. I want you to know your merit. For me to wait to hold you should help you to see how greatly I value you."

"Thank you Jean-Paul. I appreciate your respect and know it well, from your actions. Would you honor a request from me?"

"I would my sweet."

"Please place your cheeks on my breasts and your tongue behind my ear and your hand between my thighs. I request your undivided attention with your skin pressed firmly against mine. This is my desire with full understanding of your respect for me."

"Cherie, I desire you above food and water. I crave your skin, your lips, your breasts, your warmth. My wanting of you is ever present. I also desire to make you a happy woman; to see your smile, hear your laughter and know that your needs are met. However, I satisfy myself by resisting your beauty until you are my wife. Allow me to earn your respect with integrity, so that I may respect you always."

"I admire your desires, although mine are still present," I said. My heart ached for more reassurance. I wanted to melt completely in his loving embrace. With an ocean separating us from marriage, and André searching our tracks, I worried that the day might never arrive.

Chapter Fourteen: **Back in Time**

New York City, April, 1899

Jean-Paul and I talked about our wedding all the way home. During the one hour ride, we decided that we wanted to travel to France as a married couple in order to share a cabin and to avoid the chance that André could stop the wedding. All we needed now were strong men to protect us from André. We decided to tell Monsieur and Madam Batton our plans.

It began to rain as soon as we sat down for dinner. The sky darkened and rain tapped against the window panes. Madam Batton lit two more candles. Her dining room was small, but formal, with a cherry wood table of great detail. Soft upholstered cushions of fine check pattern fabric covered the seat. She served us roast, potatoes, rolls, Brussels sprouts and vanilla pudding for dessert. The room smelled divine. The food and conversation were pleasant.

Near the end of the meal, Jean-Paul shared our news. "We wish to travel as a married couple and we would like both of you to be the witnesses at our wedding," Jean-Paul explained.

"No. You must not give up a beautiful wedding and sharing this experience with your families. You've come this far. You can make it all the way back to France and do a proper wedding." Madam Batton's voice was adamantly firm.

"Madam, you're correct on all counts. Yet there's one more thing to consider. What if our plan failed in some way? What if Cherie was forced into a marriage with André? If she were already married, then she couldn't be wed again. We are simply choosing to protect the decision we have both made against the real threat that exists." Jean-Paul spoke the fears I had inside.

"He could be correct." Monsieur Batton jumped in to reassure his wife. "If a man is willing to let another man die to protect a betrothal, then you do not know what else he may try to do. Madam Martine would not have taken all of the precautions had she not been worried about the risks."

"I'm not certain that I agree. Traditions are followed for a reason. The Church has standards and requirements because of God's will," Madam Batton added. "Perhaps I shall telegraph Martine and ask her suggestion."

"Madam, please don't telegraph Martine. André found out the date and time that I was leaving through a member of Jacques's and Martine's home. André could easily get word of the telegram and contents," I begged.

Madam was quiet for a moment. "It's really not my charge to tell you two what you must do. I want only what's best for you. I will be your witness at a ceremony if you will promise me to pray to God about your choice and then do all that you can to include your families in this union."

"That seems like a fair request," Jean-Paul added, surprising me with his answer. I'd not seen Jean-Paul pray and I wondered what his prayer might say.

It took two days for Jean-Paul to get us scheduled for a marriage ceremony at the court house. I went shopping with Madam Batton and found a simple white gown. The sleeves were soft silk and flowed gracefully on my arms, caressing me with the smooth weave. The neckline was round and lined with tiny pearls. The silk dress draped from my shoulder to my feet in one elegant flowing swoop. The skirt was wide at the bottom, but you could only see how much when I turned quickly. My new shoes were dazzling white pumps with a three inch heal. I felt beautiful.

Jean-Paul borrowed a suit from Monsieur Batton that he had hadn't worn in years, but was sure he would fit into again someday. Jean-Paul wore it well, with a fine white shirt and bow tie. The formal coat fit him nicely, with tails in the back. Jean-Paul looked sharp in black. Looking at him, I wanted to leap into his arms and kiss his handsome face.

The judge who wed us looked tired and old. He hunched forward and pressed his face close to the pages to read. He didn't seem particularly interested in our wedding, not smiling or showing any concern. But then he surprised me. After the short vows he read, and Jean-Paul and I said "I do,", he spoke up in a solemn voice. "You two young people appear to be in love and serious about your vows. I caution you that the commitment you made this day is of no less value because there's no fancy band present, or cousins and flower girls. God recognized the importance of your promise today and you should too. I've been married for almost fifty years. My wife is my favorite person on earth. I would not be the man that I am today without my loving companion. Respect and honesty are the foundation of a good marriage. You will fight. You will disagree. You will become angry. Just remember the love that you feel this day. Remember why you chose to make the pledge to honor and love. If you treasure each other, it will be the greatest blessing that you have. If one of you dies before the other, God help you. If you love one another the way I love my wife, then you might die too of a broken heart when the other departs this life. That's the power of true love. Please, look at each other."

We turned from looking at the judge to face the one another.

"Put your faith in this union. Don't take it for granted. I now pronounce you husband and wife. You may kiss your new bride."

Jean-Paul slowly reached for me, watching my face as he moved. His motions were meaningful and measured, as if this was our first kiss and it meant everything in the world. He pulled me in from my waist, slowly wrapped his arms fully around my body, and began to kiss me. His lips gently met mine, then firmly sank in deeper. His lips did not move at first, as if he were savoring my warmth and scent. Then he kissed me with emotion. I felt as if this were the most important kiss I'd ever had. I lost track of the room, the witnesses and firm judge. I could have been anywhere in the moment and know only the kiss.

Following the wedding, there was complicated paperwork regarding immigration. It was written in English, so Senator Batton interpreted all of it for us and made sure that we had what we needed. I signed all of the papers as I was instructed. There was mention of dual citizenship. I wasn't sure what that entailed, but I was happy to do whatever it took to be the wife of Jean-Paul.

That night Jean-Paul and I were permitted to sleep in the same room at the home of Monsieur and Madam Batton. Jean-Paul lit the bed lamp and smiled at me as if we shared a secret again. This time I felt that we had a real secret. Our families didn't know that we were married; my family didn't even know where I was. And no one knew the magic that ensued between Jean-Paul and me when we touched each other's bare skin. That was a secret no one else would ever know.

Jean-Paul reached for me, beckoning me to come to him. I walked toward him, without an ounce of resistance. As our hands touched, I felt his warmth, his pulse, his love. Immediately I felt the surrendering begin. I wanted to give myself in every possible way to my husband, my lover.

He sat on the edge of the bed and drew me close. I stood between his parted thighs. His hand reached to my head and wrapped around my hair. He drew me in for a slow, powerful kiss that expressed, 'You're mine. I chose you. I desire you. I love you. I must have you."

I responded. My lips and tongue expressed my heart, "I belong to you. You can have me. I surrender to you. I love you. Please take me and claim me."

Jean-Paul lifted my blouse while I stood before him. He removed my corset. For a brief second he stared at my breasts he had known a month before. In the next second he engulfed my left nipple in his mouth, kissing it with his desire and appreciation and an effort to give me pleasure. My head titled back and I pressed my chest towards him, begging for more, granting him every part of me. His hand held my right breast. Soon his mouth moved from left to right, granting the right nipple the same gratification.

He removed my skirt, letting it slip to a heap on the floor. Then my undergarments fell and I stood naked before my fully dressed husband. I didn't want to change a beat of his rhythm. I feared to move without command. This was the moment where he must know my willingness to obey his desires. This is the moment where I respond to his touch instead of demand it. He was the leader, and I his willing participant. He must find his way through the maze of my body and learn each turn and each point of pleasure.

He lifted me at the waist and laid me on my back on the bed. Kneeling over me, he showered my body with kisses while using the back of his fingertips to gently caress my skin. I enjoyed my nakedness exposed to him. The vulnerability felt invigorating. Being enjoyed by my lover fully caused me to feel more beautiful. I didn't demand for his clothing to be removed. I understood deep inside that he was prolonging the pleasure that we would enjoy. There was purpose in his calculations, and I trusted them.

For a moment he didn't touch me, and I sensed that he was absorbing my nakedness. I smiled at the thought of him enjoying what my body could do for him. Then ever so slightly, his hand caressed my hair and found my cheek. I felt his lips touch mine and the rush came like a river unleashed. His excitement pulsed through me, into my lips, down my throat and deep into my loins. I didn't know if I could wait one more moment before I had to know him inside of me. I made a conscious effort to let go, be in the moment, and revel in the pleasure, like savoring dark chocolate. His warm, clothed body made its way on top of mine. The pressure felt invigorating, but I wanted his bare, warm skin. I dared not make any demands. He was fulfilling my wishes with thoughtful movements. I couldn't allow doubt to come into this moment. He always knew what served me best, which helped me to trust completely. I couldn't imagine a better place to be than lying naked below my husband, the man whom I respected most above all others. To feel wanted by this man, touched exquisitely, and cared for deeply, was the greatest experience I could possibly imagine.

Jean-Paul's kisses found their way around my body; my shoulders and elbows, my fingertips and hip bones, even my knees were graced by his powerful mouth. His hands explored me, finding every inch, tantalizing my skin with the tingling pleasure of soft caresses. My eyes remained closed, and I pictured his eyes memorizing my form that he might paint my body image on to canvas with a brush. My love was the greatest gift this man could now embrace. Suddenly I understood why he took a lot of time and care to see my body from head to toe before he dared allow his body to merge with mine.

"Open your eyes, my darling," Jean-Paul instructed me.

I looked deeply into his eyes to see what he wanted.

"Undress me my love."

I saw in his expression that he wanted me to connect with him the way he had just connected with me. I saw the request, permission and desire. I sat up next to Jean-Paul and I began to caress his cheeks with my hands. My fingertips moved down his neck to the top button on his white pressed dress shirt he had borrowed for today's occasion. I unbuttoned the top button, revealing his strong neck and my whole body quivered. I unbuttoned again and again, each time exposing more and more of his beautiful, hard pectorals. When I reached the last button, I opened his shirt, viewed the whole of his torso and I lie on top of him, breast to breast, heart to heart absorbing his love and showering him with my own.

With care, I placed kisses across his neck, shoulders and chest. I was drawn to his belly, like the pull of a magnet. I could not resist. I was ready to kiss his hips and thighs. I removed his belt, unbuttoned the top button of his trousers, and unzipped the zipper. Jean-Paul gently lifted his hips and allowed me to remove his trousers past his feet. I removed his under garments next and I was face-to-face fully exposed to his sex.

I kissed his stomach without hesitation, as if I knew what to do all along. I landed my lips firm and meaningfully on his hip bones and on his thighs. Then lastly, with intention, I placed soft, hungry lips on his hard, protruding member. I loved the way the smooth, taut skin felt on my lips. I opened my mouth and presented my tongue. It was more velvety than Jean-Paul's lips, but much firmer. It smelled sweet and delicious. I inhaled deeply, bathing in the scent of it. I licked again, with my eyes still closed. My tongue enjoyed the sensation. I licked and tasted, relishing in this pleasure shared between us. Jean-Paul's body tensed, and his back slightly arched. A small sound of pleasure escaped his lips. His arms reached for my shoulders. He wanted to pull me away up to his face. "No," I said softly. "I want to know you this well. I don't want there to be any part of you that I don't know completely."

"You have a lifetime to know me completely. Today, I want you to know how deeply I love you." Jean-Paul put his strong arms under mine and lifted me onto his body. We laid naked, face-to-face, and nose to nose. "You're the most beautiful woman I have ever seen in my life. I cannot wait to capture your beauty on canvas."

Jean-Paul wrapped his arms around me and kissed me, then firmly rolled me onto my back and began to kiss me with the vigor of a hungry man. His hips pushed against mine and I responded. His hands rubbed me everywhere that his body did not. I felt myself melting into the bed, letting go as if I sank into a sea of calm. Comfort enveloped me, with intense pleasure. My body tingled in every orifice and I wanted nothing more than to feel as if I'd melted inside Jean-Paul and we were one body.

I felt his body moving in search for the place to penetrate me. I loved the search, the excitement, the anticipation of it. I adjusted my body to assist his probing. He found his way, and entered me, as if there was nothing more important he could ever do.

Shockwaves pulsed through my body. I thought I might explode into tiny pieces, broken all over the bed on the night of my wedding. I wasn't sure I could handle the intensity of the moment, the physical force of it, the hunger, the need. I began to cry, quietly. Although I tried to hide it, Jean-Paul noticed. "What's the matter, my love?"

"Nothing could be more perfect. My tears are only because I'm overwhelmed with joy."

Jean-Paul looked deep into my soul, smiled, and began again with intense passion. It seemed to slow him down for a few moments. Then the intensity built up again and he moved inside of me as naturally as if he'd known me always.

Our bodies responded to one another, with the kisses and caresses and the waves of thrusting. When I thought it couldn't become any more pleasurable or intense, my body exploded in blissful waves of delight. Jean-Paul seemed to release at the same time as his body tensed momentarily and then relaxed. I looked at his face, which was filled with a smile and bright eyes, as relaxed as I've ever seen his face.

We lay still, embracing, smiling, warm and satisfied. The air smelled of the two of us, our sweat, and our wet skin together as one. I didn't want to ever move again. No moment in my life had I ever felt this safe. I imagined that it might be true for Jean-Paul as well. We fell asleep in our embrace. We didn't stir for many hours. The danger and challenges ahead seemed to have disappeared forever, or at least for a few hours.

Chapter Fifteen: **Dressed in White**

Le Havre, France, April, 1899

For seven days Jean-Paul and I tried to enjoy our honeymoon across the Atlantic, but it was less than romantic. The ship was far less equipped than the Deutschland and our cabin smelled like the restrooms. The food left much to be desired. Rats occasionally ran under our feet. We did our best to enjoy each other, although it challenged us both.

When we arrived in Le Havre, relief and joy of being on familiar soil brought tears to my eyes. Marion had communicated with Martine, who shared our plans with my mother. When we arrived, we were greeted with love and open arms. I saw the look in my mother's face, and I burst into tears.

"I'm sorry Mother! I didn't mean to hurt you..."

"Sh...Hush ma Cherie. My heart is bursting with love. It's I who must apologize to you. We saw the letter that André wrote. I'm sorry for your suffering. When we confronted André, he was most arrogant and accepted no responsibility. Your father and I want only for your happiness. You needn't ask for our forgiveness. We should ask for yours."

"Oh, Mother and Father, I love you both beyond words!" We embraced for many minutes while tears dampened our cheeks and clothing.

Mother and Martine had everything arranged, including giving the priest our nuptial inquiry papers, stamped with the seal from the Bishop of my parish as well as a letter from my Bishop, stating that he knows of no reason why we cannot be married in a Catholic church in Le Havre. They also brought Baptism and Confirmation certificates for each of us with the official seal. Jean-Paul did not offer any objections. They selected a local

174

priest, name Father Nolan, whom my parents had met before while visiting my grandmother.

We were to be married the following day. We slept in different rooms that night, as tradition would expect. We kept our first ceremony a secret so that our family would think that they were watching us wed for the first time. We would only share our first ceremony if we needed it to protect me from André.

The next morning Jean-Paul and I were led to a small church in the heart of town. The entire building was lined with rich, dark wood. Small stained glass windows were high on the building, and a single steeple reached upward. The structure was far simpler than most cathedrals in Paris, but the simplicity allowed the focus to be on Jean-Paul and me.

The building was graciously prepared for our ceremony and adorned with white and pink flowers tied with lots of ribbon on every available post and pew. Near the altar were giant bouquets in three matching baskets with white roses, purple tulips, pink and white carnations, pussy willows, pink and white orchids and red and pink lilies.

I walked into the bride's chambers to find a beautiful white gown made of satin, chiffon, and lace waiting for me. The skirt was wide and full with a large, hooped slip under it. The gown was covered with hundreds of pearls and embroidered flowers were attached to the dress in the center of the blossom, adding dimension as the pedals flowed freely. The sleeves were soft, woven lace with an intricate pattern of flowers and leaves. The neck line stretched low between my breasts, revealing far more than I thought my mother would approve. I didn't comment on the neckline, but thanked my mother with hugs and tear filled eyes.

Mother helped me into my gown with her eyes tearing up as well. She brushed my hair and pulled part of it up while other locks draped my shoulders. "You look beautiful darling. I'm happy that you have a good man to care for you," my mother told me. "I'm grateful that I could be here to share this day with you."

"I'm sorry that we are not getting married in the church that you and Papa were married in," I said.

"Not to worry my dear. We are both happy. Now let's get you into that chapel so that you can share your life with Jean-Paul." My mother gestured towards the chapel as she held back her tears.

Walking with my father, with my arm on his, I walked down the aisle surrounded by the people who mattered most to me. I strolled towards the man I loved; the man who could see who I really was and wanted nothing more than my happiness. As he watched me walk, I didn't feel worthy of his powerful love. Now was not the time to question if I deserved him. He was already my husband in one country, and today I wore a white dress, held pink roses and was surrounded by my loved ones supporting this union. There wasn't a girl in all of France who could have wanted anything more.

Jean-Paul and I stood at the front of the chapel with the priest in the center. Jean-Paul's cousin, Marion, stood next to me and her husband Claude stood beside Jean-Paul. My parents and Martine and Jacques sat in the pews. The priest bowed his head and everyone followed his lead.

He began with a prayer. "Grant, we pray, almighty God, that these thy servants, Jean-Paul Soule and Cherish Bourguignon, now to be joined by the Sacrament of Matrimony, may grow in the faith they profess and enrich thy Church with faithful offspring.
Through our Lord Jesus Christ, thy Son, who lives and reigns with thee in the unity of the Holy Spirit, one God, forever and ever.

Following the prayer, Martine stood and read the Romans 12: 9-18 on love.
9. Love must be sincere.
Hate what is evil; cling to what is good.
10. Be devoted to one another in brotherly love.
Honor one another above yourselves.
11. Never be lacking in zeal, but keep your spiritual fervor, serving the Lord.

13. Share with God's people who are in need. Practice hospitality.

14. Bless those who persecute you; bless and do not curse.

15. Rejoice with those who rejoice; mourn with those who mourn.

16. Live in harmony with one another. Do not be proud, but be willing to associate with people of low position.
Do not be conceited.

17. Do not repay anyone evil for evil. Be careful to do what is right in the eyes of everybody.

18. If it is possible, as far as it depends on you, live at peace with everyone."

Then she sat down, giving Jean-Paul and me each a warm smile.

After the scripture, the priest presented a brief sermon about the sanctity of marriage. Then he asked us, "Jean-Paul Soule and Cherish Bourguignon have you come here freely and without reservation to give yourselves to each other in marriage?"

"Yes," we each replied. I immediately thought how I could no answer that question the same had I stood next to André.

Before the priest spoke again, the chapel door opened and in walked André. He stood at the back of the chapel near the door for several seconds. Jean-Paul and I stared at him and our family sitting in the pews turned to look. My father stood. "Please continue Father," he said before he walked to the back of the chapel. The priest didn't say a word as we all watched.

My father held the chapel door open and offered André the opportunity to step outside. André stood firm, with his eyes fixed on me. My father grabbed his arm to pull him, and André shook him off, without moving his gaze. "Get out," my father said sternly in a lowered voice.

"I'm just here to observe. Please continue," André said with a raised voice, speaking to the priest and throwing his chin forward. He didn't look at my father.

"You were not invited," my father objected.

"Why wasn't I invited? I'm practically family."

"Sit down André. If you make a wrong move I will…"

"You will what?" André asked with a chuckle.

"Sit down." My father's tone was powerful. His words were not to be dismissed without grave consequences.

Once André was seated, my father joined my mother at the front pew, glaring in anger back at André before he was seated. With a commanding voice my father said, "Please continue Father."

My heart was in my throat and seemed to block the passage of air into my lungs. I felt faint. Jean-Paul studied my face. "Breathe, Cherie," he said. I tried. The room started to go black. I feared if I didn't stay awake something bad would happen. I fought the light-headedness. I tried to breathe. My battle was lost. Jean-Paul slipped away and I crashed silently into nothingness.

When I opened my eyes again, André's lips were on mine. He pulled back when I awoke and studied my face. "There you are he said." I didn't move or respond. Where's Jean-Paul? What happened to me? I didn't dare speak and further enrage this man.

Then I heard my mother's voice. "Cherie, darling!" She pushed André aside and embraced me as I lie on the floor.

"What happened, Mother?"

"Apparently you fainted. André has emergency training from school. He rushed forward and checked your heartbeat and breathing. You didn't appear to be breathing so André blew air into you, and here you are. Thank goodness André was here."

Painted with Love

I looked around the room. Jean-Paul stood over me with a look of fear and disappointment. It was easy to see his discomfort with André's rescue "Jean-Paul," I called. He lowered himself to me slowly and took my hand. "I'm sorry, I didn't mean to faint. I was scared."

"I felt helpless," he said angrily.

"You're my air. Without you I can't breathe. Will you still marry me?" I asked.

Jean-Paul nodded and smiled. Our family sighed in relief and returned to their seats. André assisted Jean-Paul in helping me and my large dress to standing. André held my arm and said, "I needed to know directly from you that this is what you want, and that this man is not lying and manipulating you into this union. Tell me the truth Cherie. Is this what you want, or what he wants you to do?"

I saw my childhood friend making his most heroic effort to save his ego. I had hurt this man. The truth would be no less painful. "André, it doesn't matter what you want for me, or my parents or your parents. My heart has its own will. No one can decide for my heart whom I shall love. With total commitment, my heart belongs to this man." I gestured to Jean-Paul and then reached for his hand. "The sun, moon and stars cannot make me feel differently."

André nodded firmly once. His eyes looked down. Then he looked back at me. "Can I be your second choice, in case you need one?" He paused, looked at Jean-Paul and then back at me. "You never know, this husband may expire and leave you a widow. Then you will beg for me."

I stared at André in disbelief. My head and body did not move, breathe or speak.

"Perhaps this is not a good time to decide. Please, enjoy your wedding. Don't let me stand in the way of TRUE love!" he spat.

179

André walked towards the back of the chapel and out the door, slamming his hand against it as he exited.

Jean-Paul and I turned to each other. Then we looked at the Father and nodded.

"That was a little too exciting. Where were we?" Father Nolan looked at his book. "Ahhh, here we are. Jean-Paul and Cherie, will you honor each other as man and wife for the rest of your lives?" We each said yes, together, then looked at one another and smiled. I felt my answer deeply and profoundly.

"Will you accept children lovingly from God, and bring them up according to the law of Christ and his Church?"

"I will," we said in unison.

"Would everyone please stand," asked the Father. Our family members all stood. I smiled with teary eyes, pleased that I could stand before the people I loved on this great occasion. "Since it's your intention to enter into marriage, join your right hands, and declare your consent before God and His Church."

He turned to Jean-Paul. "Do you, Jean-Paul Soule, take this woman, Cherish Bourguignon, to be your wife in the eyes of God? Do you promise to be true to her in good times and in bad, in sickness and in health? Will you love and honor her all the days of your life?"

"I will," Jean-Paul replied. A surge of excitement spun through my body. Jean-Paul looked intently at me and added his own words. "Cherie, you own my heart, today, tomorrow and always. There's nothing I will hold from you. I shall be your faithful husband forever."

I felt my heart beat firm and solid. The Father turned to me and asked, "Do you, Cherish Bourguignon, take this man, Jean-Paul Soule, to be your husband in the eyes of God? Do you promise to be true to him in good times and in bad, in sickness and in health? Will you love, honor and obey him all the days of your life."

"I do," I said proudly. I looked into Jean-Paul's eyes. I focused and spoke from my heart, "Jean-Paul, I shall give you love and care with all that I am forever and ever. Our hearts are everlastingly one and I belong to you always."

"Do you have a ring to symbolize your love?" the priest asked.

"Yes," Jean-Paul replied.

"Repeat after me, "Please take this ring as a sign of my love and faithfulness in the name of the Father, the Son, and the Holy Spirit."

Jean-Paul repeated the words as he placed the beautiful ring on my finger and looked lovingly into my eyes, "Please take this ring as a sign of my love and faithfulness in the name of the Father, the Son, and the Holy Spirit," He repeated. My heart skipped a beat as I accepted my wedding ring a second time from Jean-Paul, this time in the Church that felt familiar and before the people that mattered.

The priest handed a white taper candle to each of us. We each lit our candles from a small candle on the altar, and then together we lit the unity candle. Once the candle was lit, the priest shared a lovely prayer for the Virgin Mary. He also expressed his concern for great challenges ahead.

Jean-Paul and I looked at each other, wondering why the priest declared in his prayer that there would be trials for us. I shrugged, concluding that he didn't know us well enough and perhaps spoke his standard prayer.

Martine handed me a yellow bouquet of daisies, which I laid at the feet of Mother Mary's image at the altar.

The priest looked at our family. "May I please present, Monsieur and Madam, Jean-Paul Soule. Go in peace with Christ." We all replied in unison, "Thanks be to God."

Mother and Martine were crying as they walked to give Jean-Paul and me a warm embrace. We were surrounded by smiles and a family who loved us.

Following the ceremony, hugs and congratulations, we all left together and walked to a quaint, nearby restaurant. We sat down to a lovely meal in the private back room. Marion and her husband were there, Martine and Jacques, my mother and father, and Jean-Paul and me.

"We are delighted to see you two happy, Cherie," my father exclaimed. "How did André learn of your plans today?"

"I have no idea," I said, looking at the faces of everyone present. Marion looked around the room, as if she were pretending not to hear the question. All the other eyes were upon me. "Marion?" I asked, "Do you know how André learned of today's events?"

"Moi, why are you singling out me? What do you have against me Cherie?" Marion replied.

"I'm not singling you out. I didn't know if you heard my father's question because you were not participating with all of us."

"Look. I love Jean-Paul. He was my best friend before you came alone. I only recently met André. I don't know why you broke his heart. He seems like a kind, intelligent man."

Jean-Paul interrupted our banter. "When did you meet André?" he questioned.

"He came out to the house a couple of weeks ago when I was visiting Mother. I'm tired of being interrogated, like this whole mess is my fault. Cherie, you're the one who messed things up for everyone. This day has been hard enough already. I'm leaving." She stood quickly and excused herself from the table.

Jean-Paul and I looked at each other. His face reflected my confusion. I sat quietly wondering if André had gone to Jacque and Martine's home more than once, or if André found Marion on the day I was leaving Paris.

My father changed the subject. "We are all wondering what your plans are?"

Jean-Paul replied, "We're going to go to California to establish trade for Jacques's business. With hard work, we plan to be back in Paris in two years' time."

"Michel," Jacques spoke up for the first time during the meal. "Jean-Paul doesn't know this, but I plan to give him this part of the business. It's an excellent opportunity for him to have an income and follow his passion, which is painting. Establishing this trade destination in California will ensure their future. It has been my plan for Jean-Paul all along."

"Please bring my daughter home soon," Mother asked Jean-Paul.

The sun lit up the sky and my heart as if heaven was smiling at this special occasion. My parents were supportive, just as Jean-Paul had expected. As the party wound down, my mother pulled me aside. "Cherie, André's mother told me that André had plans to work in America. She didn't say why. She indicated that André did not give a reason. Has he talked to you about going to America before?"

"Non, he always said that he would stay in Paris, near family," I replied.

"Perhaps your travels abroad have interested him," Mother said.

"The country is big enough for the both of us, as long as he doesn't try to kill my husband." I could see the stress my words caused my mother. I quickly changed the subject.

"Thank you for telling me, Mother." I paused briefly with a look of reassurance for her. "I will miss you terribly. I will return as soon as I'm able. Thank you for your understanding and support. You've been everything to me, Mother. I know we fought a lot, and I was always head-strong, but I watched you. I always admired you. In some ways I just wanted to be different from you because we were so much alike. You're the most amazing Mother ever. I hope that my children feel at least half as much love for me as I do for you. Everything you taught me is now what I take with me. I want to be more like you."

My mother was crying. She couldn't speak. She kept nodding her head, trying to let words escape, instead more tears flowed. We embraced again. Finally, she managed to say, "I love you. I wish for your safety and happiness. You know that I can't travel that distance, so please write and come back soon." She didn't have to say any more. She had said it all through the years. I felt fortunate to be her daughter.

My father walked over to the two of us. "May I cut in?" He asked. My mother wiped her face and turned away.

"I will miss you my cherished. What's going to keep me busy when you're not here to aggravate me?" I laughed out loud. He was trying to bring a smile to our faces. "I'm proud of you daughter, for being true to yourself." I tried to speak and tell him that he taught me to be who I am, but he interrupted and continued. "I've always been proud of you. You've been in touch with your heart since you were a small child. I always admired that about you. My brain has more to say out loud while my heart stays quiet. Thank the Lord above that you're different. You allow your heart to have a voice, even when it challenges others. It's commendable. The world needs more people like you, my sweet. Remember how important learning is. Open your mind to new knowledge. When you return, you can tell me all about the new land. If I were a younger man, I would be intrigued to explore it. I will see it through your eyes."

Now, I was crying and I could not speak. I looked up at my distinguished father who loved me powerfully. He was the reason I wouldn't settle for less than Jean-Paul. I'd always been loved by a man. I understood what it meant to be respected. I could never let myself be called a wife to a man I could not hold in high regards. My father taught me many things, but above all he showed me what a man is capable of being. Because of him, I now had a husband who would revere me, make me feel safe, and I could be honored to be his wife.

"I have no words clear enough to explain my gratitude for your support, for believing in me and for showing me how to love. I wish I could say… more…" Tears flowed in streams down my cheeks. My wedding dress was becoming wet from all the tears shed by me and my parents. Jean-Paul was correct to have us come back for the wedding. I married a wise man, and today was only the beginning of exploring his love.

Martine approached me next. Her look showed pride and exuberance at once. "You're a beautiful bride," she began. "I could not have chosen a more perfect mate for Jean-Paul if God had given me the task. Now we are finally family and you can call me 'Mother' instead of Auntie." We both smiled.

"I am a bride today because of you. You saved me from doom. I owe you my life."

184

"You owe me a hug and nothing more. Go in peace now and be happy and make some babies. Nothing could be cuter than a child belonging to the two of you," she added. We had a long embrace. I felt a mutual respect and knowing between us. Our secret of my escape would forever hold her dear to me.

We spent two days in Le Havre for a brief honeymoon, soaking up France before our long voyage. Then we boarded a large vessel to cross the rough sea to our new land. During the journey back to America Jean-Paul and I were both pretty quiet as we each realized that it might be two years before we saw our family again.

The last day of the cruise I became terribly ill with fever, chills, vomiting, and fatigue. I decided I hated traveling by ship and would only take one more trip across the ocean when it was time to live again in my homeland. Jean-Paul became slightly ill as well, but cared for me as if he was strong.

Jean-Paul bought tickets to leave immediately for the west coast by train. I didn't feel like traveling any more, but I didn't want to tell Jean-Paul how ill I felt. We would need to impose on Madam and Monsieur Batton again or stay in a hotel if we didn't leave right away. Jean-Paul found a carriage ride to take us to the train station. He helped me board, and then he loaded our belongings on to the baggage car.

Jean-Paul paid for us to ride by train all the way to San Francisco to avoid traveling the last leg by wagon. I sat quietly on the coach seats of the noisy train, trying not to show Jean-Paul my terrible fatigue. I could barely hold my head up or keep my eyes open. I was weak from vomiting and no food. Twenty-two passengers had died on the ship from the dehydrating illness. I certainly felt fortunate. Jean-Paul expressed pure gratitude that I was among the strong survivors. Yet, my reserves were empty and I wondered when I would have the time to rest and regain strength.

We had ten more days of travel on the long voyage from east to west to reach our new home. Food was not readily available and restrooms were few. Jean-Paul saw the pallor in my face. He asked me what he could do to make me well. "Hold my hand and smile at me," I told him.

185

Jean-Paul decided to upgrade our ticket to a sleeping car. The cost was significantly more, but he knew that I needed the rest and privacy the car would provide. When we reached the next station, he negotiated for a sleeping car. The train was very full, but two beds were available with two other passengers in the car, both male. Jean-Paul told me it was the best he could provide, although he wished he could do more.

I laid in the bottom bunk of the car and slept for days. I woke only for soup, tea and bathroom breaks with no interest in sitting to peer out the window.

"Jean-Paul, you are kind. Thank you for caring for me. I wish I could be better company for you on this long journey," I told him before closing my eyes again.

Jean-Paul later told me about an incident that happened while I slept. He noticed one of the men in our sleeping car staring at me. Jean-Paul felt angry inside and ready to fight the man. He thought the men were probably railroad workers or miners, going from town to town, never settled and always looking for sex because they weren't responsible enough to settle down with a wife and give a good woman a home. The idea of them thinking about me in an inappropriate way infuriated Jean-Paul, although we were stuck with them in this small car for days. The two men slept most of the time and looked haggard. Jean-Paul assumed it was because they were recovering from over consumption of alcohol. Neither one of them looked as if they had enough strength to give a day's work or owned any clean clothing.

One of the men noticed Jean-Paul watching him and he broke the indignant tension Jean-Paul felt. "What happened to her? How did your wife become ill?"

"On a ship," Jean-Paul replied sharply. "We came across the Atlantic from France. Many people caught a terrible illness. A lot of people died from dehydration. I am grateful to have her alive."

"Indeed," said the weary man. "You are fortunate."

"Where are you men traveling from?" Jean-Paul asked through his anger.

"My name is Peter. This is my father André. We are the only survivors in our family. We moved to Galveston, Texas from Holland three years ago with our wives and my four children." Peter began to choke. He paused and looked at the floor before returning his gaze at Jean-Paul. "Did you hear about the hurricane?"

Jean-Paul thought for a moment. He had heard a little about a bad storm and many deaths. He nodded twice.

"We were there. There was no warning. One minute we are in our field and the next minute it's blowing and raining like there is no tomorrow. Father and I began to run for the house. The sea started to come onto land right away. Our own boat floated in the field and we ran for it through a swamp of wet crops. We both got to the boat and went to save our family." Again Peter stopped and gulped as if he were swallowing all of his pain. Peter started to cry. "The ocean came in too fast. Before we knew it, the fields were covered in three feet of water. We couldn't control the boat and get through the flood to our house." Peter held his face in his hands. He shook his head. "They're all gone; every one of them. We're the only ones left. Half the town is dead and the animals too. The place reeks of death and is flooded with the tears of the living. The place haunts us. My father and I wish we were dead with our wives. I can hardly look at a child without falling to the ground and screaming. I have nothing to live for my friend. Everything I valued in my life is gone from me. I have nothing. You are lucky that your wife survived. Take good care of her. You will be nothing if you lose her."

Jean-Paul sat quietly watching a broken man cry. His father hadn't even opened his eyes. Jean-Paul felt badly for misjudging the men. "I'm sorry for your loss, Peter. I know that doesn't help. But I am very sorry." The two men looked at each other with a sense of understanding. Peter nodded, "Thanks mister." Peter lay back down and closed his eyes again. Jean-Paul told me that Peter looked as if he were praying for his own death.

I slept through the whole conversation. Jean-Paul told me that he was glad I didn't hear the story and feel even worse than I already did. He knew then and there that he must never lose me and he must get us home to our families.

It seemed a strange coincidence to me that his father's name was André, but neither Jean-Paul nor I commented on it.

By the time we reached Oklahoma, I was feeling stronger. I sat up holding my tea, peering at the mountains and grassy valleys that passed, not saying a word. Finally, I asked, "Jean-Paul, I reviewed the maps before we came, but I didn't really understand the empty space and endless tracks. All of Europe wouldn't fill up this country."

Jean-Paul smiled. "It is good to hear your voice and see an inquisitive expression on your glowing face."

When we arrived in San Francisco, the first thing I said was with great enthusiasm, "It reminds me of Paris!" There were many rows of homes that looked much like the one I grew up in. Jean-Paul smiled back at me with relief.

Our new apartment was modest and dark, needing many items, and a woman's touch to make it more comfortable. I couldn't wait to get started.

Jean-Paul painted while I cooked and listened to the deep hum he made in his throat as he stroked the canvas with brush and paint. I smiled in gratitude and praise to God for Jean-Paul.

It was time for me to go out to shop for items the home needed. The windows were bare, offering no privacy. The cupboards didn't have cooking utensils, or enough pots and plates. There was no reason to live like a peasant. Jean-Paul had saved up more money than I expected. With the money given to us at our wedding and a generous gift of cash from my parents, we had plenty of funds to buy the essentials.

I fixed up our new home while Jean-Paul set up the new business. On the weekends we walked along the beach and enjoyed our new city, while we dreamed of returning to Paris.

Shortly after we settled in to our new life, I began to receive letters from André. Two months after we moved in, I found the first one in the mailbox. My heart nearly coiled into a permanent cramp the first time I held the envelope sent from André Monet. I feared the content, but decided I must know what he was planning. Reluctantly, I opened the letter and read the awful words.

My Dearest Cherish,

California suits me well. Once I mastered this unpleasant language they speak here, the bar exam was easy to pass. I was hired immediately by an excellent firm. Yours truly is a criminal litigator, and an excellent one, I must say. Let me make clear that money will never be a problem. Should you become my wife in the future, you will be cared for well.

As you know I am a forgiving man. I am certain that you were coerced into this marriage, manipulated by an evil suitor. This is why I don't hold my anger against you, directly. You will come to see my wisdom in time. I watched you walking yesterday. You looked beautiful, as always. I would like to buy you a new dress. Poverty doesn't suit you.

My love for you is growing, Cherish. As I mature, I realize how short and precious life it, and how quickly it can be taken away. I know that being with the woman God intended me to be with is of utmost importance before this body I hold dear is taken to the grave. I will hold you in my arms again, before my last day of life.

I will continue to write to you so that you will remember I am here suffering without you. I pray for your wellbeing.

André Monet

I crumpled the letter in anger. I hated him for trying to destroy my happiness and make me feel guilty for his feelings. He was no longer my friend. Now he was my enemy. I wondered if I should tell Jean-Paul. Perhaps I should not upset him, yet I didn't want anything hidden between us. I waited for the right opportunity.

We spent the weekends exploring the area and restaurants together. Days after the letter arrived, Jean-Paul invited me to join him for a day trip. He summoned a carriage which took us northwest, towards downtown and the mouth of the bay. Jean-Paul helped me from the carriage and carried the food, leading us towards a path. Jean-Paul walked a bit quickly. "Can we slow down, Jean-Paul? At this pace I shall tire. You must try walking quickly in this long skirt with these boots."

"Sorry, my love, I didn't realize my pace. I'm simply excited to show you something."

"Will it still be there if we arrive a half-hour later?"

"But of course, my darling. Please forgive me."

"Very well, have we much farther to walk?"

"Are you tired? Would you like to rest?"

"Um, a little."

"Let's rest over here." Jean-Paul directed us to a patch of wild grass where we sat to rest. Jean-Paul looked around to see if we were alone. With no one in sight, he leaned in to offer me a kiss. "Pardon me my lovely wife, I find your lips completely irresistible." I accepted his advance with pleasure. We both withdrew after one passionate kiss, knowing that if we lingered close together too long, an interlude would surely follow.

"Cherie, darling," Jean-Paul began, "I want to be a father."

"My love, I am excited and ready to bear and love our children. I desire to give you sons and daughters that I may bathe, feed and dress. But most of all, beyond anything else, I shall show them how much I love you and teach them how great you are."

"How's it possible that you're not impregnated already? I make love to you every day, sometimes twice. Will it take long?"

"Sweet, Jean-Paul, sometimes these things take time. Your Auntie Martine would say, 'In God's time.' It will happen. Be patient."

"So true. Thank you, love."

"For what?"

"For being you and loving me."

"You're most welcome." I smiled the most loving smile I could muster.

"Could a man be luckier than this?" Jean-Paul asked.

"Could a woman be more appreciated?" I asked. We both smiled in gratitude of each other.

"Darling, I have some news."

"Good news I hope," Jean-Paul said. The sun lit his hair and the wind blew it wildly. I wanted only to see him smile and not deliver this news.

"Not really good news. When the mail arrived this week, there was a letter from André." Jean-Paul's eyes widened and then I saw a hint of anger. He didn't speak. "The letter said that he passed the bar in California."

"What else did he say?!"

"Nothing worth mentioning. He didn't announce why he was here and not Paris, or in what city he was dwelling." I paused briefly to see if Jean-Paul wished to comment. "He has a way of threatening, between the lines. It's his way to intimidate. He is trying to come between us. We cannot allow him to win this game."

"How could he possibly have our address, Cherie?!"

"Jean-Paul, there's no need to be angry with me. You know that I would not give it to him. How could you question me in this tone?"

"Then who?" Jean-Paul had not raised his voice to me before now.

"I believe that it's Marion," I said.

"Marion? Never. What motive would she have to share this information?"

"This is only a guess, but it seems to me that deep down she wants to be more than best friends with you. She loves you more than a friend or cousin."

"What?"

"Jean-Paul, at our reception dinner I watched her carefully. I saw how she looks at you. She met André at Martine's home. I believe she told André about me getting on the boat to leave Paris. She must have overheard my conversation with Martine. She didn't know that I changed from servants clothes into a golden gown."

"She's married."

"She's not happy," I replied. Jean-Paul studied my face. "A woman sees these things." The sun disappeared behind a cloud, the air cooled and the cold ground gave me a chill. A quick shiver shot up my spine.

Jean-Paul was silent, as if contemplating Marion's behavior towards him over the years. His eyes moved around in many directions, perhaps searching for answers.

192

Jean-Paul stood and reached for my hand. He lifted me to my feet and turned to continue our walk. We walked together in silence. I regretted sharing the letter on our walk.

An hour later we reached the destination Jean-Paul had directed us to. Jean-Paul spoke, avoiding the subject of André. "We are here. The water before us is the Pacific Ocean. In town you see the bay. This is the ocean." I looked out in wonderment. I had floated across the Atlantic, but not peered upon the Pacific. Before us stretched a vast body of water, one that my parents, and most Europeans, would never see. It extended out until it disappeared into the horizon of mist and clouds. It was soft blue, with almost a white sparkle over the surface. It was massive, yet alluring and friendly, almost welcoming.

Jean-Paul explained more, but with a tight tone, hiding emotions he didn't want to show me. "This area is called the Presidio. It was named el Presidio by the Spanish leader Lieutenant Colonel Juan Bautista de Anza who arrived here in 1776 with a small group of men to establish the northern- most outpost of the growing Spanish empire. Their rule here didn't last long though. Soon it fell under Mexico's control. The United States took control of the Presidio in 1846 and made it into a strong western army post. Before Europeans arrived here, the native people, called the Ohlone, lived here for more than one thousand years. They fished as their main source of meat."

"Thank you for taking me here Jean-Paul. This is magnificent. Where did you learn this history?"

"One of my new buyers of tea is a colonel who lives here. He gave me a little tour and the history. He showed me that this is the best viewing point to see the Pacific and told me when to look for whales migrating through." These words comforted him some, because his voice lightened up slightly and he almost seemed happy.

"Maybe you could paint it Jean-Paul, and send it back to Europe. Your eyes and paint strokes would show others the unique beauty of this massive water. I wish we could live on this bluff, and look at this sea every day." I tried to cheer him with my joy, and hide my fear of André. More than anything, I wanted him to promise me that we were safe.

193

Jean-Paul studied me as I looked out to sea.

"Will you take me here again Jean-Paul? I will make us a lovely picnic and we shall sit here together for hours and you can bring your pens or your paints. Please, Jean-Paul?"

"Of course, anything you wish." His promise lacked his usual enthusiasm, but I knew he meant it.

Jean-Paul and I reached home just before dark. "Cherie," Jean-Paul said with seriousness, "Let's make a baby tonight."

I smiled and felt happy he wanted me.

Jean-Paul picked me up in his arms roughly, as if saving me from a burning building. He quickly carried me into our small bedroom and tossed me on the bed roughly. He stood looking at me for a moment, while I studied his expression. His face was concentrated. I didn't know if his thoughts were on conception or André's letter. Vigorously he unbuttoned my blouse and began kissing my neck and breasts with firm, short kisses. His intent was focused and determined, yet emotionally distant. I didn't know if I wanted to make a baby with him so absent. If I asked him to stop, it could upset him further. With reluctance, I gave into his will, wondering what drove it forward.

As he penetrated me, he stared into my eyes. He released his semen quickly and watched my face. I felt that he was communicating to me that his semen was impregnating my womb at that moment and his will would make it so.

He watched me for a full minute after his release. Then he rolled onto his back and stared at the ceiling. It felt as if he had left the house. I felt alone. Inside of me, big emotions stirred. It wasn't clear to me how to interpret the pain in my heart or the tightening in my throat. I wanted to sob, but not in front of Jean-Paul. There were no words to comfort us. Once again André had come between me and my love.

Two months later, the signs were certain. A child was conceived in our disconnected lovemaking. I wrote a letter to my mother and father to share news.

Dearest Mother and Father,

I'm pleased to share with you that I'm pregnant. I feel well and the baby should come before early next year. I look

194

forward to bringing the child home to Paris to meet his wonderful grandparents.

The San Francisco Bay area is perfectly lovely. You would enjoy it here. In many ways it reminds me of Paris, although it's encumbered with hills and steep roadways. Walking around the city requires much effort.

I wish I could see you both. I have no idea how to be a Mother myself. Does it come naturally? What can you tell me? Will I be a good Mother? I want nothing more than to bear Jean-Paul's children and to be a good wife. My life feels complete. Sometimes I wonder if it's really fair. Do I deserve to be this happy?

I love you always Mother and Father.

From my heart, Cherie"

I waited patiently for my mother's reply. When the letter came, I nearly cried while trying to open it. Then I read with tear filled eyes.

My dearest Cherie,

Your letter arrived today and my heart leapt from the sight of it. Then when I began to read it and I learned that you're with child, my initial joy turned to exuberance. Tears are flowing as I try to see the paper and pen to write to you. My heart is bursting with love for you and with happiness for us all. I shall be a grandmother.

My life has been beautiful and full of love. However, the most spectacular joy I could imagine to have before I go home to our Lord, is to be a grandmother. You and Jean-Paul have given me the greatest gift.

I pray that you will be back in Paris while the child is very young and I may teach the baby the same songs that I taught to you. I wish to help with the child and bounce it on my knee. We can all go on outings to the park. I shall begin gathering things we will need at the house for the little one.

I shall write you a full letter on the best foods to consume and best practices to preserve the wellbeing of the child. I wish I were with you. For now, I will wait anxiously for your letters.

I miss you. You have missed much activity in Paris. I wish you and Jean-Paul could have delayed your departure just a year. The World's Fair is changing many things about this city. With the influence of countries from all over the globe, Frenchmen are opening their minds a little to the possibilities that the French don't know everything. There are two new museums built for the Fair filled with art from all over the world. If only Jean-Paul's art could be displayed among the paintings by extraordinary men from America and China. The three new train stations are complete as well as a spectacular new bridge. You saw them working on it before you left but you should see it now. It looks more like a work of art than a bridge. They are calling it Pont AlexAndré III. Your father and I went to the Musee d'Orsay. It is beautiful with glass ceilings. I imagined Jean-Paul's work displayed in the main hall.

We also attended many of the Olympic Games. One can scarcely get around Paris from all of the extra travelers who have come to watch the competition. The French are touting that because it is the year 1900 the Olympics will be the biggest ever. The turn of the century brings such excitement with it! Your father took me to see the first women tennis players in the Olympics. Then he took me to see the first women Olympic golf players. I found the golf rather difficult to enjoy because we stood at one place and watched different players hit the ball from the same place. We didn't get to follow the players around the course as I would have liked. It was exciting to see women participate. Your father said that he wanted you to know that you could do great things, just as these women were doing. He also said he expected much of you. I wish you could have been there. Many of the events were poorly scheduled causing low attendance. The organizers had difficultly notifying players when they were scheduled to compete. Some athletes missed their events due to inaccurate and incomplete information. But I had a marvelous time.

Marion told Martine that André moved to America. She also said that he still loves you. Perhaps it is the childhood love that never dies. I hope that he doesn't try to interfere in your marriage. Your father and I treasure Jean-Paul.

I fear for your wellbeing constantly. It doesn't seem safe to me to have you so far from home. Please be careful. Mother's

intuition is very strong, and mine says caution. Keep sending your letters, Cherie. My love and heart are with you.
   All my love,
   Mother

Chapter Sixteen: **It isn't Fair**

San Francisco, November, 1901

Pregnancy and childbirth were not easy without my mother close-by. I missed asking her questions and having her help with my new baby boy, Little Jean. I wrote to her often and gleaned as much knowledge as I could. I wanted to show her our son as soon as possible. His big eyes and round face were just what my mother would love.

Being a mother filled me with joy each day; nursing, singing, rocking and loving my baby. I threw myself into the task full heartedly. I felt important to two men, one little and one big. I had everything that I could imagine, except for my parents.

Instead of having my mother near me, I had my new best friend, Juliette. We became inseparable. I leaned on her like the big sister that I never had. She always seemed wiser and knew what to do. I would have felt lost without her. She was also from Paris. Her aunt and uncle moved to the area to run a hotel that they bought from another family member. Juliette loved to visit them often. She invited me on several occasions to join them, and I always declined. On one cold November night, when her husband George could not accompany her, she begged me to come with her. Jean-Paul insisted that I go, despite our terrible fight hours earlier after the mail arrived. He assured me that he would care for our son at home and welcomed the evening at home with Little Jean. Reluctantly I left the house with Juliette, and headed for the pier in the foggy night.

Juliette and I walked aboard the San Rafael just moments before she slowly pulled away from the dock fully loaded with passengers to cross the bay from San Francisco to Sausalito on November 30, 1901. The San Rafael had a great reputation as one of the last great steamboats built with her hull design. I read about her in the San Francisco Call Newspaper which reported that she was, "by far the prettiest boat that ever cleft the waters of

San Francisco Bay." I hadn't been on a ferryboat before, but I agreed that she was beautiful and magnificent.

This was my first trip across the bay and my first time back on a boat since I was terribly ill coming across the Atlantic. I watched the passengers curiously as they stirred about the fanciest boat to glide across the cold, dark bay. The ferry moved smoothly, as if without effort. Juliette grabbed my hand. "Come here, Cherie. Look at the fog. I've never seen it this dense."

"How can the captain know where we are going?"

"It's always foggy in the bay. The captain knows what he's doing. We are perfectly safe. Thank you for coming with me to see my aunt and uncle."

"I'm excited to meet your relatives. You're lucky to have family near you. I wish I could see my parents. I miss them terribly. I want them to meet my baby."

"I would enjoy visiting my aunt and uncle more often. It makes me feel at home. My uncle loves to talk with my husband. He will be disappointed to learn that George had a labor meeting tonight. I wish Jean-Paul would have come to entertain him."

"He decided last minute not to join us. I almost didn't come as well, because Jean-Paul and I had a terrible fight tonight."

"What about?"

"I received another letter from André. He proclaimed his love again. I haven't responded to his letters and I don't know how to make him stop. He's upsetting Jean-Paul more and more. He's trying to build a wedge between us. I think it is working."

"Is that why Jean-Paul decided not to come tonight?"

"Yes," I said sadly.

"And he wanted Little Jean to stay home as well?"

"Yes, because of the cold night," I replied with my head bowed.

"What did the letter say?" Juliette asked in a quiet voice.

"The same stuff he has said before. He says that he still loves me. That God designed for us to be together. I made the wrong choice, but he will forgive me one day. He always ends by saying that we will be together one day."

"Don't worry. Your love with Jean-Paul is strong enough to survive this. Let it pass. Tonight you're here with *me*. Isn't that enough? You shall see your handsome family soon and kiss away Jean-Paul's anger." Juliette teased me playfully with a hint of exaggeration in her voice.

"Oh Juliette, I love being here with you. I won't let André spoil this night for us. I'm delighted that we've been in this exciting city together for this past year. I've enjoyed the holidays and celebrations together. I don't know how I could have survived it without you."

"I feel the same about you." We each smiled. "How's Jean-Paul's artwork going?"

"Jean-Paul is more distant lately. Perhaps it's because he only gets to focus a few hours a week on his art. I want him to get to do what he loves and not have to work such long days. He comes home drained of all strength. I can never get enough of him. I miss him. Maybe he's falling out of love with me. Maybe André's letters are coming between us."

"You're over reacting, Cherie. Settle yourself down."

I took a deep breath. "Thank you for inviting me tonight Juliette. This is just what I needed. Did you know that I was terrified of ships until I sailed across an ocean? After sailing on a large vessel three times, I found them to be much safer than I thought."

We stared into the dense, misty fog. Leaning against the rail, I enjoyed the wind rushing by my face, whipping my hair in un-patterned waves. "Isn't it haunting? I can't see a thing."

A young child laughed nearby. Several children played near their parents. I turned to see an older sibling teasing a baby to make the child smile. I pictured Jean-Paul and me walking hand in hand on a ferry with our new little boy in tow.

"Cherie," a voice said as a hand came down on my left forearm. Chills sent shockwaves up my spine which exploded in my head. André's voice registered, and my whole body tightened.

"Don't look so worried," he said turning me around. "Are you not pleased to see me?" he said with a sly smile. "I have a few questions for you, since you have not responded to my letters." He looked at Juliette who stared in shock. "I need to borrow your friend for a moment. I will bring her back." He pulled on my arm which he held tightly. "Come, Cherie, I must speak with you. Don't you think you owe me that?"

I was ready to face André and tell him directly to stop writing to me and upsetting my family. I yanked my arm from his grasp and looked firmly in his eyes. "Yes, I wish to have a few words with you as well."

We walked down narrow steps into the well-appointed dining room below deck. Several people were enjoying dinner and others were sipping warm drinks. He selected a table at the far end of the room and we each sat down.

"You look good. Motherhood agrees with you."

A sense of shock drew me back.

André noticed my face and replied, "Yes. I heard. Don't worry. If your husband is not able to take care of you, through death or for some other reason, I will provide for you and your son."

Again I stared in disbelief.

André replied, "Are you surprised that I would be so generous and still love you with another man's offspring? You will soon understand that my love for you will never die. I'm a patient man…and I don't give up a good fight." He paused and stared at me. "Are you going to say anything?"

"André, your constant threat and lurking around are deplorable. You're inconsiderate and selfish. I'm a happily married woman. Leave me be."

"Happy are you? Are you sure that your husband is happy? He communicated by letter with family in Paris. He doesn't always express happiness. You know that if I don't do it, God will surely punish him for stealing the woman who belonged to me."

I thought for a moment. He writes to Jacques and Martine and occasionally he writes to Marion. Marion must be the one feeding information to André.

"My affairs are none of your business. Go back to Paris and leave me alone!" I was firm. It felt good to confront André.

"You don't understand, but you will. I will not be going back to Paris…as long as you are married to Jean-Paul." André stared at me with a coy smile.

I glared back in disgust. "I want you out of my life André, for good. I'm married. I don't love…"

A loud explosion cut off my words. I flew out of my chair and smashed into a metal pole behind me. I fell to the floor dizzy with blackness veiling my eyes.

For moments I lie in shock unaware if what caused the loud blast. I tried to sit up and noticed my balance falter. Passengers around me started to panic and scream. I felt swishing in my head and gravity pulling me sideways. I looked for André, but I couldn't see him. People were moving everywhere.

"Get off the boat," A man shouted, but it sounded like a dream. I was dazed, confused and could not move my body.

I looked again for André. He was walking about the room bleeding with his right ear dangling from his head. He was shouting things that didn't register to me, as he walked in a circle. Finally he saw me and walked straight towards me.

"There you are Cherish." André said. The boat tipped, or perhaps my head just felt a tipping, I couldn't be sure. The floor quickly filled with water. My body slid across the wet carpet.

I heard screaming and shouting. "The boat is sinking fast!" said a man. "Get up on deck. Lifeboats! Get in the lifeboats!" People were pushing and shoving to get up the narrow staircase to the deck.

The large ferry began to tilt. I slid with passengers across the floor and we piled on top of each other. Water continued to fill the dining room. I finally focused my eyes. What I saw didn't make sense. Something had ripped the hull open to the cold San Francisco Bay.

I touched my head and felt a bump, but I didn't feel any pain. I became more disoriented and confused. *"Ships are safe."*

"Oh Cherish. Everything happens for a reason. We could leave this boat and sneak off together, and no one would know if we were dead or alive. You see, where's your husband now? It's me who saved you at your wedding. I must save you again!" André stood above me with water sloshing above his ankles, bleeding from where his ear once was attached. He walked as if he were drunk, faltering in the deepening water. He reached his hands to help me. I didn't want him to have the satisfaction of helping me, but I knew that I needed help. I reached for his hands. Moving forward, I felt my head swirl as if I floated in a rough sea. My eyes would not focus. I closed my eyes and felt panic. With my eyes closed I tried to stand.

"Ouch!" I screamed. "My leg!"

André bent down and knelt in the frigid water. "Cherish, I will carry you to the deck, but first I want to hear you say that you need me." André studied my face. I stared in disbelief. The room was emptying out quickly. Soon I would be alone with André in this room of water below the water's surface. His game was working. I had to need him to be rescued.

"At this moment, I need your help to get off this boat. Please help me André."

"That is not exactly what I was asking for Cherish." He paused then added, "Tell me that you love me."

It didn't matter what I said if I never saw Jean-Paul and little Jean again. I knew they were my priority. I had to live to see them again. I had to lie to André to get to Jean-Paul. "I love you, André," I said a simply as I could.

"Well done, Cherish. Tonight, everything changes." I didn't know what he meant, but I felt uneasy about his statement. André helped me stand and quickly placed me in his arms. My face was inches from his dangling ear, which he seemed not to notice. "Wrap your arms around me. Hold on tightly," he said. Then he added, "It's good to hold you again." Slightly faltering, he carried me up the stairs to the deck. "The life boats are already in the water. You need to jump into the water and swim to a lifeboat. They will pull you in. Can you swim?"

"NO!" I cried.

"Then you will have to trust me, Cherish. You trust me don't you? You broke a covenant to me and ran after another man, but you can trust that I will do what's best for you." His voice was calculated and spiteful. I didn't know what I could do to get off the boat and away from André. "Perhaps we will be together forever, sooner than I thought." André was silent for just a moment, lost in some evil thought of his. Then he looked intently into my eyes. "I will lower you into the water, and then I will jump in after you."

A sudden grip of fear clenched my jaw. I swallowed hard. What would André feel I owed him for saving my life again?

The deck of the ferry was emptying of people. The remaining people on deck were afraid to get in the water. I understood how they felt. Most passengers had already climbed into the life boats. The screams echoed up from the water, calling for the large ferry that struck our boat, to rescue them. "Help! We are over here. We have no paddle."

It felt as if André and I were alone on the large vessel. André picked up a rope and untied it from a cleat. He wrapped the large line around my waist and tied it very snuggly.

"This rope is heavy and too tight," I objected.

"The rope will float, so it won't feel heavy in the water. Look at me! Trust me." He hung me over the rail of the sinking ship with a rope around my waist. The cable cut into my stomach and squished my ribs. I could barely breathe.

"Hold on tightly," he instructed me. After I cleared the railing, the rope slipped from his hands or he intentionally dropped me. My body fell through the air for a quiet second. I hit the water with a firm splash.

Suddenly I felt the cold, dark ocean bay. Water filled my nose and mouth. My head pounded with pain. My skin burned wildly from the freezing water.

I flung out my arms to reach the surface and get some air. I looked for André, but he was not there. I tried to scream, but my body shook hard and my mouth filled again with water. I reached for the surface to cry for help. As I reached the cool, foggy air, panic scared me enough that I could hardly take a breath or make a sound.

I focused on getting air. Heavy, wet boots weighed me down. The rope around my waist tangled around my long skirt and feet, making it impossible to keep my head above the surface. My injured leg barely moved enough to kick, so I tried to float on my back, as I'd seen others do.

I shouted, "André!" and sank again below the water.

As I emerged, I filled my lungs with air, while water splashed into my mouth. Then my tired, trembling body sank again in the dark sea while I fought to ignore the frigid temperature and pounding pain. I swung my arms and kicked my good leg hard to get more air. My head felt heavy.

"André!" I called again.

Fatigue overcame me like a heavy blanket falling over my eyes. I gasped for air and my lips shivered before I closed them tightly, while my exhausted frame sank down in the frigid seawater.

When I emerged, I heard a passenger in a nearby life boat. "There's a woman in the water! I can hear her over there!"

The dense fog prevented me from seeing them and them from seeing me splashing at the surface. I called for help again. "Over here." I felt I could hold on a little longer if I could just lose my boots. I took a deep breath and bent myself to reach my laces. The cold water seemed to numb the dull pain in my right leg. I unlaced my boot and began to kick it free. Suddenly something pulled on the rope tied around my waist, dragging me quickly away from the surface. I held my breath, hoping somehow I could make it back to the top. The fatigue and reality set in. The blanket of exhaustion weighed heavy. The fight to stay warm stole the balance of my strength.

As my body sank further in the cold ocean water, I kicked my good leg as hard as I could while reaching my arms frantically towards air. I didn't move closer to the surface. As I struggled with no progress, anger overcame me.

This is not fair, I screamed in my mind. *I want to live! God, help me! Don't let me die! Jean-Paul, Mother, I love you. It isn't fair!*

Darkness overtook me as my body ran out of oxygen and sank towards the ocean floor.

Chapter Seventeen: To See or Not to See

Nairobi, November, 2005

I woke with a start, gasping for air. My eyes opened, but I couldn't make out anything. All I could see was white light and mild shadows. *Where am I? Did I drown? Am I in heaven?* I wondered frantically. "Help! André. I'm drowning!" I called.

Suddenly I heard a woman shouting in a strong accent. "Doctor, de patient is being awake. Doctor, please, quickly!"

"Dee? Can you hear me? It's Brian. Are you back with us?"

"André, help me, I can't breathe," I cried.

"Dee, you're not drowning. There is no water. There is no André. You're having a bad dream. You're here in Kenya with me. I will take care of you. You will be fine."

"Just a moment ago I was sinking to the bottom of the ocean. It felt real. Where am I? What day is it?" My tongue wouldn't work right and my words slurred together.

"You are speaking so well. That's wonderful. Okay, today's Tuesday. You're in Nairobi, Kenya. It's November 10th, 2005. You live in Seattle. You have three daughters. You're a photographer. Do you remember anything?"

I looked in the direction of the voice. I saw a shadow of light brown that must have been the head belonging to the voice. The room seemed bright. White and gray, shadows were everywhere I looked. "Why can't I see?" I asked in an angry tone.

"You hit your head, Dee. The doctor has a plan for surgery. He's going to explain it to you."

"Will I be able to see again?" I asked.

"He thinks so. Think positive," Brian reassured.

"I can't handle this. It's too much," I cried.

"Dee, be strong. I will help you. You have me now…"

"Der is Miss Dee. We are happy dat you have the open eyes this sunny day. I'm Doctor Patel," said the Indian man with a strong accent. "I shall check a few tings Miss Dee. Do not be worrying. You be improving berry well."

"I can't see anyone. Does anybody get that? What the hell. Am I blind? Tell me right now." I burst into tears. I tried to stop crying to hear their reply. I gulped air, hoping that someone was going to wake me from this nightmare.

"Miss Dee, you have de swelling at de base of you skull. You must have de surgery to alleviate some swelling and tissue damage. When this swelling has subsided, your vision may possibly return. We don't know if you will be experiencing any of de permanent damage. The very good news is, Ms. Dee, dat I called the very good surgeon, Dr. Larry Bryant, from San Francisco, who does de specializing in this exact surgery that you be needing. I explained to him all of your information. The good doctor is waiting for you to be well and travel to see him."

"San Francisco?" I blurted out. "Are you God damn kidding me?"

"Dee?" Brian shouted. "What's wrong?"

"I'm going crazy. I woke up feeling like I was drowning in the San Francisco Bay. When I open my eyes I'm blind and this crazy doctor wants to send me to San Francisco for surgery. I'm scared out of my mind right now."

For a moment, no one spoke. I imagined them all staring at me, while I couldn't see their faces. A hand came down on my right hand. I nearly flinched and pulled away. "Dee, I will get you through this. Put your trust in me. I love you."

You...you...love me? I don't even know who you are. I recognized Brian's voice, but I couldn't recall what he looked like. I certainly didn't feel like I loved him, in a romantic way. I began to sob like a lost child. I felt such relief as I let tears pour from my heart. I cried for Cherie, lying at the bottom of the bay. I cried for my eye sight and the pain in my heart that I couldn't identify.

"When can I go home?" I asked to anyone listening.

"Miss Dee, you must go to Doctor Larry Bryant at once and have de surgery to help you see. Dis must be your most important priority. We are watching all tings for you to know when you ready for the air travel. The very good Mr. Brian can assist you to be going right away."

Again there was silence. Tears were still falling fast and soaking my hair and pillow. Brian rubbed my hand.

"I got you, Dee. We can leave soon and get you well," Brian said.

I took a couple of deep breaths and worked on appreciating what I could at that moment. I looked in the direction of Brian's voice. "Thank you for being willing to help me. I know I can't go alone." Those words tore a hole in my chest, like a real wound. "I would like to call my daughters. When can I do that?"

"Anytime," the doctor said.

"Are you sure that you feel up to that? You just woke up. I could tell them that you're awake and flying to San Francisco," Brian offered.

"I want to talk to them."

"Okay, I will take care of that for you."

The next twenty-four hours were busy. I spoke to my daughters and did my best to reassure them I would be home sometime soon. I sat with the doctor as he wrote out prescriptions and gave me instructions and discharged me from the hospital. I dealt with payment arrangements and details of my condition, without being able to see and without remembering much of the past. Brian was helpful and acted as my guardian. He seemed to enjoy being involved a little too much. Then Brian took me to the airport where I was transported by gurney to the plane and sat in first class with a lot of attention from Brian and the flight attendant.

Traveling without being able to see the passengers around me, or the sky outside the airplane window, was very disheartening. I felt depressed and feared what would happen if my eyesight did not return. We arrived in San Francisco, and I was taken directly to San Francisco General Hospital. My appointment with Dr. Brandt was the following day

Brian never left my side. He saw to every detail as if I were a child. "Okay Dee, did you get that? Tomorrow morning Doctor Bryant will come in to see you."

"My ears are working fine, thank you."

"Great, I'm just checking. I'm going to order you some lunch and then I will read you the paper. You can sleep anytime you want."

"What's on the menu? I want to order my own lunch. I haven't eaten a real meal in months."

"I know what you like."

"Brian?"

"You want me to read you the menu to you?"

"Yes."

"Okay, but I know what you will order."

"Maybe you know what I would order Brian, but I don't. I can't remember my favorite foods." I suddenly felt sorry for myself again. I hated being dependent on anyone. I needed him for sure, and that made me more frustrated.

I pouted a lot the rest of the day, feeling depressed. Brian left me alone, and was patient with my disposition.

The next morning the Doctor came in early. "Ms. Coulter? I'm Doctor Bryant. Nice to meet you," he said finding my right hand and holding it briefly, rather than giving it a standard shake.

"Hello, Doctor."

Then he addressed Brian. "Are you her husband," the doctor asked.

"No!" I replied a bit too loud and quickly.

"I'm her partner. I'm here for her."

"It's great that she has support right now. For this first appointment, I would like to talk to her alone, if that's okay with you Miss Coulter."

"That's fine with me," I replied.

"I need her to answer some very personal questions." The doctor explained. "Thank you for your understanding."

"I'd like to be here. I want to know everything doc," Brian insisted.

"She can tell you all about it after I meet with her. Please step out for a few minutes," the doctor politely instructed.

"Okay. I will wait right out here."

After Brian closed the door the doctor said, "He's a persistent fellow, isn't he?"

I offered a tight lipped smile as an apology.

"All of your files have been forwarded to me. I have spoken with Doctor Patel in Nairobi several times. I know everyone else's account of how you're doing and what happened. What's your account of the events?" he asked politely.

"I don't remember the accident. I vaguely remember taking pictures and...maybe there was a jeep behind us. Many details feel like a dream fading away." I paused. "I can't recall anything else. Is that okay?"

"That's enough information. Thank you. I like to assess your mental acuity, recall, and other cognitive functions. I need to look for other damage that perhaps the MRI won't show. I want to know how much of your memory was affected. Do you remember anything in the days preceding the accident?"

"When I think about the past, it feels vague and sporadic. It's hard to tell my past from fantasy. None of my past is strong and clear right now, but I have had a few short memories come to me that were very clear."

"Good. That likely will continue to happen. Do you remember any dreams while you were unconscious?"

"Dreams?"

"Yes. Many patients have elaborate dreams while they are unconscious. It just provides me another piece of information."

"I...I...um...I did have a dream of..." I paused. My mind recalled Jean-Paul's smile and tender touch. I recalled our home in San Francisco, one hundred years ago. *Where should I start?* How could I tell this neurologist that I dreamed I drowned in the San Francisco Bay? "You really want to know my dream?"

"Yes. Did you have one dream or many? Often patients have dreams related to what their body is experiencing, although the dream does not make sense. Yet it can feel very real."

"Real? How real?"

"You tell me." He paused. Perhaps he saw the distress on my face. "I only need to know if you had dreams. You don't have to share the details."

"Oh, okay, well, I dreamed. Yes, I did."

"Could you feel anything in your dreams; pain, touch or hear sounds?"

You mean like Jean-Paul making love to me for the first time? Like hiding in a wooden box on a long country ride into Paris? Or André throwing me into the ocean and letting me drown? "Yes. I could feel things in my dream."

"When you woke up, in Nairobi, did you know where you were and remember who you were?" he asked.

"When I woke…I was confused. I thought I was drowning."

"Confusion is not uncommon when you wake up. Your brain was adjusting to being conscious." He paused and looked at my watery eyes. "You're doing great. I have a few more questions. What do you see right now as you look around?"

"Shadows. Just light and shadows."

"Can you see my hand in front of you?" he asked.

"Not really. I see a light, vague shadow."

"You see my hand as a light shadow?"

"Yes."

"What color?"

"Mmm, it's kind of gray."

"That's helpful information, Ms. Coulter."

"Doctor? Could you please call me Dee?"

"Yes, I can." I couldn't see his face, but it felt like he was smiling.

"I need to look at the back of your head, your neck and shoulders. Could you slip your gown down to just below your shoulders and sit up for me?" He examined my head and looked carefully around my ears, neck, upper back and shoulders. He pressed on lymph nodes, pressed on skin and then examined it for color and asked me if I had any pain.

"Thank you, Dee. You can lie back now." He became more sober and gave me more details about my condition. "What you have is neurological vision impairment, which is loss of vision resulting from your brain injury. Medically we refer to this as ABI VI. Other terms that the medical community used to use are cortical visual impairment and cortical blindness. This simply means that you have damage to the area of your brain that's responsible for your sight."

"Okay, I sort of understood all of that. You're the expert that can repair the damage, right Doctor?" I asked.

"I can relieve the pressure and repair damaged vessels supplying blood to the area. You may have some permanent damage because of lack of oxygen to a critical portion of your brain that processes vision. We won't understand the extent of the damage until after your surgery."

"Tell me straight. What do you think right now?" I asked.

"I have high hopes that you will experience some improvement in your vision. Once I repair the damage that I can, and the swelling goes down, you should experience more details. It's impossible to say at this point what the extent of the damage is or how your vision will be."

"I was hoping for better news."

"I wish I had some. I need to prepare you for the possibilities and probabilities. With the cause of this condition being a head injury from two months ago, it's likely that there is permanent damage."

Suddenly I felt nauseated. I thought I might need to throw up.

Dr. Bryant continued. "I'm going to order some cognitive tests for you to take today. They are simple and short. My guess is that the only damage to repair in your brain is some swelling surrounding nerves that feed information from your eyes to your brain. I arranged for you to have the surgery tomorrow. Are you ready for this?"

"I'm ready to see again."

He laughed gently. "I'm sure you are. I will do my very best."

"Thank you, Doctor."

"You're welcome." The doctor left and Brian walked in.

"What did he say? Good news?" Brian asked.

"Not really the news I was hoping for. He said I probably have permanent damage to my brain and eye sight."

"God damn it. Is that really what he said?"

"Yes."

"Damn. No way. Oh God, Dee. Are you okay? What do you want me to do? Can I help you in anyway? I don't know what to say." Brian rambled in short sentences as his thoughts spewed from his mouth.

"I want to be alone."

"Yeah, I got it. If that's what you want. I'll be back in a little while." Brian walked out. I wanted to cry. I expected tears, but all I felt was shock and disbelief. I was blind. I may never see again. How could this be true?

I spent the day in a blur of mixed emotions and confusion. If I had permanent blindness, I would lose my profession, my income and my ability to live fully independently. I sat in bed terrified with my thoughts alternating between denial and suicide. In those moments of terror, I couldn't imagine living my life without a face to photograph or sunsets to quiet my mind.

An invisible, heavy weight pressed against my chest. I felt sorry for myself and longed for sympathy and distraction. I didn't want to call my daughters in tears and tell them what the doctor had said. I decided to make a phone call that I had been avoiding. I needed to call Paul Brown. He didn't know why my art hadn't arrived for the exhibition. The last time he heard from me was when I called from Nairobi. I could only imagine what he thought after he didn't hear from me or receive my photos. Worrying about it made my stomach sick, yet I needed to call and explain what happened.

While Brian was on his walk, I felt around until I found the phone. I picked up the receiver and heard a dial tone. Then an attendant said, "Reception desk. May I help you?"

"Hello, this is Dee Coulter. Could you please dial Gallery Paul Brown for me? I can't see the phone."

"Certainly, hold one moment."

The phone sputtered an obnoxious ring and my stomach tightened further. "Gallery Paul Brown," a female voice answered.

"May I please speak to Paul?"

"I will see if he's available. May I say who's calling?"

"Dee Coulter."

"Oh," the woman said with surprised tone in her voice. The phone clicked over to background music while I waited.

"This is Paul," I heard a moment later.

"Hi Paul, this is Dee Coulter."

"Yes, I know. How may I help you, Dee?"

I blurted out as quickly as I could, "I have a very good reason why my work was not present at your October exhibition."

"I'm sure you have a great reason." His voice was light and teasing. "You don't seem like the type of woman that would just leave a guy hanging on the line for an art show after he spent a lot of time and effort promoting it. Please, do tell."

Thankfully, the witty rapport was still present and I desperately wanted to mend the relationship, even if he never displayed my art again. "I was injured in Nairobi. I've been in a coma for two months. I am in San Francisco by coincidence to have brain surgery to repair my…" I couldn't say it. If I admitted my blindness to Paul, I couldn't pretend it wasn't real. I held back my tears and swallowed hard.

The hospital intercom announced a code red. Loud beeping and the sound of people running interrupted my focus and reinforced my concerns about my surgery tomorrow.

"Dee? Are you okay?" Paul asked.

Paul's words brought me back to the moment. I took in a deep breath. "I'm having surgery tomorrow." I couldn't make myself convey the specifics.

"I'm sorry to hear about your accident. I'm relieved to hear your voice and know that you are going to be okay. Thank you for calling. After your phone call from Nairobi, I was looking forward to meeting you. I couldn't imagine why you hadn't called back. I would never have guess that you…. I'm sorry. At least I know now that I didn't scare you off." Paul sounded as if he was trying to hold back emotions.

More loud sirens filled the hallway. I wondered about the current emergency.

"I'm truly sorry …"

"There is no need to explain anything," Paul replied. "Did you travel to San Francisco alone?" he asked concerned.

"No, Brian is with me…" A nurse entered my room to take my vitals. I gave her a look of desperation that I needed to finish my call.

"Good. I'm glad you have someone to help you. I hope our paths cross again."

"I would love to talk about my work," I said. "I will be at San Francisco General Hospital for two weeks. Perhaps we can meet before I fly home."

"Perhaps, but it sounds like you have a full plate right now. Focus on getting well, so that you can take more pictures in the future. Thank you for calling, Dee."

"Brian is not my boyfriend," I said loudly and abruptly. It didn't come out the way I wanted, but I felt the opportunity to speak up slipping away. The nurse took my right arm and stared at me with a look of confusion. I tried to reassure her with a few nods. She shrugged her shoulders and placed a blood pressure cuff on me.

"Excuse me?" Paul asked.

"I am not dating Brian. He is not my boyfriend. He wants to be together, but I do not." I paused briefly, then I changed my tone. "I would love to have dinner with you…after my surgery."

"Well, that's great news. Please call me when you are recovered and you feel up to enjoying a divine meal with an enthusiastic host."

"I look forward to it," I said.

"Not more than I," Paul assured.

I smiled. "Bye for now, Paul."

"Good-bye lovely Dee. May your surgery go well."

"Thank you."

The phone clicked and he was gone. The nurse looked at me again with raised eyebrows.

"It's a long story," I said.

She replied with another questioning glance. "He's a really nice guy."

"Who," she asked. "Brian or the guy on the phone?" She must have thought that the ever-present Brian was my boyfriend. She raised her eyebrows again, typed something on my electronic chart and left the room.

I lay back on the bed and lost myself in thought to find distraction from reality. I relived the details from the life of Cherie; the sight of Jean-Paul's hair drifting in the wind, his soft kisses and gentle touch. I soaked in the calm, wet air of San Francisco, content, in love and optimistic. Only my pending drowning could damper the magic in my thoughts regarding Jean-Paul, his strong hand holding mine and his throaty hum when he painted small details. I found myself more intrigued to be in my dream than to be in my hospital room. I remembered loving him, and how he cared for how I felt. I saw him holding our son and placing a brush in his awkward grasp. Cherie's memories I could recall, yet I couldn't remember my past as Dee Coulter.

When the door opened, I was jarred fully awake, shocked at the contrast of how shaken I felt compared to my previous moments of relaxation. My life seemed pale in comparison to the story of Cherie.

"I brought you some sushi. Are you hungry?"

"Yes I am. Thank you, Brian. You're thoughtful."

"I have been trying to tell you that I'm a great guy. Right now you have an excuse for not seeing what's right before your eyes. But when you're well again, I won't cut you as much slack."

I couldn't think of a reply. I didn't respond, and Brian let it go. *Where was my protective wit when I needed it? Why can't I feel love the way Cherie did?*

The next morning I found myself sick to my stomach. It didn't help that I couldn't eat before the surgery and hadn't eaten for twelve hours. My nervousness was mixed with hunger, thirst and fear. I wasn't afraid of having my head shaved and cut into. I was terrified of waking up and still not being able to see. I'd barely spoken to my daughters. I found it challenging to reassure them. We just sat on the phone and cried together. No one knew how to comfort me and I certainly didn't have the wit about me

216

to comfort anyone else. I prayed that later today I would call them to tell them that I could see and would be home shortly to take pictures of the wedding and my grandson.

"Are you ready for this Dee?" Doctor Bryant asked.

"Fix me up, Doc. I want to go home."

The mask came down on my face with light, fresh oxygen flowing as anesthesia dripped into my vein. The lights faded. Darkness blanketed me as I fell into a dreamless sleep.

What seemed like moments later, I woke groggy and disoriented.

My mouth felt as if it were filled with cotton. "Ahhh." I let out the only noise that my saliva free mouth could utter. Then I mustered up another sound, "Water! Water!"

A nurse came and stood over me. *Oh my God*, I could see the outline of her round, puffy face. I could see where her eyes and mouth were, though quite blurry. I smiled and I tried to speak again, but my tongue stuck to the roof of my mouth. I wondered if this was as good as I would see, or if it would improve. I tried to calm the panic building in my body.

"How do you feel? Are you nauseated, Ms. Coulter?" she asked me.

"No."

"We want to make sure you don't drink water until your stomach is settled. You have a lot of stitches and vomiting is not great for stitches. We are giving you some IV fluids. The anesthesia gives you a dry mouth."

"Please?"

"Soon, we need to wait about an hour, maybe less before we fill your stomach."

My terrible thirst somehow reminded me of lacking air while I sank from a foggy surface in the cold bay. A slight hysteria agitated my nerves.

After an agonizing time in the recovery area, I was wheeled to a private room. Dr. Bryant showed up an hour later. "It went really well, Dee. There were no complications and I was able to remove some damaged tissue and fluids and repair some badly damage blood vessels. Although you have some permanent damage, I would like to check your eye sight. Can you see more right now than you could this morning?"

"Yes. Things are blurry, but I can see more shadows. Will my sight improve any further? You said that it could improve after swelling from the surgery subsided, right?"

"We can expect some improvement in the next week or two. We removed a lot of pressure from the nerve pathways to your eyes and increased circulation to the area. Some swelling will remain for a short time from the intervention of the surgery. Only time will tell us. Tell me as much detail as you can see about my face."

I looked intently at the doctor. "Well, I can tell where your eyes and your mouth are. I can see the outline of your face. I can see that you have brown hair and brown eyebrows. Ahhh, I can barely see your nose, but it shows up as a different shade than your cheeks."

"What color are my eyes?"

"Um, I'm not sure. Every few minutes I see everything in double for a minute or two. Will that go away? Please tell me it will get better."

"I don't know Dee. Double vision is another common problem with these injuries. Sometimes special glasses with prisms help with double vision. Today is a good indication of what you will have. We will know more in the coming days."

"Will prescription glasses help my eye sight?"

"Unfortunately they won't. This is not an eye problem. It's a brain issue."

"Oh my God. I can't believe this. This is not fair. I finally received the recognition I have worked hard for with my photos. I will have to give up my life's passion. This can't be happening to me."

"You survived a terrible injury. You're lucky to be here. You have children, right?"

I nodded.

"You have people who love you. Try to stay positive. You're lucky to be alive."

I'd rather be dead than blind.

Painted with Love

I sat somberly. Dr. Bryant performed some more eye tests and encouraged me to rest. Then he left.

Ten minutes later, a nurse entered the room with someone in tow.

"Dee?" I heard the voice say.

"Who's this handsome man," I blurted out as I looked in his direction.

"You can see? Really? How well can you see?" Brian asked.

"I can see that you're wearing a red and white Cat in the Hat cap on your head and a wetsuit. Why are you wearing a wet suit? You're blurry. You're not normally this blurry, right? Is this just a bad day for you?"

"Oh my God, Dee, it's you! Your sarcastic attempt at humor is refreshing. You haven't given me any shit since you hit your head. I thought the bump changed your personality, although, if we are all lucky, your jokes will get better."

I smirked back at him.

The nurse that brought Brian in checked my IV entry point and then the bag level. She fussed with some buttons on the new monitor at my bedside and then walked out.

"How do you feel?" Brian asked.

"I feel good. I will take some more of that Oxycodone please!"

"Oh, it's the drugs talking. That explains a lot."

"Ha! Very funny."

"When do you get out? Should I break you out?" Brian chuckled.

"The warden said they might let me out in two weeks."

"Oh boy, more hospital stays. Well, this time will be easier, because you won't be in a coma and I won't have to talk to your silence." The monitor beside me suddenly made an annoying beeping sound as Brian finished his sentence. We both looked at it, and waited for a nurse to come check the machine and turn off the noise. When no one showed up, Brian went into the hallway to find my nurse. A few moments later, she entered the room with Brian.

"Your blood pressure is very low," she told me. "Are you light headed?"

"No, my mouth is really dry and I feel sleepy. I feel some pressure in my head, but not light headed," I replied.

"I will let the doctor know and see what he wants to do. I am going to lower your head and ask you to remain level until I hear back from the doctor." She lowered the head of my bed and removed one of my pillows. She pushed some buttons on the monitor and left the room.

I looked at Brian and let out a big sigh. "Listen, Brian, I really appreciate everything that you have done for me. I really do. You're a gem. But you don't need to stay here. You need to get back to your life."

"Dee, you're my life. It is written in the stars that we are a match. Trust me on this. You will come to know it over time."

"I don't want to do this to you."

"Do what?"

"André, I appreciate you…as a friend, but you deserve a whole woman. I'm…"

"Who the hell is André?"

My left hand quickly covered my mouth. "Oh. Oops. Sorry about that," I said with my fingertips still over my top lip.

"You are acting strange. Where did the enormous arrangement of flowers come from?" Brian asked, changing the subject. Are they from your daughters?" Brian asked.

"I thought I smelled flowers," I said, looking in the direction of the scent. "I don't know who they are from," I replied.

Brian walked to the window ledge and must have retrieved a card from the bouquet. "I can't believe you didn't notice these." Brian read the card aloud. "Thinking of you. Rest well and recover soon. Paul.''

"Oh, that was thoughtful," I replied.

"Who is Paul? André, Paul…how can you even keep track? What's up, Dee?"

"Paul Brown, the gallery owner. I called him to tell him why my art didn't show up."

"Oh yes. Don't you find it odd that he's buying you expensive flowers?"

"Not really. I'm really tired. The drugs, you know. I need to rest now," I said. My head felt heavy and sleep pushed my eyelids closed. My arms felt as if they were tied to the bed and a headache was building.

"Do you care about me?"

"Yes," I said with my eyes closed, "as a friend. Now I'm your blind friend that wants a little rest and space to process things."

"What do you mean blind friend? …how well can you see?"

"Oh, you want to talk about that huh? Well, I see more shadows than I did before. I see outlines of people. I see that there are objects in this room." I opened my eyes and looked around, scanning my surroundings, wishing I knew what the objects were.

"Are you kidding? You still can't see? What did the doc say? Will you get better?"

"He doesn't know. But it's not likely to improve much. What I see is what I got. I'm practically fully dependent." I closed my eyes again, yearning for rest. I spoke softly as I started to drift off. "I can't drive a car again or be a photographer. How damn depressing is that?" I peeked at Brian who was silent.

Brian sat quietly with his head bowed. He shook his head a couple of times without looking up. Finally he looked up at me. "This is bad news."

"No kidding." I wasn't sure if he meant for me or for him. I let my eyes close again and my muscles relax. My arms and legs felt itchy, but I was too tired to move. My mouth felt as if it were filled with cotton that sucked every morsel of moisture out of me. "Go back to Seattle Brian. You have a life."

"You really shouldn't make decisions right now Dee. You're compromised. I've known you for two years. Let me decide what's best for you right now."

"No way, I'm in charge of my life. I can manage just fine!" I replied raising my head and my voice.

"Dee, this is not a time to be stubborn. I can take care of you. I did for the past two months. Please don't forget that? I declared my love for you. Does that not count for anything? Are you interested in another guy, André or Paul? Is that it? I'm the best thing you got. I know you and love you." He paused and put his head in his hands. "I need some time to think. I want to hear it from the doctor. Maybe there's some hope that I can have the old Dee back." Brian paced the room with his head down.

I talked through the drug induced drowsiness, using all my strength to reply. "This is it. I'm a blind woman now! I should have died in that accident. Why didn't you let me die André? I don't want to be Dee. I don't want to be blind."

"My name is not André, it's Brian here! Don't give up, Dee. You're stronger than this."

"Right now I need rest and quiet. I don't need to argue with you."

The room started to become part of a dream, including Brian's reply. "I'm not going home, Dee. We are going to talk about this later. Just get better baby. It's all going to be fine. We will get your eyes fixed. I will get you a new doctor. The next surgery will go better. This guy is the wrong doctor." Brian looked at my face in silence, but I couldn't make out his expression. Then he spoke. "I'm your man, Dee. Remember that. Nothin's changed."

His last remarks stirred me from my dreamy state and I forced out the words that popped into my head, "The whole world is different as I see it. Nothing is the same…is more accurate for me."

"We'll see." Brian kissed my hand and walked out. I fell into blissful unawareness, while I wished that my life wasn't real.

Chapter Eighteen: **Relativity**

San Francisco December 2005

The next morning Brian spoke to Doctor Bryant. He argued with the doctor that my eye sight was not acceptable and he wanted a new neurologist to fix what Doctor Bryant couldn't. The doctor was patient with Brian and explained that I had permanent damage where oxygen was deprived from an area of my brain for too long. I heard him say that there was a slight chance that new neural pathways could form and my eye sight could improve more over time, perhaps years. Once reality hit Brian, he walked around like a lost puppy. He stewed for an hour or two, then stood beside by my bed. "It doesn't matter to me that you're blind. You need me more than ever now. You can't live without me."

"André please, I need time to absorb all that has happened."

"Damn it, Dee. Who the hell is André? Have you lost your mind too?"

"Yes, as a matter of fact I have. Thanks for reminding me. I almost forgot I had memory loss and brain damage!" Brian paced around the room not sure what to do. It looked like there were three or six silhouettes of him walking back and forth. I could hardly keep track of the real Brian that stood in the middle of his repeated profiles. At the same time I could see his energy in a new way. I could see his mood as moving color, patterns and waves of light in silhouettes of Brian. It allowed me to watch in awe and not be upset by his mood.

"This is just a bit stressful for you, which makes you more guarded. You always keep me at a distance. You have done it since we met. You're so independent and won't allow a man to love you. You're going to live your life alone and lonely unless you let me in. Let me in, Dee, please? How will you date other men if you can't see?"

"Thanks Brian for the lecture. How much do I owe you?"

"You're cute even when you're so stubborn." He chuckled a little. "Hum, why I put up with you?" I could tell he was smiling and sensed that he wasn't giving up on me.

For the next ten days, life was a daily routine of conversations with Brian, eye tests, physical therapy and quiet crying. The most tolerable part of my hospital stay was when my youngest and oldest daughters flew down to see me. My middle daughter stayed in Seattle because she didn't want to travel with her new baby.

I spent hours with my girls, talking and trying to remember the past. I heard all about their lives, which gave me a glimmer of desire to live.

My eye sight improved slightly after a few days, but double vision still came often and details were not clear. I couldn't read, or identify my pants from my shirt hanging in the closet, except by color or touch. I couldn't see my shoe laces to tie them. I learned to do a lot by feel. I didn't express it aloud, but I feared dependence more than death.

It was a Tuesday. I had permission from the doctor to do light activity, which meant I could go for a walk outside and have lunch in the cafeteria with my daughters. We sat and talked about the upcoming wedding and what was happening in their lives. I wished I could see their faces better.

We returned to my room smiling to find a man waiting inside. I assumed it was Brian from first glance. "Whatcha doing...?" I started to say. As I got closer I realized that it wasn't Brian. It was someone I didn't know. I could see that his shape and the energy around him appeared far different from Brian's. I held my breath and felt a warm wave pass through me.

"Hello, Dee." He walked towards me and extended his hand.

I could see his blurry arm and I reached for his hand, looking down to help my weak vision. "Hello. To whom am I speaking?"

"Paul Brown."

A lump rose up and into my throat. "Oh." I swallowed. "Hello Paul." I looked at his face to make out his features. We had spoken on the phone many times and exchanged several emails, but I hadn't met him in person. He stared at me for a few moments without a word. "Excuse me," I said. "This is my daughter Jessica and my daughter Clair." Paul and my daughters exchanged greetings. "I need to speak to them in the hallway. I will be right back," I said to Paul.

The girls and I stepped into the hall and shut the door. "How do I look girls?" I asked.

"You look great mom. We fixed you up before we left your room, remember?" Jessica said.

"Do I have food in my teeth or lip stick smeared?" I asked.

"No," Clair chuckled. "Who is the guy? Why are you so nervous?"

"I don't know why I am nervous. We spoke several times about my work. I don't know why he is here. He was always flirtatious. I just... Never mind, I am being silly." I said, although my body was reacting in ways I couldn't control. I rubbed my lips together and smoothed my hair. I took a deep breath and tried to look relaxed.

"Sounds like you need to talk with him and see what is going on between you. We will go for a walk, Mom, unless you want us to stay?"

"I'm fine girls. Go get some fresh air. But nothing is going on..."

My daughters walked away and I opened the door to my room. Paul stood as I entered. "Have a seat, Paul," I said as casually as I could. He sat back in the chair and I sat on the bed. "What brings you to see me?"

"Oh, yes," he began before a long pause. "Forgive me for staring; you just look incredibly...familiar."

His words seemed to have some significance as my body felt a sense of relief as he spoke. I shook off the feeling and replied, "Perhaps from my website photo?"

"Ahhh...never mind." He closed his eyes and shook his head before he continued, "I waited for a phone call from you to

225

say that you were feeling better and ready to have dinner with me. When I didn't receive a call, I thought perhaps something was wrong. I hesitated to come uninvited, but I had to know if you were okay."

"Oh yes. I'm sorry that I didn't call, Paul. The surgery didn't go as well as I had hoped." I paused as I took in that statement realizing the weight of its meaning. "I am still recovering physically, as well as mentally and emotionally. But I'm glad you are here. Your visit gives me a reason to smile."

"You look fantastic. What problems are you experiencing," he asked.

There was that question. I knew I would have to answer it many times over the coming months and years. Why did I have to answer it first with a handsome, flirtatious, successful art dealer? If I didn't tell Paul I was blind, perhaps he would continue to find me attractive and we could flirt on the phone as if everything was normal. As soon as he knew I couldn't see, certainly I would lose my appeal in his eyes. But he was right before me now. I couldn't lie to him. I took a deep breath and let it out. "The surgery intended to repair my eyesight." I wondered if my hat was covering my shaved head completely and if my clothes were flattering my figure. I adjusted my pose on the bed to look relaxed and feminine. I sat up and leaned back against the raised bed and crossed my legs.

Paul didn't respond for several seconds. "Your eyesight? Wow, I'm sorry, Dee. I had no idea."

"I know you didn't. I didn't mention that my sight was affected because I didn't even want to say the words out loud."

"I understand." Paul paused for a moment. He looked down at the floor with his right fist pressing against his forehead. "I wish I knew how to help you."

I smiled with tight closed lips and nodded my head. I sighed and then placed another pillow behind my back and adjusted my position on the bed.

"Are you going to be okay?"

"That depends on your definition of okay. I will live."

"Are you going to be able to keep taking pictures?"

"No." I shook my head with a tiny side-to-side movement.

"Dee? That's terrible. You're so good."

I choked back my tears and nodded. I swallowed hard, but couldn't reply. I cleared my throat and reached for the water bottle. Instead of grabbing the bottle I knocked it over. Quickly I stood it upright, stumbling with my awkward hand-eye coordination. Embarrassed for displaying my handicap, I opted to play it off. "Darn bottle nearly escaped. Good thing I'm so quick on the draw."

Paul seemed to not notice. "Your eyes…they look incredibly beautiful. You're looking at me as if you can see me."

"I can see you, just not the details." I stared at Paul while we were both silent. I noticed that I could see, or feel, a sense about him. Without visual minutiae distracting me, I was more aware of his posture, which felt very safe, almost familiar. His tone of voice was more apparent to me, and seemed both playful and caring. Suddenly I recalled shaking hands with Paul moments ago, and the warmth that traveled from his palm into my body.

Paul broke the silence in a lighthearted tone, "Details are not as good on me as they were a few years ago. You're better off not seeing them."

I smiled, understanding well how the years had worn my fair skin.

"When will you be released?"

"Soon, I hope."

"I would love to take you to dinner and discuss an exhibition of your work, if you will allow me another chance to show off your talent."

"Yes! That sounds great." I wanted to burst into tears. At least my previous work could be shown, even if I never took another photo. "I would love to see your gallery sometime," I replied. Paul didn't respond, so I added. "I can see shadows and get a feel for the space. Objects come into a little bit of focus occasionally. I just can't hold a focus for very long. I see a lot of double and triple vision too."

"I would be honored to give you a tour of the gallery. Will your eyesight improve with time?"

"Not likely," I said with a tight mouth.

"Humm, perhaps your world will become more beautiful without the minutiae. You could see as Monet did, with a broader stroke." He paused again for a minute and my mind raced to a dream with a fiancé named André Monet.

"When would you like to see the gallery?"

His words interrupted my maddening thoughts which were running in five directions at once to find the meaning of this strange juxtaposition of names. Claude Monet was the right age to be a father or uncle to the André Monet of my dream. I snapped back quickly as if I hadn't left this world for another time and place.

"I'm on strict orders to rest. No jumping on trampolines, running marathons or water polo games for at least a month." I smiled wide and adjusted my position again. I scratched my head which itched wildly from healing skin and hair beginning to grow back around my incision.

"I can imagine. I will take it easy on you." Paul smiled, then stood and walked towards me. I rose from the bed and walked to the foot of it. "I could pick you up when the doctor gives the okay, and take you on a short tour before dinner. I would have you back resting in three hours. You tell me when."

"I can't turn down an offer to go somewhere other than this hospital. I will call you at the gallery when I get the okay."

"Here's my cell phone number. I'm not always at the gallery. Call me direct," Paul said stepping in very closely as he passed me his business card. I could feel his breath on my face and could smell his salty, spicy scent. I breathed in his exhalation and aroma, allowing it to excite me and calm me all at once.

"Thank you, Paul. I look forward a personal tour."

"I can't think of a lovelier way to spend an afternoon."

"I will call you soon."

Paul stared at me again, without a word. Then he added softly, "Please do."

I didn't understand why I suddenly felt flustered. Perhaps it was his deep voice and the ocean breeze mixing with the fragrance flowing off his skin. Paul turned towards the door as

Brian walked in. I couldn't make out Brian's expression, but the room suddenly felt tense.

"Who are you?" Brian asked Paul.

"Paul Brown. A pleasure to meet you."

"Oh you're the gallery guy. Nice of you to stop by."

Paul seemed to stand taller to meet Brian's subtle jealousy. "I will be showing Dee's work at my gallery." Paul said as he raised his chin towards Brian.

"Her past work you mean? She is not planning on taking more photos." Brian stuck his chest forward and put both hands in his trouser pockets.

"Any work she will let me show," Paul said confidently.

"That's great. So, Dee is on medication right now. She needs lots of rest. I have been taking care of her for two and a half months. She can give you a call when she is feeling better."

"Excuse me," I interrupted as I moved between the two men. "Talking about an exhibit is the most exciting thing that has happened to me since I woke from a coma. It's enough to make me smile. Plus seeing my daughters," I said.

"What about me. Haven't I given you a reason to smile?" Brian asked.

I put my lips tightly together with compassion for Brian. "You've been awesome, Brian. Who else could put up with my sour disposition?"

He appeared to smile. "Exactly. That's why you need me. You should get some rest baby," Brian said in a softer tone.

"Brian, we are friends," I relied firmly.

He grabbed both of my shoulders and looked in my eyes. "But you are still in shock over your…stuff. You will come around. I know it," Brian assured me. Brian turned to Paul. "If you want to show her photos, that's great. She will call you."

Paul gave Brian a hard glare before turning to speak to me. "Call me when you want to see the gallery, Dee. I will exhibit your art and do everything I can to show your talent," he said kindly.

"Thank you, Paul. I will call you soon."

Paul left the room. When I heard the door close I spoke immediately to Brian. "Would you please go too?"

"I was…"

"Please?" I asked.

Brian walked out and closed the door behind him.

Two days later, Doctor Bryant gave the all clear for me to have an afternoon outing. He gave me a thorough check-up before I left with several instructions and symptoms to watch for.

"If you have any symptoms, return to the hospital or call for an ambulance. I don't expect any complications; otherwise, I wouldn't let you leave."

Paul picked me up in a silver, convertible Mustang. As we drove the busy streets of San Francisco, I tried to see what I could. Sometimes when I stared at an object for several minutes, my brain registered it more clearly with greater focus. But as we flew by buildings, cars, a park and stop lights, I could often decipher what objects were, but missed any particulars.

We arrived at his gallery and Paul lead me inside. The gallery was spacious with stark, white walls and concrete floors. It was neatly appointed with pieces of art and sculptures of large variety, although I could only make out details of the art if I starred and concentrated. When my double vision showed up, I enjoyed the art twice or more at the same moment. Paul gave me a tour, with a short description about each artist and why he chose to display them.

"Why did you choose to show my work?" I asked.

"That's easy. I appreciate the way you capture emotions of people all over the world. We have so much wealth, and you show us the hardships of real people, and happy families with little or nothing; poverty, community, tradition, need and the stories of people thriving with so little. I feel like I step into their world. Your pictures stir a sense of guilt for not being more grateful. I like art that stirs such powerful feelings."

"Thank you. My purpose is to connect the world by helping people see that no matter where we live, or what we have, we all share the same emotions. We are all human and one race, the human race. My intention is not to make people feel guilty."

"Perhaps that is just me, feeling guilty that I don't smile enough when I have so much."

Painted with Love

After the tour Paul said, "I brought in a painting from my personal collection that I thought you might find interesting. It's in this small viewing area, through here." Paul led me to a small doorway that opened to another part of the gallery. As I entered the new space I felt immediately different; almost transformed as if I was visiting another era. A spot light shown-down on a rear wall that was blocked by a screen standing on the floor that may have been made of bamboo or wood. I couldn't tell.

I walked straight towards the screen and back wall, as if something was calling me. Rounding the screen, I looked at the display. Instantly my heart reacted by thumping hard and fast. Quivers rose up my spine and my breathing stopped. An electric buzzing and a déjà vu feeling swept over me.

On the back wall hung a large portrait of a beautiful young woman portrayed in exquisite detail. It wasn't clear at first, but as I stared, mesmerized, it came more into focus for brief seconds. It seemed as if the woman sat there, on the wall, holding still before me, in real form. Every painted stroke gave life to her two-dimensions. Shadows, color and lines brought her into existence. Her smile was playful, her eyes seductive, her pose flirtatious. The brightness of her countenance glowed around her body, subtly, to share her warmth and delightful air with the viewer. She wore a simple, white gown. Her small frame complimented the dress more than it flattered her. She appeared genuinely happy. Everything about the painting seemed lively, radiant and telling.

I took a step closer, tempted to touch her and somehow become her.

I recognized those brush strokes. I knew the artist and the powerful way he could conveys a face. Suddenly I was back in France standing in Jean-Paul's studio looking at another painting; of a woman in sorrow who looked much like the woman I am today. That woman's grief was something I knew all too well today.

"She's beautiful isn't she?" Paul said from behind me.

I spun quickly, startled to realize that he was directly behind me. For a couple of moments I'd felt between two worlds. "Oh, my! Yes," I said recovering my composure.

"I didn't mean to interrupt your experience." He paused and looked at me. I returned his gaze. I saw him more clearly for the first time. He was a handsome man with blue eyes and strong features. He was tall, with a gentle smile and polite demeanor. I tried to pull my gaze away, but it seemed magnetically fixed. "Can you see why I bought this piece?" he asked.

I nodded.

"I find her mesmerizing," he added. "Interestingly enough, your eyes look like hers. Did you notice?"

I didn't know what he was talking about, and didn't respond. I simply looked at his face.

"That's why I had to show you this piece." He paused, waiting for my response. After more silence, he asked, "What do you think? Do you see the resemblance?"

"Well, no. I'm not sure. She comes into focus for a moment and then fades into a blur again." I still had goose bumps and an overwhelming feeling of knowing something profound about this painting, or woman. Standing between Paul and the artwork felt like a familiar place. With my skin tingling and a heightened sense of alertness, I also felt reassured. I had to know more. "Where did you get this portrait?" I asked.

"Do you have time for a story," he asked.

"I have two hours until I'm back in the ward," as I jokingly called it.

"Very well." Paul smiled and then continued. "Have a seat," he offered, gesturing to a bench behind the screen. He guided me by my arm and sat down beside me. "Twenty years ago. I walked into a very small gallery near the waterfront. When I saw this woman, I was instantly mesmerized. I stood locked in place, fixed on her eyes. Those eyes; it was as if she looked right into my soul. I couldn't hide from her and I felt ashamed for every great thing that I hadn't done. I could see in her gaze that she expected more of me, and I didn't measure up.

"A déjà vu feeling swelled up inside me. My body tingled." As Paul spoke, I nearly laughed spontaneously from the coincidence. I held in my amusement so he didn't think I was giggling at him.

"Within ten minutes I offered the owner one hundred thousand dollars for this painting. I had to have it. He quietly told me that it wasn't for sale. I told him to name his price. He told me that he could never sell this painting. For him it was all that remained of the memory of his mother. He would never part with it.

"When I left the gallery, I felt empty. I realized that all of my success did not give me the one thing that I truly wanted; a woman who would look at me with that gaze. I went back the next day and sat before the painting. Perhaps she told me to quit my job, or maybe I dreamed up that part. I asked the gallery owner, John, if I could work at his gallery for free. I've been an art dealer ever since."

Every word that Paul spoke caused my heart to increase its pace and my breath to quicken. I tried desperately not to let him see my growing excitement.

"Am I boring you? Are you sure you have time for all of this."

"It's fascinating. What is it that draws you to her?" I asked.

"She just speaks to me in such a profound way. I'd never had that feeling before or since…until now." He looked at me intently, staring quietly at my face as if we shared a deep secret.

"Excuse me? What do you mean…until now?" I asked.

"I feel a déjà vu around you, perhaps because your eyes remind me of hers." He paused.

I didn't respond. This man was hitting chords in me I didn't know that I had. Something was happening that I didn't understand. A magic in his presence took away my defenses and tore down my walls. This feeling was strange to me.

"How did she die?" I blurted out.

"Oh, it's unfortunate. She drowned in an accident as a young woman."

My head swirled for a moment, like the slow spin of water. A slight pressure squeezed my chest and stomach. I sat quietly, wondering if God had a sense of humor.

"Are you okay, Dee? You look a little green. Do I need to get you back to the hospital?"

233

"I'm fine, I think. I'm just trying to...take all of this in."

I looked closely at him to detect his expression. It was hard to contain my feelings; being around him made my body tingle. His voice tone delighted me and his scent held me fixed in place. I gathered my composure and said, "This portrait is quite profound."

Paul stared into my eyes as he responded. "The artist truly loved this woman. He painted her to keep her alive, hoping that perhaps one day she would be standing right before him in all of her radiance and beauty, looking at him with her cheerful eyes and generous smile. He hoped that once again he would feel the same deep love in his heart and realize that nothing else mattered as much as looking into her soul. He longed for her magnificence to overwhelm him once again; just as it did when they met for the very first time." Paul continued to stare at me, studying my reaction.

I knew more than he realized. His words caused me to know what I already suspected.

I looked back at Paul. I searched deep into his eyes, which were fixed on mine. This man was easy and familiar to me. My body wanted to be close to him. I craved his gaze upon me. For a moment I imagined loving him and being adored in return, fixing him meals, rubbing his back, listening to his day. I quickly snapped out of that thought and remembered that I was legally blind. I couldn't possibly be enough of a woman for him. I could never be what Cherie was to Jean-Paul. It wouldn't be fair to let him love me when he could have a woman with eye sight.

"Dee?" Paul broke the silence expecting a response from me. I couldn't answer. He waited a few more seconds before he continued. "Do you want to know what I think?"

Something in his tone made me know what he meant. I couldn't possibly respond positively to his realization. If he knew that I dreamed I was this woman, and that perhaps we shared a life together in another time, I wasn't prepared to break his heart again at this moment, even if it was what I must do. Fear froze me in place. "I'm not sure that I do."

Paul took my shoulders in his hands. I held myself stiffly and feared his words. He turned my body square with his. "Dee."

I closed my eyes as if I could shut out his answer. Paul didn't speak. Several seconds went by. Slowly I opened my eyes, looking up from my lowered head. Paul slowly said, "It can wait until later."

Whew. I sighed. I needed time to decide how I could protect him from a future he didn't really want.

"Would you like to see a picture of John, the son of this woman?" he asked.

I swallowed hard. I knew what that meant. I may be looking upon the son of Cherie. "Okay" I replied slowly.

He opened his wallet and turned a picture towards me and held it close for my inspection. "I don't know why I still carry it really. He's been gone a long time." I looked at the picture with an effort to focus my eyes. "He was ninety when this picture was taken. He was born in 1901," Paul explained.

The two men stood side-by-side in the photo with water behind them. I couldn't make out much detail. A deep sense of love and compassion flooded my heart as I felt the boy who lost his mother. In my mind I saw a child watch his father cry and paint. This friend of Paul's was a part of my dream, or maybe he was more than that. I studied the picture and concentrated to see details. *What did he look like as a young man? What did he like to do?*

"He was a dear friend to you?" I asked.

"He was indeed. We needed each other. I don't really know how else to explain it." Paul looked at his watch. "I promised to get you back to the hospital on time. We need to get going." We both stood and he offered me his arm again to guide me. "I may be too forward, but may I ask you a question?" He paused and turned towards me. I held my breath. "Could we discuss the exhibit over dinner tonight? I will bring you a San Francisco delectable meal to your room. You must be tired of hospital food by now."

"Are you crazy? Does anyone get tired of pudding cups and soup from a packet? Yum!" I smiled and then said, "Another offer too good to refuse."

"What would you like to eat?"

"Surprise me."

"Okay. It's a date," he paused holding his breath.

I smiled and he released a sigh. Then I added, "But the purpose of this 'date' is to talk business. Do we agree?"

"Sure," Paul said quickly.

Paul took me back to my hospital room and said goodbye, agreeing to bring me dinner at 7:00 pm.

Brian walked up the hallway just as Paul was leaving.

Paul said, "Hello Brian," as he walked by him.

Brian raised his chin in a perfunctory nod as Paul walked past and disappeared into another hallway. "How did the gallery tour go?" Brian asked.

"I like his gallery. He is going to do a show as soon as possible. We are going to talk about it more tonight."

"Hmmm," Brian accused. "Where are you meeting?"

"Here. It's a great opportunity," I added. "Please support me in this. He is coming tonight at seven. Please be polite and let us talk."

"Okay. I'm going for a walk," he said and then he turned to leave. I knew he felt jealous and I hated to see him sad.

I sat alone in my room looking forward to a good meal and more talk about business with Paul. But the attraction between us needed to be extinguished. I didn't want to mislead him or encourage him. He deserved to have a whole woman; not a damaged one. It wasn't fair to him to allow the love he felt for the woman in the painting to bind him to a future with my impairment.

Chapter Nineteen: Discovery

San Francisco, December, 2005

That afternoon my daughters and I visited. We took a stroll together around the hospital grounds and they became more acquainted with my limits in walking around by myself. My oldest daughter was hoping to stay in San Francisco until I was ready to leave, so she could assist me with travel. We were both hoping that I would be released soon so she didn't miss more work.

Then Jessica asked the question I didn't want to answer. "So Mom, tell us about Paul," she asked smiling.

"Yes," added Clair, "you seemed quite infatuated."

"What? You're so wrong. He is just a gallery owner excited about my work. I wanted to make a good impression."

"Whatever, you can't fool us. We saw your reaction. Does he like you?" Clair asked.

"I don't know. It doesn't matter anyway, he lives here, and I live in Seattle and…"

"So what? People move. And what else Mom?" asked Clair.

"I am blind," I said quietly. We all stood there quietly for a moment, as if we had almost forgotten.

"You don't seem blind, Mom. You are still beautiful and engaging," Jessica replied.

"I can't drive, read, work or cook dinner. I'm dependent on someone else for navigating around. In time I will learn to walk with that stupid stick the therapist is trying to teach me to use. I don't want to be that woman. I don't want the man who adores me to be…burdened."

"Don't you think he is old enough to decide these things for himself? Do you really think that he needs you to protect him from his choices?"

"In this case…I think maybe I do need to protect him. He may be interested in me…because I remind him of someone else."

"Who?" Clair asked.

I paused, wishing that it made sense to someone else besides me. "I can't explain it right now. But no one knows what the new me will be like until I have time to adjust to life without normal eyesight. Until I know me, Paul is safer to keep his distance."

My girls were both silent. We all felt the heaviness of the subject. My life was more complicated now. It was a fact we needed to face. Bringing Paul into that mix would only complicate things further, for me and for him.

After talking with my daughters, I felt homesick. I wanted to be in my house where I could safely pout about my challenges ahead.

The girls left about an hour before Paul was scheduled to arrive. I shuffled through my closet looking for another outfit to wear. My daughter had brought me clothes from home and the therapist taught me how to dress with poor eye sight. I wanted to look nice for Paul. Then I changed my mind and decided to not look like I was trying. There was no need to encourage him to hope for the impossible. I chose a red blouse and jeans to keep it simple and casual.

Brian hung around before dinner pacing like a lost cat. He tried to engage me in conversation and make me laugh. His efforts were transparent. I could have reassured him not to be jealous, but I didn't.

Paul arrived with dinner promptly at 7:00 p.m. Brian stood directly in front of Paul and asked him why he brought food.

"I wasn't willing to share her hospital meal, so I thought the polite thing to do was bring dinner from a real restaurant," Paul said.

Brian turned towards me and said, "I'm only a phone call away if you need me, honey. I'll be back in an hour." He left the room reluctantly.

"It smells divine. What did you bring me?" I asked. "French cuisine from Fleur de Lys. Chef Hubert Keller is one of the best chefs in the city."

"French?" I asked.

"Yes. I fell in love with it when I was in Paris."

"I'm excited. What a thoughtful choice."

"I'm happy that you approve. Have you been to France?" Paul asked.

"Yes," I said slowly, remembering my dream and how beautiful Paris was. "I was in Paris last February."

"Really? What took you to Paris?"

"I can barely recall the details. I think I was photographing in Turkey and I felt drawn to go to France. I remember going to the Eiffel Tower and watching the sun setting. It was quite impressive."

"Where were you on your last photo shoot?" Paul asked.

"I was in Kenya taking photos of a Masai tribe. I don't remember much about it. Brian told me about the trip. My camera was damaged in the crash and I haven't had the opportunity to see if the photos are accessible."

"Brian was on the trip with you?" Paul asked with a slightly elevated voice.

"Yes. He invited me to take the pictures for his project."

"Are you and Brian...involved?"

"Oh, he thinks so. I can't really remember what our relationship was before my accident. I only remember bits and pieces. In the memories I recall, we were just friends. Now he says we are a couple, but I don't have feelings for him and I have no desire to be in a relationship right now."

"Not even with the right man?"

"No." We were both silent.

Paul set a plate before me which smelled divine. I noticed that he cut the meat before he left a fork and knife beside my plate.

"Bon appetit," he said.

239

Painted with Love

My filet mignon was decorated in shallots and fresh sprouts. Paul had duck breast served on eggplant with olives. The smells were more intense due to my nose making up for what my eyes lacked. Each bite was delectable. After two weeks of hospital food and two month on IV fluid, I had to remind myself to eat slowly and not gulp the savory meal. Eating with Paul felt lovely, as if we had done this for years. I watched him cut his duck and bring his food to his lips.

"How's your meal," Paul asked.

"Umm, divine, thank you."

"Excellent. Mine as well. I love their menu. It reminds me of…" Paul stopped with no apparent intention of finishing his sentence.

"Reminds you of what," I asked.

"Oh, well, when John and I visited Paris, we dined at a small bistro on Rue Street. I found the place utterly charming, and ghostly familiar." He paused as if lost in thought. "I enjoy the restaurant because it reminds me of that experience."

I found Paul to be genuine and alluring; even irresistible.

"Well this is a lovely meal," I replied.

"Dee, do you mind if I share something very personal with you?"

"I suppose," I replied. I drew in a quick breath, gasping quietly.

"When I look at you I feel an overwhelming sense of excitement and contentment all at once." Paul studied my face.

I nodded my head slowly, over and over. I looked around the room with my eyes, holding my head still, absorbing his words.

"I was afraid to share my feelings with you Dee, but I was also afraid not to. You're the only woman that has ever made an enormous impact on me. My life will seem empty without you around."

"Paul, I appreciate your honesty, but I don't feel that it's a good time for me to date anyone right now. My memory is spotty, I'm depressed. I haven't figured out how I will make a living. I need to focus on healing and evaluating my future. I'm a legally blind photographer, who lives in Seattle, who just met you, and I'm not interested in starting a relationship. I would love to have you show my work. I'm sure that you're an amazing man, but I can't see myself learning to live with this handicap while starting a new relationship. It's too much for me right now." I felt the lies leaving my lips and landing like a quiet bomb of destruction on the kind man across the table from me. It seemed like the right thing to do, but on some level it also felt wrong. When is a lie honorable? I wanted Paul to love me, but I couldn't expect it or ask him to give up his life and enter my limited world.

"I can respect how you feel, even if I don't agree." He paused, as if contemplating his words. Then he continued. "How can you be so beautiful, warm, engaging and charming?"

"It's a curse," I said with a smile.

"Yes it is, on me," Paul replied. He paused. "I would love to provide an exhibition for you and show any other work you have available. It would be my pleasure. I will help to retrieve the pictures off your camera and have them printed, if you would like my assistance." Paul smiled again. His smile was infectious and I found myself smiling in return.

"Thank you for loving my work and being willing to show it." I held my breath wondering if I should share what I was feeling. Then it slipped out. "I would be lying to myself if I didn't admit that I felt a connection with you. But I just don't feel comfortable dating right now. How could you possibly be interested in taking on a project like myself?"

"Perhaps it doesn't make sense, but when is logic a prerequisite to love?" Paul said softly with a slight sigh. He stared at me. I found myself staring back, seeing glimpses of him in focus and often two or more of him at once. "I would love to get to know you and keep in contact," he added.

"That's fine, but I don't want to mislead you. One day at a time. That's about as far as I can look ahead right now," I replied.

"I understand. When are you going home?"

"As soon as the doctor will discharge me. My daughter, Jessica, is getting married in a few weeks in Seattle. I will host the reception, with a lot of help. I have a new grandson whom I will meet for the first time when I return home. His name is David Luke."

Paul looked intently. "You're a remarkable woman."

I felt myself blushing. I looked down, breaking the unfaltering gaze.

We enjoyed our meal with light, warm conversation. Paul was easy to talk to and his love for collecting art was fascinating.

As the meal concluded, Paul said, "I look forward to learning more about you. I should go so you can rest. It has been a big day."

Our plates were mostly empty and I'd finished all that I could. I passed on the offer for the dessert he brought.

"If you feel up to it before you go home, I would enjoy taking you to the waterfront. There's a nice park on the bay."

My heart jumped when he said 'the bay.' My mind flashed back to the image of a dark night covered in fog and the frigid water that held me in its grip. Going back to look at the bay may lend me answers and healing. I swallowed hard and decided to face my ghosts. "Actually, I would love to go down to the water before I go home. That would be great."

"Excellent. You tell me when and I will make it happen."

"The doctor told me that I could have a four hour excursion next, and he would evaluate how I did before I go home."

"Four hours? Well that gives us time for some pampering as well. How about joining me for a healthy breakfast tomorrow and the best coffee San Francisco offers?"

"You mean I would pass up this lovely hospital brew, so contrasting to my Seattle coffee?"

"This coffee rivals what you serve in Seattle."

"Oh, a competition, and you seem so confident. Now I'm intrigued. Where do you find this excellent brew?"

"Breakfast and coffee will be served at my home, which overlooks the Pacific Ocean on the south side of the Presidio. Then we will find our way down to the bay."

"It sounds acceptable. What time is coffee served?"

"How about if I pick you up at 7:00 a.m.? Does that give you enough time to prepare for a luxurious morning followed by a gentle walk in the park?"

"You really know how to make a girl smile."

"I enjoy making you smile, for selfish reasons." His tone was soft, with light-hearted humor.

"You're in luck. I enjoy smiling."

Paul chuckled aloud, as if I'd truly delighted him. Paul left with a thoughtful good-night and a wave. After he was gone, I wondered if I was too encouraging. I didn't want to embolden his interest. My heart felt sick with the idea of being a liability. My eye sight would compromise my self-reliance and limit my options, but I didn't have to impose that on a man. I preferred to be handicapped without an audience.

I didn't sleep well that night. I woke a few times, forgetting what city I was sleeping in. When I woke, I remembered one short dream. I dreamt that I was Cherie, returning from the market with groceries. I'd become lost and couldn't find my way back to our apartment. Jean-Paul found me wandering on the streets and said, "Never fear ma petite. For wherever you travel, I shall always find you. I have a nose for you like a hound dog. I shall paint you the clues and guide you back to me." I woke with a sense of relief.

I dressed in the most flattering outfit I could find in my limited wardrobe. I asked myself why I was trying to look nice for Paul. I argued back to myself that a woman has a right to look nice always, because women love to look beautiful.

It took longer to dress than I expected. I was still putting on my socks when Paul showed up. "Good morning. You look refreshed and lovely. Did you sleep well?" I caught a glimpse of his eyes and my dream flashed before me.

"I slept like a dream," I assured.

After he observed me tie my shoes without looking at my laces, Paul walked me to his car with my hand on his arm. He opened my door and guided me into his car with his left hand on my back and his right hand holding mine. We drove west, through the Haight-Ashbury District. As we neared the end of the land, I saw glimpses of the sea meeting the sky.

Paul slowed the Mustang more and more. The homes were impressive and the ocean view even more so. Although I couldn't make out detail with the car in motion, I realized the large stature of the homes and their respective estates. Fog hung in the air in patches. I could see hints of ocean far away and wondered what the distance was from the land to the water's surface below. Paul guided the car into a driveway made of stone pavers and parked under a porte-cochere.

"Welcome," he announced casually.

"Thank you," I replied without revealing my amazement. His home was expansive with exceptional quality. It was modern, with large windows and a gentle sloping roof. The exterior was soft grey, but I couldn't make out the material.

We stepped inside the front door. The interior was immaculately clean and attractively furnished. His décor was simple, with no clutter, which appealed to me. I wished I could see the specifics. I noticed a painting near the doorway. I looked closer and discovered a beautiful sunrise. As I stared at the painting, Paul stood behind me and said, "I am always drawn to sunset and sunrises. They stir me in an unusual way. I can't explain it."

My mind raced back to Cherie's first sunrise with Jean-Paul. I drew in a deep breath. "I've had similar experiences," I said.

A woman walked up to us and Paul turned to stand between us. "Dee, this is Mechel," he said introducing a small, older woman dressed casually. I didn't understand if she was his wife, lover, housemaid or relative. No explanation was offered. I was too embarrassed to ask.

"Nice to meet you," I said. She bowed slightly and extended her hand to take my jacket. "Oh, thank you," I said, handing her the only jacket my daughter brought from Seattle.

"Are you ready for the best coffee south of Seattle?" Paul asked.

"Well, that's quite a promise. I can't turn down the opportunity to decide if your tale is true."

"Very well, make yourself comfortable," he said walking me into a living area with large windows and an ocean view. Then he guided me to a seat.

Paul returned with a tray adorned with numerous items in elaborate style. I stared carefully, turning my head slightly from side to side, which helped me get more of the particulars. My double vision made it appear more beautiful, as if a soft, white glow surrounded each item. A silver, ornate coffee pot sat in the center with two delicate china cups to the side. Cut vanilla beans protruded from a tall cup. What appeared to be handmade white and dark chocolate truffles sat on silver colored paper cups. Fresh made whipped cream filled a bowl with a small spoon held in place by the thickness. A tiny pitcher of honey and wooden sticks covered in crystalized sugar provide a way to sweeten the fragrant elixir. This was by far the most extravagant way I'd ever seen coffee served. Although the details were blurred, I was impressed with my ability to discern what each item was.

"Well, I certainly can't complain so far."

"Let your palate be the judge," Paul suggested as he poured me a steaming cup full of dark liquid.

"Thank you," I said as he handed me the drink. I was slow to find each item. I tilted my head in odd angles for better vision. Paul waited patiently. I spooned some whipped cream into the top of the cup and stirred in a bit of honey. I stirred the combination with a vanilla bean. Then I brought the fragrant brew to my lips. I sipped the hot liquid, coating my upper lip with a small amount of cream, which I removed with my tongue. The flavor of the coffee sat perched in my mouth, delighting my taste buds. My eyes closed as I focused. Whether from mere presentation or perhaps from the unique bean and way the coffee was processed, this cup was certainly my all-time favorite. "Mmmm," I announced.

"So you approve? How does it compare to the Seattle-brew that made the latte an American compulsion?"

"I would say that Seattle is consuming an abundant amount of quality blends, while this is a feast of the passion for the morning ritual. I much prefer this indulgence, although it could be too early for truffles."

"One never knows the mood of a woman and the hour at which chocolate is a necessity. Luck favors the prepared."

"I see. You're hoping for luck today?" I smirked, narrowly avoiding saying, 'hoping to get lucky.'

"Indeed. If I cause abundant smiles to grace your lips, I shall be a lucky man."

His response caused me to pause. Fortunately I did not release the wit that came to mind. My efforts to keep things light and superficial were thrown off by his meaningful kindness and genuine caring.

"You're off to a good start. I'm smiling already."

"There are more smiles in your future, I predict. After we dine on the magnificent creation of Mechel, then we'll walk below to the water's edge. There's a gentle trail, a little long, if you're up for the walk." He paused, looking for my approval.

"I feel well. A walk to the beach sounds inviting."

"Of course, I have some warm attire for you. It's a bit brisk this time of year; most of the year, actually." Paul smiled.

My cell phone rang. The caller ID identified Brian's number.

"Excuse me, Paul," I said before I answered. "Hello?"

"Where are you?" Brian asked, obviously upset.

"Relax, Brian. I'm sorry I didn't tell you I would be gone this morning."

"I came to the hospital and you were gone with no explanation. I asked the nurse and she said you left with Paul to go to breakfast. I haven't even taken you to breakfast since you woke up."

"Brian, I'm sorry. We are having breakfast. I will be back around noon."

"You're having breakfast until noon?"

"It's just breakfast. Nothing's going on, with you and me or with Paul and me."

"Dee..."

"I'll be back later. Bye." I hung up the phone frustrated and worried about Brian.

"Is everything okay?" Paul asked.

I took a deep breath. "Sure."

Paul looked at me in disbelief.

"It's nothing. Brian just won't give up on the idea of being a couple. I tell him no and he keeps at it, like I'm going to change my mind. He acts as if what I want doesn't matter. He's driving me crazy. Let's forget it and try to enjoy the morning," I said.

"I like that idea," Paul replied smiling. "After we take in the sounds of the crashing waves, I thought we would head over to a beach on the bay, before I take you back."

"Great," I replied.

"Please tell me if you feel the slightest bit tired."

"Thank you, I will."

Paul and I enjoyed an exquisite breakfast of eggs benedict and fresh fruit. We sipped some more coffee and then Mechel presented me with some warm attire for the walk. We thanked her for the delicious meal and stepped out the patio door and descended down a few steps towards a gently sloping path. The walkway was broken occasionally by more steps, all descending the side of a steep cliff connecting the land to the sea. Paul kept his left arm firmly bent for my grasp and protection. As we neared the bottom of the trail and reached the sand leading to the waves, we encountered a few washed up logs blocking our path. Paul walked in front and offered me his hand to assist my climb. I held Paul's hand and delighted in the warmth and comfort I felt from his touch. For an instant, I felt a feeling of never wanting to let go. Then guilt reminded me of my plight.

As I finished my climb over the log, I tried to let go of Paul's hand. He adjusted his grip to carefully fit my hand in his as he led me to the water's edge. I felt a natural instinct to pull away and not allow his intimacy. With some uneasiness, I allowed my hand to be held and my body to be lead. As soon as we stopped at the edge of the wet sand, I pulled my hand away.

"I love to come down here," Paul told me.

"It's beautiful," I replied. I saw the ocean in a way I'd never seen it before. My multifaceted vision made the ripples on the waves look multilayered. The sun looked like six suns almost in one place, but each ball of light slightly offset. It seemed as if I could see the energy of the sun leaking from her edges. The fuzzy sky looked surreal, with translucent strata and rainbow essence.

Paul interrupted my daydream. "Yes. It's peaceful, far from the reaches of the masses. But it's more than that. There's magic in the water. She's mysterious. I throw my heartaches to the sea and I call to her to rescue me from what's missing."

"What's missing?" I asked.

"Nothing is missing at this moment," he replied looking at me.

His words were non-threatening. I didn't hear any demands or manipulation. He didn't look for a promise, or an immediate knowing. He wanted a safe place to open his heart. He found it with me on this beach.

We walked on the sand along the water with my hand on his arm. He offered his hand, and I declined politely. The waves made a beautiful sound, crashing in powerful rhythm as if they hammered a secret code.

Paul broke our silent listening. His voice was serious and meaningful. "They came to the water often."

"Who?" I asked.

"John's parents."

"Oh." I replied. Something inside me told me he was right. We kept walking. The breeze blew a hard gust and I turned my face into Paul's shoulder.

"I know why he painted life size portraits of her," he continued.

"Oh, really? Why?" I asked.

"So that he would never forget her. To keep her memory alive." Paul stared as if to see if I understood. We both held that thought, as if contemplating it would reveal the meaning of life or love.

"Are you sure of all of this?"

Paul stopped walking. He turned me toward him. "I've never been this sure of anything in my life. At the risk of seeming like I didn't hear your request to keep us just friends, I'm going to share something with you." He paused and looked at me, raising my chin with his index finger so I would meet his eyes. "Everything that I thought I knew in my life came to a standstill when I saw you. I felt things that I could never deny. I understand now that love is something that travels with us. Love breaks the barrier of death and distance, and time. Love is bigger than what we can describe with words or paint or show to someone special. Love lives beyond our bodies in some eternal realm we cannot see, but perhaps we get small glimpses of it, or touch the very edge of it. You showed me this. I've walked the earth in this life unable to let my heart go to a woman. I walked in fear of what pain I might have if I opened love's door.

"When I saw her in paint on canvas, I loved her, and it made me want to love a woman. But there wasn't a lady who kept my attention for very long. Then you came along. I know, without any doubt, that you're the woman who owned my heart in another time and perhaps many lifetimes. You're the exact woman whom I painted, because my heart would have shattered into pieces if I couldn't look at your smile and see those eyes." Paul pointed to my eyes. "You're the woman who completed me, and when I made love to my soul mate, every doubt of the possibility of love was chased away. You're not the woman I dreamt of; you're the woman my dreams are made of, and my soul must live forever, just so that I might love you once again."

I tried to stop myself, but I couldn't. I didn't want Paul to see my vulnerability, but my ability to hide from this man was impossible. I cried and let my huge tears well up in my eyes and fall to the ground. All my life I wanted to believe in the power of deep love. As long as I could remember I would tell myself that love is only about two people needing each other and that the fairy tale was a joke to keep us hoping for something more. For the first time, in my forty six years, there was a man telling me that he loved me; not my body, my hair color or my charm, but me. He loved my soul. He pined for me before he met me. He remembered me even when death had separated us.

I slid to my knees and sat on the sand. Paul joined me and wrapped his arm around my shoulder, pulling me in to rest my head.

"I never stopped loving you," he said.

More tears fell. I felt overwhelmed by his tenderness and my pain. I wondered if it was poetic justice to be taken away

249

from him and then find him again. When I wanted him, I was swept away by the sea. When I couldn't be a good wife, he's right before me.

Paul and I gazed out at the ocean, while my head rested on his shoulder. He brushed my hair with his hand and took a deep breath. I stopped crying, although tears were just below the surface ready to flood forth again. He turned his head to look at me with kind and gentle eyes.

I broke the silence, pulling away from too much closeness. "Well, I need to get home and see my daughters. I must have a barrel full of mail and bills to address. I have to sell my car and learn my way around the city on foot. You understand? I have to go home."

"Dee, couldn't you give me a chance to love you?"

"I don't know Paul..."

"I want to take care of you, not that you can't do it without me, but I want to share my life with you."

"You don't really want to love a blind woman," I said.

"I already do," he announced.

My head flung back with surprise.

"Dee, you're a radiant woman with an irresistible glow. I'm lucky to bask in your luminescence."

I wanted to believe everything that he said and not feel the need to protect this man from my problems. Reluctantly I replied, "I'll think about it."

His face softened with a smile. Slowly we ascended the path and returned to the house. After a glass of fresh lemonade, we climbed into Paul's car. He drove me near the Golden Gate Bridge and down to the water. We parked by the waterfront and walked over a small wooden bridge leading into a protected area for birds and wildlife.

When we reached the edge of the water, he reached for my hand again. With hesitation, I allowed him to hold mine. We looked at the water. I gazed at the formidable bay, remembering a dream of the dark, biting water holding me away from air, love and life. I shivered from the memory. I closed my eyes to shut it out. When I opened my eyes Paul was staring at me.

Painted with Love

I felt it coming before he moved. I became paralyzed against the flow of his energy. He drew in closer and landed a soft, meaningful kiss across my lips. I allowed his advance and received his gift. I responded in kind with salty lips and my windblown hair brushing both our cheeks. His kiss sent waves of familiar joy through my body. I knew this man. I'd felt this sunshine, this air, this beach, these wave sounds and this tingling in my soul before today. I kissed back with more delight, surrendering to the bliss, succumbing to his desires.

I fell into it completely, forgetting where I was, the day, Nairobi or Seattle. I melted into a moment that existed on an eternal realm. It was a moment of forever. There was no time, no names, no beach, and no hearts. There was only the meeting of two souls, connecting, giving, uniting, reuniting, and exploding pleasure in every direction. For a moment I didn't have a body. This beautiful man was opening my heart. His kiss was powerful enough to part the seas of my disbelief, and convince me that life going forward is a journey worth traveling. With the touch of our lips, I felt more than lifetimes could ever tell. While time stood still, the deep wounds and dry painful cracks in my heart healed.

Following the kiss, we shared a long gaze and knowing. It felt as if Paul had just pulled me out of the frigid, black water. Moments earlier I was a woman drowning in heartache. He rescued me from dark, cold loneliness and suffering. With one intimate connection, the bay was less daunting.

We left the water to return to my hospital room. After he walked me to my room, his right hand reached for my left ear and brushed my hair behind it. "You're truly beautiful."

"Thank you," I replied.

Paul reached his arms forward and invited me to come closer. I followed his lead. I closed my eyes as Paul enclosed me in his embrace. I wrapped my arms around his waist and let my breath escape and my facade relax into the comfort of his warmth and safety. His touch felt timeless, as if it was always there when I closed my eyes and wished for it. I wanted nothing more than to feel this comforted. My heart told me that I could trust this man.

"Dee, I want to move slowly going forward. I don't want to rush us. The exciting mystery of Paul meets Dee is still unfolding. The soul inside of you excites my being. I want to savor every delicious morsel of this story. I will court you and buy you chocolate. I will surprise you and meticulously learn your preferences and history as Dee Coulter. I will fall deeply in love with the essence of you, and enjoy every moment. I will not take any of it for granted or forgo any opportunities to fully taste, smell, see, hear and feel you from beginning to end. The deliciousness of you will be enjoyed more than nine course meal, with pleasure, patience and delight. Will you allow this?"

I smiled, and nodded slowly.

"For now, I will bid you good rest," Paul added.

I studied his face under the florescent light with my arms still around his waist. He was serious, yet kind. I wanted to beg him for his touch, the way Cherie demanded of Jean-Paul, but I would not ask Paul to compromise his poetic discovery of our future together. I could see myself being loved and cared for, giving my heart and love in return.

"Dee!" I heard Brian's voice from behind Paul. I peered around Paul, dropping my hands from his waist. "What's going on?" he asked.

"Brian, um, it's complicated. I can't really explain..." How could I explain to Brian that one kiss held me in its grasp for so long that I would only feel whole when those lips kissed me again?

Brian took two giant steps towards us and stood inches from Paul, eye-to-eye. Glaring at Paul he said. "I had a feeling he would try to steal you from me."

"Brian, please. I've been trying to tell you."

Brian put his hands on his hips and waited with a look of anger.

I spoke slowly. "I don't have romantic feelings for you. All of your doting and smothering will not change that."

Brian turned toward me and softened his shoulders. "Not true, Dee. Things will be different when we get home. You will need me. You can live at my place. Look, you owe me. I saved you. I took care of you. You can't leave me after all I have done for you."

Paul spoke quietly to me, "Do you mind if I step in?" he asked.

I gestured with my arms open wide for him to go ahead.

"This is between Dee and me," Brian interrupted. Brian looked at me. "You belong to me, Dee."

Gently, Paul spoke. "I know that you understand that women do not belong to us. Even our soul mate is not our possession. Each person makes a choice every day to be together. Not one person, but both. Love is respect. They are one and the same. To love a woman is to respect her decisions and honor her soul's journey."

"Are you through with your lecture?" Brian asked.

"I'm not quite through." Brian took another step toward Paul, but Paul's countenance was calmly strong, with truth on his side. Brian remained in place. "You did an honorable thing as a man and friend to stand by Dee. Only a good man would give such devotion. No doubt you love her."

"Dang right, I do."

"You want her to love you in return?" Paul asked.

"Yep." Brian shifted his weight from one leg to the other, impatiently listening.

"But you can't force love." The room was silent as Paul's words hung in the air.

Brian looked at Paul, then turned to me. "Do you love me, Dee?"

"Only as a friend."

Brian looked around the room searching for a way to win. His body turned from side to side, looking for his next move. He put on his ball cap and said, "I will see you back in Seattle. This guy won't be waiting for you when you get home, ready to take you in. But I will."

Brian turned to Paul. "She's in no shape for any funny business, buddy. You are wasting your time. You don't know anything about this woman. It isn't fair for you to make her think you are someone special, 'cause you're not."

"Some things are not as they appear."

"And some things are!" Brian brushed by Paul without looking at him as he exited the room.

The tension in the room slowly relaxed, like the air slipping out of a balloon. Paul turned toward me and lightly placed his hands on my upper arms. "Are you okay," he asked looking closely.

With a big exhale I said, "Yeah, thanks for your help."

He embraced me tenderly, then pulled back to see my face. I sighed and smiled with delight. His face glowed in the faint light with his features accentuated by the shadows. His eyes were blurry and occasionally there were two or six of each eye. But I felt his soul and emotion more than I saw his gaze clearly. I closed my eyes to memorize the expression imbued in his mysterious façade. The lack of details couldn't hide the feeling his look created, but it increased my natural intuition to see without eyes. *If only I could capture on film what I feel from his gaze.* Instantly I felt a quick shock shoot straight through my chest as that thought entered my mind. I tingled from head to toe. *I must capture this sense of instinctive vision with my camera.* My new view of the world was blurry, poetic, shrouded in obscurity, and full of evolving insight. Looking at the world from a different perspective, I saw life in a way I'd never discovered before. I want to share my perspective with others. I will find a way to create pictures that show meaning more clearly than visual minutiae.

Paul leaned down and gave me a sweet, soft kiss. "I'm going to take care of you. All you need to focus on is sharing yourself with your daughters and family. I will not leave you alone. You're stuck with me now." He smiled and waited for my approval. Then he continued. "Your job is to embrace this new chapter of your life. You were just given a second chance to see the world in a new way and live your life with all of the people who love you. That's your task. Let me handle everything that I can for you."

I was starting to see that perhaps I did have a reframed purpose with the latest limits of my body. This evolving chapter may be a spectacular one. "I will do my best to embrace the gifts and love all around me," I replied.

"You're amazing," Paul said smiling. "I will bid you good-bye for now. There are important preparations I need to make. Call me if you need anything. I will visit you in Seattle as soon as you're ready for me."

I smiled wide, excited about my future photography and future relationship. "Good-bye, Paul. Thank you for a lovely morning."

"It was my pleasure. I look forward to many more mornings of coffee with you."

Paul left my room. I sat quietly on the edge of the bed. My life was beginning anew. There were challenges ahead for sure, but perhaps my eyes were just beginning to really see.

About the Author

    This romantic adventure was inspired by a déjà vu encounter Karen Diana Montee experienced while visiting Paris. When she is not writing steamy love scenes, she can be found on her mountain bike, hiking, snow skiing or water skiing. She enjoys activities with her close-knit family and partner, as well as their loving support. Born and raised in Idaho, Diana is more comfortable alone on a mountain than driving in traffic.